An
Uncommon
Protector

A LONE STAR HERO'S LOVE STORY

SHELLEY SHEPARD GRAY

ZONDERVAN®

ZONDERVAN

An Uncommon Protector

Copyright © 2017 by Shelley Shepard Gray

This title is also available as a Zondervan e-book. Visit www.zondervan.com.

Requests for information should be addressed to:

Zondervan, *Grand Rapids, Michigan* 49546

Library of Congress Cataloging-in-Publication Data

Names: Gray, Shelley Shepard, author.
Title: An uncommon protector / Shelley Shepard Gray.
Description: Grand Rapids, Michigan : Zondervan, [2017] | Series: Lone star
   hero's love story ; 2
Identifiers: LCCN 2016039195 | ISBN 9780310345428 (paperback)
Subjects: | GSAFD: Love stories. | Christian fiction.
Classification: LCC PS3607.R3966 U53 2017 | DDC 813/.6--dc23 LC record
available at https://lccn.loc.gov/2016039195

Scripture quotations marked NLT are from the *Holy Bible*, New Living Translation.
© 1996, 2004, 2007, 2013 by Tyndale House Foundation. Used by permission of
Tyndale House Publishers, Inc., Carol Stream, Illinois 60188. All rights reserved.

Printed in the United States of America

17 18 19 20 21 / LSC / 20 19 18 17 16 15 14 13 12 11 10 9 8 7 6 5 4 3 2 1

For my Thomas, Tom Sabga

*I promise this very day that I will repay two
blessings for each of your troubles.*

ZECHARIAH 9:12 NLT

It is well that war is so terrible, or we would grow too fond of it.

ROBERT E. LEE

PROLOGUE

Johnson's Island, Ohio
Confederate States of America Officers POW Camp
July 1865

IT WAS HOT. AS HOT AS JULY. WIPING THE SWEAT FROM HIS brow, Sergeant Thomas Baker gazed out at the waters of Lake Erie and watched the waves leisurely lap its banks. It was a peaceful sight since the lake was so calm. Its surface was smooth, reminding him of a sparkling pane of glass. For once, not a boat or craft was in sight or in hearing distance.

Indeed, it was peaceful. Tranquil.

So much so that Thomas could almost imagine he was out and about, taking a turn along the shore with a lady friend to enjoy a bit of warm weather. She'd have one delicate hand on his arm, and her hand would be bare, allowing him to admire her soft, pale skin. His goal would be to encourage her to smile at him. And because his intentions weren't all that good, his next goal would be to pull her closer. Close enough to smell her sweet scent. Close enough to brush his lips along the smooth nape of her neck. Just to see her shiver.

He stretched his right arm and imagined taking her on an

outing in a little rowboat, nothing fancy. Once he rowed them out a ways, he would lay down the oars and encourage her to lean against him. Then there she'd be, trailing her fingertips in the water as the current lazily moved them along. They wouldn't be hungry or cold. They wouldn't be afraid of death or pain or rats.

They would simply be at peace.

That moment would be perfect.

"Baker? What ails you?" a guard called out, his voice as coarse and biting as his accent.

Thomas didn't bother to reply. Instead, he knelt down into the mud. Pain shot through his knee as it hit the soggy ground. He ignored it, though. Just as he'd learned to ignore most aches and discomforts over the years.

He hadn't had an easy life. Losing his family at far too young an age had marked him. Fighting battle after battle in this never-ending war had been filled with its own fears and challenges.

But gardening while confined in a prisoner of war camp in the middle of Lake Erie certainly held its own brand of torture.

Especially for a man like him who wasn't finding much success while doing it.

In an effort to keep his men occupied, Captain Monroe had somehow managed to talk one of their guards into allowing them to plant the pouch of fruit and vegetable seeds one of the captain's admirers had sent him.

Not surprisingly—after all, their guards were a dim-witted, lazy lot—no one could think of a single reason not to let the officer prisoners plant a garden. Looking pleased as punch, the captain had allocated a good section of their yard for the effort.

As the guards stood by, the captain had a group of them hoeing hard dirt and clay, planting seeds, and carefully watering and

ACCLAIM FOR SHELLEY SHEPARD GRAY

"Be still my heart! Shelley Shepherd Gray has masterfully married the romance of the Old West with rich post-Civil War history to create a truly unique tale unlike any you have ever read. Without question, *An Uncommon Protector* is an uncommon love story that will steal both your heart and your sleep."

—JULIE LESSMAN, AWARD-WINNING AUTHOR OF *THE DAUGHTERS OF BOSTON*, *WINDS OF CHANGE*, AND *HEART OF SAN FRANCISCO* SERIES

"Gray is a master at integrating rich details and historical accuracies to create an engaging tale that will take the reader back in time. Strong secondary characters are well integrated. It is a shame to see this series end."

—*RT* BOOK REVIEWS, 4-STAR REVIEW OF *WHISPERS IN THE READING ROOM*

"Shelley Gray writes a well-paced story full of historical detail that will invite you into the romance, the glamour . . . and the mystery surrounding the Chicago World's Fair."

—COLLEEN COBLE, *USA TODAY* BESTSELLING AUTHOR OF *ROSEMARY COTTAGE* AND THE HOPE BEACH SERIES ON *SECRETS OF SLOANE HOUSE*

"*Downton Abbey* comes to Chicago in Shelley Gray's delightful romantic suspense, *Secrets of Sloane House*. Gray's novel is rich in description and historical detail while asking thought-provoking questions about faith and one's place in society."

—ELIZABETH MUSSER, NOVELIST, *THE SWAN HOUSE*, *THE SWEETEST THING*, THE SECRETS OF THE CROSS TRILOGY

"Full of vivid descriptions and beautiful prose, Gray has a way of making readers feel like they are actually in Chicago during the World's Fair . . . the mystery surrounding the 'Slasher' keeps the reader engaged throughout."

—*RT* BOOK REVIEWS, 4-STAR REVIEW OF *DECEPTION ON SABLE HILL*

AN
Uncommon
Protector

tending the seedlings as though they were newborn babes. Now the plants had borne fruit, and every afternoon a couple of men knelt in the dirt or mud, fought off grasshoppers and mosquitoes, and weeded.

Thomas wasn't sure why he was continually on weeding detail, but since it was a far sight better than latrine digging, he went about the task without complaint.

He enjoyed being near the water, liked looking out into the expanse of it and letting his thoughts drift like one of the paddle-boats he spied from time to time. It was a gift to look at something so serene while toiling in the soil.

Except on days like today, when the humidity rose from Lake Erie like a specter and he was sweating like a racehorse in August. Feeling as though his cotton shirt was suffocating him, he began unbuttoning it.

"Baker?" the guard called out again. "What are you doing?"

Mentally, Thomas rolled his eyes. The Lord had given Clyde Carson both a big mouth and a small brain.

"Taking off my shirt!" he said as his fingers worked the buttons. Again mentally, he added his pet name for the guard—*Taking off my shirt, Clay*—on account of the man being so slow.

But he had probably said too much, even without the name. Been too free with his tone. It really was no wonder the Yankees had festooned him off in the middle of the Great Lakes. He never had learned to control his mouth.

When the guard stared at him suspiciously, Thomas held up his arm. "It was getting soiled."

"Oh. All right. But be quick about it."

Like it even mattered whether he stripped quickly or slowly. They had nothing but time to kill on this island.

After he removed his oft-mended shirt, he knelt down again

and pulled at a clump of weeds. It was muggy enough that he had to wipe the sweat from his brow every five minutes.

He grunted. When they got out of here, he was going to high-tail it back to Texas, back to Fort Worth. He wasn't sure what he was going to do, but he sure wasn't ever going to weed again if he could help it.

The men around him—his fellow prisoners—grinned at him. One or two even laughed at his grimace. His total dislike of gardening was a constant source of amusement for the lot of them.

"You ever grow anything before, Baker?" Major Ethan Kelly asked from about two yards away.

Thomas glanced up from his row of string beans to meet the major's eye.

As usual, their elegant major was handling the chore with ease. He still had on his cotton shirt. It looked clean and fresh. Actually, the only indication of the major's physical exertions was two neatly rolled sleeves. "No, sir. You?"

The major chuckled as he walked over to the next row of plants, then crouched down. "Never. But I'm finding digging in the dirt rather restful." Fingering the small green clump of tomatoes on one of the vines, he said, "I have a feeling these are going to be the best tomatoes I've ever eaten."

"I bet they will be . . . if you get to eat them. Old Philly over there is looking like he's already planning his next meal."

Major Kelly sat back on his haunches. "You and your names," he scoffed. "One day the guards are going to overhear your made-up names for them and you'll pay for the disrespect."

"Probably," Thomas said, agreeing easily. But that was the thing, he supposed. His mouth always had gotten him into trouble. He reckoned it always would, until something happened that taught him to learn from his mistakes once and for all.

But that was no matter. He was already so used to hardship and scrambling for everything that he wasn't sure how to handle easy days with no hint of despair. Only in his dreams did he act like a gentleman.

Then, as he remembered the direction of the daydream he'd just had, he reckoned he wasn't much of a gentleman there either.

Eager to get back to the task at hand, he moved down his row, pulling weeds and swatting away mosquitoes.

When he stood up to wipe the back of his neck, Old Philly cackled. "What's wrong, Sergeant? That scar of yours paining you?"

He stilled. Though he knew he shouldn't, he traced a finger along the thick, raised line that ran down the back of his neck to a couple of inches above his shoulder blade. Even after all these years, the skin felt sensitive and burned.

Old Philly scoffed, "Looks like one of our boys got you good. With what? A bayonet?"

Comments like that made Thomas sure they were being guarded by the worst soldiers the Union army had to offer. Only a man who had never been up close and personal with a bayonet would think that type of blade would leave such a fine scar.

And only a man who had never had to fight for food and shelter would ever think a scar like the one on his neck could heal so quickly.

Resentment boiled in him. How was it that he'd constantly had to fight and scrape to survive while men like Old Philly simply coasted through?

Furious, he turned to the man. "My scar sure ain't from some blasted Yankee bayonet. If you had ever held one, you might even know that."

Philly's smirk vanished abruptly. "What did you just say to me?"

"Watch your mouth, Sergeant," Major Kelly muttered under his breath.

But the warning came too late. His mouth had gotten the best of him yet again. And because he was sweaty and mosquito bitten, and there was little to no chance he'd ever escort a fine lady around any body of water in his lifetime, he let his temper fly.

"You heard me," Thomas jeered. "I swear, every time you open your mouth, I have more respect for Yankees. No wonder they have you guarding a bunch of injured officers instead of fighting. You'd be worthless on the field. This scar is well on twelve years old."

Old Philly was now tromping toward him, passing the rest of the Confederate officers who had stopped working to watch his implosion with various degrees of regret and dismay. "What did you do to get sliced like that when you were a kid, then? Steal something?"

Now, how he got his scar was something he never talked about. Only a masochist would revisit the night his brother and parents were killed. And while Thomas Travis Baker was a lot of things, he sure wasn't the type to sit around and feel sorry for himself. "You need to stop talking."

Old Philly stiffened and his eyes bugged out. He looked so fired up, he was about to turn purple. "Did you just tell me to stop talking?"

"I did. But was that too difficult to understand?" he taunted. And while his brain was telling him to be quiet, his mouth—like always—couldn't seem to listen. "Can you not understand simple words either?"

Phillip Markham, Thomas's lieutenant, cursed under his breath.

Pulling out handcuffs, Old Philly restrained Thomas's hands.

Then, with a rough pull and a shove, he marched him to the stocks by the barracks. "Five lashes for insubordination!" he called out.

Thomas felt a shudder race up his spine. Yet again he'd gone too far.

Clay and one other guard stepped forward, grabbed his wrists, and carted him toward the whipping post. As they jerked him forward and tied him to the six-foot pole, they didn't seem to notice he wasn't putting up a bit of protest.

As other men gathered around and sweat poured off him, Thomas braced himself for the pain that was coming.

Tried to concentrate on the present.

Because even though it was a bad place to be, it was easier to bear than the dark, frantic thoughts filling his head. Easier than remembering the last thing his father told him before he pushed Thomas away and told him to hide.

For once in your life, do what you're told without argument, Thomas. Go to the secret crawl space under the kitchen. Go there now. Do it, son! Crawl in there, and don't come out. No matter what you hear, don't come out.

To his everlasting shame, Thomas had done just that. He'd torn open the tender skin on his neck when it met a protruding nail as he crawled under the cabinet. It had bled for what felt like hours as he remained folded into a small ball in a dark hole in the ground. It bled as he heard his mother scream and his older brother beg for mercy. It bled as he heard his father being stabbed repeatedly. It bled as he heard men rummage through their house, steal their horses, and at last run off.

By the time Thomas came out, the wound had clotted and the blood on his clothes had dried.

When he saw what his family had endured at the hands of the Comanche while he stayed hidden, Thomas had known one thing.

Never again would he follow instructions he didn't agree with.

As the first lash cut into his back, he welcomed the pain. Then he stared out at the water and imagined he was back in that rowboat with the sweet woman. Where everything was peaceful and lovely.

It likely would never happen, but he allowed himself to dream.

1

July 1867

EVERYONE SAID THEY WERE DANGEROUS. LAUREL ASSUMED it must be true.

But that didn't stop her from taking another peek out her open sitting room window at one specific prisoner. One of the men currently repairing the fence framing her yard, the one so close she could see more detail than ever before. Without the benefit of a hat, he was squinting as he bent over a split piece of rotted wood. Though he had an iron shackle on his right ankle, he seemed unperturbed by the weight of the heavy metal.

Instead, he concentrated on the task at hand, positioning a fresh piece of lumber in the ruined wood's place. The sharp lines of his face framed deeply tanned skin and brown hair that was already bleached by the sun.

The guard who stood by his side wasn't Ollie. He was the stranger. In contrast to the prisoner, his skin was flushed and damp with sweat under his Stetson. He seemed both bored and ill at ease.

The prisoner, however, continued to set the wood into its slot, then hammer it into place. He was now perched on one knee, his

9

expression quietly intent on his job. As with his shackle, he didn't look uncomfortable or even that bothered by the oppressive heat.

Laurel craned her neck and looked at him even more closely. He had to be hot. Terribly hot, actually. His sleeves were rolled up to his elbows, revealing darkly tanned forearms lined with veins and more than a couple of scars.

He shifted, giving her a new view of his body. A line of perspiration trickled down his neck, right along a long scar that disappeared under the collar of his shirt. That perspiration made the thin fabric of his shirt stick to his skin, revealing just how muscular he was.

She knew she should look away. Her staring wasn't seemly. Then, too, there wasn't really anything to see that she hadn't viewed before. But for the life of her, Laurel couldn't seem to help herself. There was something about the man that had caught her regard and held on tight.

The ragtag team had been here for three days now. It was a charity mission, the idea of Sheriff Jackson. He'd served in the war with Laurel's father and was a distant cousin of her mother's. Laurel knew the sheriff felt sorry for her, essentially living on her own the way she was.

After all, she was attempting to run what was left of a pitiful cattle operation with barely twenty head, little money for alfalfa for them to graze on, and far too many squatters in the area. She was exhausted and beginning to think she was never going to be able to keep the ranch going. No matter how hard she tried, there were never enough hours in the day to do everything that needed to be done.

After she'd said as much to Will Jackson at church, he'd offered to send out a team of prisoners from the jail to repair her fence line.

Laurel was grateful her longtime friend was now the sheriff and could help her out. She was grateful for the prisoners' help too. Would have been even more glad of it if the team hadn't been overseen by Ollie Burnside—a man who hadn't been much of a worker when he was a teen and seemed to have grown lazier with each year.

He also, Laurel decided, wasn't very good at managing convicts.

Otherwise Ollie would have noticed those men were hot and thirsty. Parched. Even she knew men worked a lot better if they were given water breaks every now and then.

Unable to stop herself, her gaze fastened again on the man with the scars. He was working as industriously as ever, but his movements had slowed.

He was no doubt suffering from the heat. Her heart broke for him. All men—even criminals—deserved kindness. Giving one a sip of water in this heat was surely the least anyone could do.

And since the pair of guards seemed incapable of doing such a thing, Laurel knew that bit of kindness needed to come from her.

Yes. That was something her parents would have expected her to do.

But what would the prisoner with the scars do if she brought him a ladle of water? Would he snatch it from her, scare her half to death, and make her wish she'd never contemplated such a kindness?

Or would he take it gratefully?

Picturing the moment, she let her imagination fly. Perhaps he would take the ladle, meeting her gaze when their fingertips brushed. Smile knowingly when she shivered from the tingles of awareness sliding through her body as he brought the ladle to his lips.

Or would he look at the proffered water and speak? Maybe he would simply thank her. Maybe he would say something more.

And what would she do if he did speak? Would she reply? Dare to smile? Lost in her dreams, in her thoughts about the two of them meeting at last, she shivered.

"Laurel, step away from the window this minute!" Bess called, startling her.

Laurel jerked upright so abruptly that she knocked a book off the table next to her. It landed on the floor with a resounding *thud*.

Bess yelped.

Which no doubt startled the whole chain gang working in her yard. Laurel knew because more than one man had straightened and was now staring her way.

Oh! Had she ever been so mortified?

"Laurel, you really must present yourself in a more genteel manner," Bess chastised. "Why, those men out there are going to see you ogling them!"

Laurel was pretty sure they already had. But, unwilling to share that fact, she concentrated on saving what little bit of self-respect she had. "I wasn't gawking at them." After all, she was only ogling *one* man.

"Whatever you were doing, it wasn't seemly."

Laurel supposed Bess was right. She'd thought so herself just moments ago. But coming from Bess . . .

Here she was an orphan, barely hanging on to what little bit of property she had. Bess and Jerome, her stepsiblings who'd arrived a little more than six months ago, didn't help much. Actually, they didn't seem to be interested in Red Roan Ranch at all. Unless they were discussing how much it was worth, what could be gained by selling it. Frustrated with the whole situation, Laurel slapped her hand against the glass.

Which drew the men's attention back to her yet again.

Feeling her face catch on fire, Laurel turned away, but not before sensing her prisoner's scorching gaze.

Finally, after three days of watching him, she met his eyes.

He stared at her intently. As if he had all the time in the world to stare at her. As if he couldn't look away.

Her lips opened in wonder.

"Laurel!"

Resolutely, she shut her mouth before she caught flies, then turned to face her bossy stepsister. Bess was still glaring at her hard enough to sour buttermilk.

"Stop yelling at me, Bess. I'm not doing anything wrong."

"You're creating a spectacle of yourself, watching the prisoners like a loose woman. It's improper."

"I think not."

As Bess always did when Laurel didn't back down immediately, she harrumphed and then walked away, but not before flicking her dark-green taffeta skirts in disgust.

Once again alone in the sitting room, Laurel wondered how much longer she was going to be able to handle her stepsister's so-called help. At times like this, she feared she wouldn't make it another day.

Laurel's father had died in the war, and after a whole interminable year of mourning, her mother had remarried three years ago. Wayne Vance had been a good man, a kind man, and Laurel had been happy for her mother. He'd also had his own land, a sprawling estate two towns over. So he'd had no issue with her mother making sure Red Roan Ranch went directly to Laurel in the unlikely event of her death, especially since Laurel's brother, Anderson, had also died in the war.

But then, when both her mother and stepfather died in last

winter's influenza epidemic, everything Laurel had never wanted to happen had. She was the sole owner of a thousand acres of prime land just south of Fort Worth, near the small town of Sweetwater. It not only had a creek and several ponds, but it was also fertile farmland.

Bess and Jerome were supposed to have been happy with their father's land. But instead of holding on to it, they sold their inheritance the moment they could and, Laurel heard, for far less than it was worth. Then they'd gone down to New Orleans and Jackson, Mississippi, and spent every last dime.

Which was why they were now living with Laurel.

Almost daily someone came and offered to buy her land. Though her stepsiblings kept pressuring her to sell, she'd refused. Not only would selling make her homeless, but she'd have to figure out what else to do with her life.

She didn't have other goals. She liked her ranch. She wanted to keep it, wanted to live there. She wanted to increase her herd, send some to market. The land and cattle were her links to her identity. Her reminders that war and disease hadn't ruined everything in her life. Only most of it.

That was why, when Will mentioned that a crew of six men who were serving short jail terms for minor infractions needed work, and that he was thinking they maybe could do some work on her property, she said she'd be happy for their assistance.

Bess and Jerome had been up in arms when she told them.

But then she pointed out that no impropriety would be taking place since the men would be chained and guarded. She also took care to point out that the work needed to be done either by the men or by them.

They'd given in easily enough then.

She was starting to understand why her mother had never had

much respect for them. She'd said time and again that there were some folks who did and others who waited for things to be done for them.

For Red Roan Ranch to stay hers, it had to make a profit. Since she needed strong men like these prisoners who could work hard to help make that happen, she needed them hydrated at the very least.

Grateful to have come to a decision at last, she strode out to the kitchen that was slightly detached from the house, poured some cool water into a pail, added two chunks of precious ice, and took hold of a large ladle.

She was going to do it.

She was going to stop staring out windows, open up her front door, and walk outside. She was going to approach those men and offer them some water.

After smoothing her hair back off her face, she opened the door and walked toward the group of men. The walk was a short distance. But as each man stilled and watched her progress, Laurel felt as though she were walking two miles.

Now that she was outside and away from the shade of her house, trickles of perspiration slid along her spine.

The second guard, the stranger, the one who was most definitely not Ollie, strode to her side. He greeted her with an oily smile and the smallest of respectful nods. "Miss Tracey. What can I do for you?"

"Sir—"

"It's Foster Howell," he interjected. "Surely you remember? We met at the party on the square three years ago."

She didn't remember that party. Mr. Howell wasn't anyone she would have remembered speaking to if they had. He was rather coarse and crude. But since she couldn't very well admit such a thing, she played her part. "Yes, yes, of course, Mr. Howell. It's a pleasure to see you again."

"Indeed, miss."

Casting a glance at the line of men still staring at her, she held up her pail and ladle. "It's so warm. I thought I'd bring the men some water."

Looking eager, he reached for the pail's handle. "That is too kind of you. Thank you."

A sixth sense told her he wouldn't share the water with the convicts. Besides, she'd seen him and Ollie sip from flasks from time to time.

"Mr. Howell, I don't mind giving it to them myself."

The man looked appalled by the idea. "Certainly not, Miss Tracey. A lady like you needs to stay far away from these men. I believe Mr. Burnside told you they could be dangerous."

She glanced at the line of men again. "Sheriff Jackson said they weren't dangerous. That some were only convicted because of money owed."

"All men are dangerous. Especially around a woman like you."

A flicker of unease slid down her spine. Foster Howell could, indeed, be right. The war had taught them all that much could happen to the best of people under the worst of circumstances.

The right thing to do would be to hand him the pail and leave. To go back inside and busy herself with chores, then sit in silence and wait for the hours to pass. To try to converse with Bess about things that didn't matter. To hold her tongue when Jerome sat at her father's desk and attempted to look important.

But she couldn't do that for another day.

"My mother taught me to treat others as I would like to be treated, Mr. Howell. I'll take my chances now." Before he could caution her to stay away yet again, Laurel approached the line of men.

Now not one of them was even pretending to work on the fence. Suddenly, they seemed larger, more foreboding, and harder than she'd previously thought.

They were dirty and stained. They smelled of grime and sweat and disappointment. Upon closer inspection, she noticed their cheeks were hollow and their expressions as varied as their appearances. Some of them looked wary, others eager. All, however, looked terribly thirsty.

Telling herself she was merely doing a good deed, she walked to the man closest to her, the man who had consumed her thoughts and vision for the last three days. He straightened when she got close. When she stopped, he inclined his head respectfully.

"Miss."

His voice was deep and gravelly. Better than she had imagined. "Sir. I . . . I brought you men some water. Would you care for any?"

After a pause, he spoke again. "I would at that, miss," he replied in a slow drawl. "This is kind of you."

He was so mannerly. Even out in the heat fixing fences with an iron shackle cutting into his ankle. And his eyes . . . well, they were proving to be even more mesmerizing up close. He had blue eyes. Not gray blue. Not pale blue. Blue like bluebonnets. Blue like the summer sky in July.

Beautiful, piercing blue eyes framed by dark eyelashes. Fastened directly on her.

"Y'all are fixing my fence in the hot July sun. It's the least I could do."

Those blue eyes gleamed. "It ain't the least. It's more than we expected. And, I must admit, much appreciated."

She smiled at him before remembering she shouldn't do such

a thing. Hoping he didn't notice her hands were shaking, she held the pail toward him, allowing him to pick up the ladle and quench his thirst without her assistance.

He closed his eyes with the first sip, then sipped again.

One, two droplets of water remained on his bottom lip. The beads stayed there, taunting her.

When he swiped his lip with his tongue, she inhaled sharply.

While the other men snickered softly, her convict grinned, showing a truly fine set of teeth.

"Watch yourself, Baker," Mr. Howell called out. "You ain't out yet." Sounding gleeful, he added, "And there's no guarantee anyone is even going to want you tomorrow."

Ignoring the threat, the man—Baker—dipped the ladle into the pail again, then brought the water to his parched lips. Laurel watched each movement with bated breath.

After he released the ladle's handle, giving her leave to attend to the next prisoner, he said, "He's right, you know."

"About what?"

"You shouldn't be out here. A woman like you shouldn't be anywhere near a rough lot like us."

"You . . . you seem all right, Mr. Baker."

"I am all right." Looking amused, he smiled, triggering the startling appearance of twin dimples. "But that don't mean you should be anywhere near me."

Before she could respond to that, Ollie strode forward. "Quiet, Baker, or you'll feel the mark of my whip."

Like lightning, Baker turned on him. "Don't threaten me," he bit out, his voice hard and sharp. As far from the gentlemanly drawl as was possible.

To Laurel's surprise, Ollie stopped in his tracks.

Moving on to the next prisoner, she handed him the ladle.

As he drank his fill, she looked back at Baker. Pointedly ignoring Ollie's irritation, she said, "Mr. Baker, what did he mean about someone wanting you tomorrow?"

"Tomorrow is the first day I'm eligible to be released."

She smiled at him. "Why, that's wonderful."

He didn't smile in return. "It's only wonderful if I can get hired. That's the terms of it. Someone has to hire me tomorrow for me to be released."

Moving down the line, she smiled at the convict who greeted her with a head bob and a low "Miss" before passing on the ladle. While the man sipped gratefully, she continued her conversation with Baker. "And if no one does?"

"Then I might have the good fortune to be doing more chores for you in the future."

Feeling a bit speechless, she stared at him in wonder.

Just a bit too long.

"Bring it over here, miss," another convict called out. His voice suggestive and low, he added, "I'll take a sip of whatever you got."

Baker tensed. "Just give that pail to Watters there, miss," he said quietly. "We'll take care of ourselves now. One of the guards can set it outside your door when we leave. Go on in now."

"But—"

While the man she'd been giving water to held out his hands for the pail, her convict said, "What's your name, miss?"

"Laurel," she whispered. "Laurel Tracey."

"Miss Tracey, beg pardon, but you are a distraction. And I fear too much temptation for the likes of us. Go on in now."

"I'm not afraid."

"You should be. Now, go."

Her mind spinning, she did as he bid. She gave the pail to the prisoner and turned away. As she walked back to the house, she heard the low murmur of masculine voices, followed by the *clank* of the ladle against the pail. But she also sensed eyes watching her departure.

Tilting her chin down, she made sure to keep her pace steady. And tried not to think about how one man's attention could rattle her so much.

2

With a wince and a curse under his breath, Thomas Baker stretched out on his bunk. He'd known Howell was going to enjoy doling out his punishment, but Thomas hadn't counted on the guard enjoying it quite so much.

Propped on his elbows, his cellmate, Bert Watters, watched from his own bunk with concern. "Yer back is bleeding. Blood's soaking through yer shirt."

"Figured as much." He left it at that. After all, what else was there to say?

"How many strikes did Howell get in?"

"I'm thinking at least eight."

Bert curled his lip. "I used to save all my hate for the Yankees, but I hate Howell too."

Thomas wasn't sure he hated the guard, but he reckoned if he didn't, he was mighty close to feeling that way. "He's definitely no good. Kind of a simpleton too."

Bert raised his thick, dark eyebrows. "You're a piece of work, Baker. That man took off a good portion of your skin for no reason and you only call him a simpleton." He shook his head. "Can't say I understand how yer mind works."

Thinking back to the more than eight months spent in the

Confederate Officers Camp on Johnson's Island, Thomas weighed his words. "I've had my fair share of cruel guards. Howell is bad, but he ain't one of the worst."

"I forgot you were up on Johnson's Island." After a moment, Bert continued. "You don't talk about it much."

"No reason to. It's over." Besides, the memories hurt too much.

"Makes sense."

Thomas hoped Bert did understand. But what he probably didn't understand was that it wasn't the pain or the boredom or the hunger that was so hard to remember. It was the realization that the friendships he'd made there were likely to be the best of his life. He'd had the dubious honor of being imprisoned with some of the finest men he'd ever met. Because of that, he'd found himself both hating and loving every minute of his imprisonment there.

No man should ever be so desperate.

"Lots of you die up there while you were shut away?" Bert asked, his voice sharp in the silence.

Thinking of Phillip Markham, his lieutenant who had suffered so much before his death, Thomas nodded. "Yep. But not all." Far more had died on the battlefield.

Leaning closer, Bert said, "I heard you served under Captain Monroe. Is that true?"

"It is."

"Really? What was he like? Were you with him on Johnson's Island?"

He respected Captain Monroe far too much to discuss him. "I was on the island with him, but I don't talk about the captain."

"Why not? War's over."

"The war's over, but my admiration for the captain hasn't dimmed."

Bert's mouth went slack before he collected himself. "So the rumors are true? He really was that good?"

"Yeah. He was." In fact, he was so good that if Thomas had contacted him about needing funds—or told him he had been imprisoned for his lack of funds—Captain Monroe would have paid his debts immediately. But Thomas wasn't going to take advantage of him like that. It was better to simply deal with his situation. Somehow, some way, his life was going to get better. He was going to make sure of it.

Bert sighed. He shifted, then flopped around on his thin, uncomfortable mattress like a fish flopping on dry land. In contrast, Thomas concentrated on attempting to stay perfectly still. If he didn't move, there was a halfway decent chance he wasn't going to start crying out in pain.

Minutes passed. Little by little his body relaxed. His back still burned, but at least he was now able to breathe in and out without agonizing pain.

"Hey, Thomas?"

"Hmm?"

"You remember that woman today? The one who gave us water?" As if Thomas had been in contact with any other woman in days.

"What about her?"

"She was something, wasn't she?"

"She was." She was more than that. She'd been the prettiest thing he'd had the pleasure of seeing in years. About his age, golden hair, light-brown eyes, full cheeks that made a man ache to see her smile. She had a figure that was as rich as it was alluring.

Perfect.

Though Thomas had cautioned himself to erase Miss Tracey from his mind, he couldn't help but dwell on her again. He just knew holding her in his arms would feel like heaven. He'd seen too many starving men and women during the war. The women who now tried to have minuscule waists and an air of angelic reed-thinness only made him feel ill.

"I keep thinking about her, and her name too. Laurel Tracey," Bert said around a sigh. "Pretty, ain't it?"

"Yeah." Pretty and feminine. Just like her.

"I think Howell aims to have her. It seems she owns some prime land out there."

"I can think of a lot of other reasons to pursue her."

Bert coughed. "It's that kind of talk that can get you into trouble, Thomas. You shouldn't be thinking about her like that. You really shouldn't have talked to her."

"I was only being polite. She spoke to me first."

Bert chuckled. "You did more than that. I saw how you looked at her."

"All of us watched her. She's a fetching thing. I couldn't help it. Besides, Howell was looking for an excuse to handle that whip."

"Maybe so, but I meant Howell wants her something awful," Bert continued in a low voice. "Two men were talking about it in the yard after supper. They said Howell intends to take more prisoners back to her place next week."

"Though that seems like an odd way to gain a female's favor, that doesn't surprise me. I can't imagine him spending much effort actually going courting."

"That's why he beat you good today. Howell doesn't want you anywhere near her." Bert snickered. "I guess he considers you a rival."

"I'm not much of anything at the moment." He certainly wasn't a rival. Howell was an idiot and liked to inflict pain on people who couldn't defend themselves. "But I can pretty much assure you Howell won't be choosing me to be within two miles of her ranch ever again."

"I don't think he'll be allowing you to get real close again either. No offense, but I sure hope the good Lord intends for me to be in Miss Tracey's vicinity again real soon."

Jealousy hit him hard, though it made no sense. But he did know that she was too pretty and too vulnerable to be the focus of a bunch of prisoners' minds.

With effort, he pushed those thoughts away. "You're from here. What do you know about her? Was she married? Is she a widow?"

"I am from here, but my kin never mixed with hers much. I know she never married, though."

"Surprising."

"Some say she had a sweetheart who went off to fight, but I don't know who."

"Most men married their sweethearts." He'd never done such a thing, of course, but he'd heard a hundred stories of men who married in haste before going off to battle.

"Well, no one married her. Don't know why."

She's young, beautiful, owns land, and seems to be in need of a man to help her manage that ranch. All of those things tugged on his heart. Thomas had never been one for compassion, but even he couldn't deny the appeal of a beautiful woman who was in need of a protector.

"I wonder what's wrong with all the men in this town," he murmured. If he'd been a different type of man—one who was actually worth something—he would have been pursuing her with everything he had. She was not only everything Bert had said, but she'd offered convicts water. Women like that were hard to find and even harder to claim.

"If they're all like Howell, it ain't no surprise she's still a miss," Bert said.

"I can't fault that reasoning. He would have fit in real well with the guards at Johnson's Island."

"If they had been working for the Yankees, us Rebs might have had a fighting chance."

A bark of laughter jolted through him, pulling on his skin, stretching the wounds on his back. Against his will, he cried out in pain.

Bert jumped to his feet. "You're sure in a bad way. You ain't still thinking about getting put up to bid in the morning, are you?"

The town had a tradition of giving prisoners who weren't violent the option of becoming a good citizen's indentured servant for a year. Sheriff Jackson had approached him about it that morning before the guards marched them out to Miss Tracey's ranch. He'd quietly told Thomas it might be the best thing for him.

Thomas had agreed.

Howell had overheard.

That, Thomas knew, was the main reason Howell had beaten him to within an inch of his life. There had been a chance that he was going to be out of this small-town jail in less than twenty-four hours. And if Thomas left, Howell would no longer have his whipping boy.

"I don't have a choice. I've got to get out of here."

"But you're in sorry shape. Real bad."

"No one's going to hire me for my looks." All he had to do was stand there on two feet until someone saw something of worth in him. Though he feared there might not be anything to find, not with injuries that could affect his ability to work, Thomas intended to pretend there was. "I'll be fine."

"They stick you in a cage, you know. You'll be standing in the hot sun like a caged bird. Your back's going to burn and blister something fierce."

He hadn't heard about the cage. Glad for the dim light of the cell, Thomas grimaced. "Probably so. But I still have to try."

After surviving too many battles and skirmishes to count, he'd survived his time on Johnson's Island too. There he'd learned to control his temper and tried to become the man his father had no doubt intended him to be.

But in the year or so after his release, he'd made mistake after mistake. He quit a good-paying ranch job in Oklahoma because they abused their horseflesh. In Abilene he'd been hired on as a guard for a group of men who were unscrupulous and no better than lying carpetbaggers.

Then he'd gone and gambled what little money he had in a card game with two well-known citizens of Fort Worth. Well, everyone knew who they were but him. When Thomas lost, he lost big . . . and ended up owing those men more money than he could ever repay.

And since one of them was Judge Orbison's kin, Thomas had ended up in Sweetwater's jail. Serving time for poker debts.

Thomas had had enough. Enough of making mistakes. Enough of trusting the wrong people and misjudging the right ones. Enough of simply trying to survive. Now he was willing to do whatever he could to never wake up to metal bars again.

All he had to do was hope that morning would come sooner than later and that he wouldn't be too much worse for wear when dawn did break.

⁂

It was faint, but Laurel could see it. The squatters in the north pasture had a campfire going again. Glancing at her timepiece, she saw it was close to midnight. At this hour, all she could do was hope and pray the wind didn't pick up and burn her fields and cattle.

Squatters were the bane of her and any good rancher's existence. They wreaked havoc on land that didn't belong to them. Over the years, she'd seen their destruction. Sometimes it was merely in the waste they left behind. Other times it was the damage they did to barbed-wire fencing. Or the thieving they did.

Now, here in the middle of summer, she lived in fear that one of their campfires was going to burn out of control and scorch her land. If that happened? No doubt they'd skulk off and she'd face the consequences alone.

During the war, she'd put up with some of the vagrants, mainly because she'd been too afraid to confront them. Deserters from both sides had run rampant. Having nothing to lose, they'd preyed on women trying to survive while living essentially alone. Sometimes literally alone.

But now something had to change. She needed to grow her herd, get some to market, and build on from there. Since Bess and Jerome weren't going to help her, she had to find someone who was strong enough to take on these squatters. She couldn't do it alone. She needed a man who was tough and hard and didn't frighten easily.

She was pretty sure Thomas Baker fit the bill.

Glad that she'd made her decision, she turned away from the window and climbed into bed. She needed to rest. Come morning, she was going to hitch up Velvet, drive herself into town, and bid on the prisoner.

Closing her eyes, she prayed Thomas Baker really was everything she hoped he was.

If he wasn't, she could be making her terrible situation even worse.

3

"I FIRED FOSTER HOWELL AN HOUR AGO," SHERIFF JACKSON said to Thomas the next morning after he'd escorted Thomas into his office himself.

Thomas wasn't sure how he was supposed to reply. His back felt as if it were now home to dozens of sharp nails, each determined to make mincemeat out of the raw marks the whip had made on his skin. When he'd first opened his eyes, he'd yearned to cry out in pain.

He'd made do with allowing his cellmate to dip part of his shirt in some water and dab at his burning skin.

Soon after Bert helped him put on his shirt, Jackson had appeared at their cell's door. "Come on out, Baker," he'd said gruffly.

Then he'd led the way to his office, not even bothering to handcuff Thomas. Thomas had been surprised by that but hadn't complained. Once they were in the office, Jackson gestured for Thomas to sit as he took a fortifying sip of coffee.

But even though Jackson seemed like an upstanding man, Thomas was afraid to let down his guard. "Is Howell's firing supposed to mean something to me?"

"Maybe." As the sheriff continued to stare at Thomas over his mug, he looked increasingly disgruntled. "He whipped you like you were a blasted slave. Idiot."

Thomas agreed with him, of course, but he knew better than to disparage one of the guards. The sheriff might not think highly of Howell, but the man hadn't been a prisoner. Thomas certainly was.

"How bad are you, Baker? And don't tell me no tales. I want the truth."

"Not bad." It wasn't the truth, but it was going to take more than a few lash marks to stop him from doing everything he could to get out of jail as soon as possible.

Still looking at him skeptically, the sheriff said, "Do I need to send for Doc? I only found out what happened about two hours ago."

"You don't need to send for anyone." Especially not some doctor. He'd seen the worst of what those sawbones could do on the battlefield and wanted no part of them.

Sheriff Jackson didn't look so sure. "The back of your shirt don't look fine, but I won't push. Now, what do you want to do about today's proceedings? I gotta warn you that today might not be the best opportunity for you, son. Anyone who comes to bid wants an able worker—"

"I want to participate, sir." As long as there was the slightest chance to get hired on and out of jail, Thomas was willing to take it.

Jackson drained the last of his coffee, then set down the mug with a regretful look. "Yesterday morning I thought you might stand a chance of getting hired on, you're so able-bodied. But now?" He shook his head. "I just don't know. I should warn you there's not a lot of hope for freedom. So far, the only man who ever paid for prisoners was Kevin Oberlee, and he's gone now."

Thomas knew he wasn't much of a prize, but he had nothing to lose. "I'll take my chances."

"You sure? 'Cause the only thing you might get out of this is some food and a whole lotta cruel treatment tossed your way."

He was a man, not a child. He'd fought for the Confederacy and had been held prisoner on a forsaken island in the middle of Lake Erie. "I understand, sir."

"All right, let's do this, then." Pulling out a pair of metal handcuffs from his jacket pocket, he reached for Thomas's hands and securely cuffed them in front of his body. Then he gripped his elbow and led him out the front of the jail and into the town square.

Squinting in the sun, Thomas was surprised to see the area was fairly crowded with men, women, and children. Some looked at the cage in the middle of the square with doleful expressions. Others looked positively gleeful.

Thomas had thought nothing could ever surprise him, but it turned out he was wrong. It seemed for some people criminals garnered the same sort of lurid fascination that battlefields and human suffering did for others.

An almost carnival atmosphere prevailed. Folks were dressed in their Sunday best, chatting with each other. Laughing. One enterprising man was selling pickles from a makeshift cart. Above all of it was an air of expectation. The crowd was anticipating something out of the ordinary. Did they sense something the sheriff didn't?

Thomas stared at them, even going so far as to look several in the eye. Women tittered behind handkerchiefs and men blanched and gripped their children's hands. Through it all, Jackson kept his hand firmly on Thomas's elbow as they weaved their way through the crowd.

"It always this way, Sheriff?" Thomas asked.

"No. Maybe they heard about the whipping. Maybe they think you're something special to see. I have no idea." Jackson's voice was flat as he walked him up four steps to a pedestal of some sort. Sitting in the middle of it was a rectangular iron cage. It was tall enough for Thomas to stand upright, but barely.

It looked hot and uncomfortable and made him suddenly feel sorry for the animals carted around in the carnivals that toured the country from time to time.

Jackson sighed. "Here's what's gonna happen, Baker. I'm gonna lock you in this cage. You'll remain here for two hours or until someone makes an offer for your services."

"And until that time?"

"Until then, folks will mill around and get a good look at you. Judge Orbison will offer you up to the highest bidder."

"Until then, I wait."

"Yep. You wait. I'll be nearby, so no one should get too close. Burnside will be too. But prepare yourself, son. It ain't pleasant."

Thomas said nothing, but he was pretty sure the sheriff had just uttered a heck of an understatement. However, all he had to do was concentrate on the way his back burned and pained him—all he needed to remind himself was that some circumstances were definitely worse than others.

Since it didn't look as though anyone was about to whip him today for simply being alive, Thomas figured he could handle whatever was to come.

Jackson unlocked the cage, sent Thomas inside, then locked the barred door again.

The minute Sheriff Jackson stepped off the platform and moved to the side, the crowd inched closer from all sides. Thomas felt their disdain for him like a tangible thing. More than one person gasped at the blood that had seeped through his shirt.

Judge Orbison walked forward. Looking displeased to be out in the blazing sun in his three-piece black suit, he pulled out a spoon and clanged it against Thomas's bars.

The jarring sound, together with the vibrations the motion set off, made Thomas flinch.

At least the crowd immediately quieted.

"Citizens of Sweetwater, by now you probably know the drill. I've got a prisoner here, a Mr. . . . uh . . ." The judge turned to him. "Name, son?"

"Thomas Baker."

"Mr. Thomas Baker." As if he suddenly remembered something, the judge pulled out a sheet of paper from a vest pocket. "Ah. Here we go. This man here was once a sergeant in the CSA. He fought with honor and was captured and spent the last of the war in captivity up in Johnson's Island. By all accounts, he served bravely and was held in high esteem by one and all."

Thomas had no time to wonder where the judge had come across all that information before a thin farmer called out, "Then how come he's in jail?"

The judge glanced at his paper again. "Man couldn't pay his debts." Meeting Thomas's gaze, the judge raised an eyebrow. "That right?"

"Yes, sir." He decided to leave out the fact that the men he owed money to had been playing in a poker game.

To Thomas's dismay, the judge's account of his good character seemed a bit of a letdown for the assemblage. Perhaps they were hoping he'd done something far more dangerous or terrible.

"If he's only jailed 'cause he couldn't pay his debts, how come he was whipped?" another man asked.

"Foster Howell did that," Sheriff Jackson called out as he lit a cheroot. "He shouldn't have."

Judge Orbison motioned for Thomas to show him his back. After he took a good look at it, he frowned. "This ain't good, Jackson," he said to the sheriff, as if they were sitting in some gambling hall and talking about the weather. "Baker here might owe money, but I just received a telegram from a man about him this very morning. He's got some powerful friends. They aren't going to take it kindly when they discover how badly he's been treated while staying in our facilities."

Thomas stiffened. Who was the judge speaking of? He hadn't let anyone know he was here, especially not his friends from Johnson's Island. He looked over at the sheriff, waiting for him to ask the judge who it was. But Sheriff Jackson didn't look all that concerned.

Leaning toward him, Judge Orbison asked, "You need anything right now, son? Water maybe?"

There was no way he was going to sip water while half the town looked on. "I only need someone to offer me a job, sir."

"That would certainly fix things. We'll see what we can do." He inhaled, then turned back toward the crowd. "Alrighty. For those of you who might have forgotten, here's how our prisoner auctions work. This man here will be on display for two hours. If you have questions, deliver them to me or Sheriff Jackson." He cleared his throat. "If you are interested in hiring him on, come directly to me."

A hush fell over the crowd as more than one person approached, then turned away. After another twenty minutes passed, the square began to empty.

As the sun beat down on him, Thomas's optimism faltered. It had been a long shot, of course, but now it seemed he was doomed to spend many more nights in captivity. Even his "friends in high places"—or whoever had sent the telegram—couldn't gain him early freedom. Not merely with some good words. He wouldn't ask his friends for anything more anyway.

He passed time by staring out into the distance, much like he'd done on Johnson's Island. If he concentrated hard enough, he could imagine he was someplace else. Someplace better, more peaceful. Where his back didn't burn and he could sit down.

An hour went by.

He'd just pressed his chapped lips together and was considering asking for that sip of water when the lingering crowd parted and two rough-looking ranchers approached. Their faces were craggy from years spent out in the elements on horseback. Sharp eyes examined him as though he were livestock.

Thomas straightened and stared back. He wasn't afraid of hard work and he wasn't afraid of work-hardened men. But that didn't mean he was going to let them imagine they'd be getting a greenhorn if they freed him.

Time seemed to still. One of them nodded.

"I hope I'm not too late?" a sweet voice called out.

Immediately, everyone's focus changed. Thomas moved his head to the right and blinked.

Because there was Miss Laurel Tracey. She was moving gracefully through the crowd, dressed in a rather complicated-looking green calico and a straw bonnet with a bright-yellow ribbon threaded around its brim.

The bonnet set off her face and brown eyes. The dress was worn but in good repair. It had a bustle that emphasized her small waist.

She looked clean and fresh and perfect. Completely out of place.

Thomas tried not to stare, because, well, he was already standing in the hot sun in a cage with his back burning like the devil himself had set his pitchfork on it. The last thing he needed was to get punished for being disrespectful.

But Lord Almighty, she was a sight to see. Pretty and curvy and oh so innocent looking. She also had a little lift to her chin that said no one should make the mistake of thinking she didn't have a backbone.

Men and women moved to the side as she continued to walk toward him. Judge Orbison lifted his hat. Sheriff Jackson extinguished his cheroot and moved to her side.

"Miss Tracey," Judge Orbison said. "Afternoon."

"Sir." She smiled more brightly at the sheriff. "Will, hello."

"Miss Laurel. Good to see you," Sheriff Jackson greeted in a smooth tone, giving her a small bow. "What brings you here?" he asked, looking worried. "Are you having some kind of problem at the ranch?"

"I am, but it's nothing this man can't fix." Turning to Thomas, she smiled.

Sure he hadn't heard right, Thomas gripped two bars and leaned as close as his cage allowed.

Jackson pushed back the rim of his Stetson a couple of inches. "I understand he's been part of the crew that's been working on your fencing. Do you need them back?"

"Oh, I don't want that crew back. No offense, but I, well, I don't care for Mr. Howell's company much."

Judge Orbison stepped closer to her. "Did Foster Howell harm you, Miss Laurel?"

"Oh, no. It's just . . ." She opened her mouth and shut it with a firm shake of her head. "I don't think it matters anymore, does it? I mean, not if I'm here to hire Mr. Baker."

Thomas exhaled. Tried not to smile. Not because he wasn't pleased about what she was offering him. No, it was more like he wasn't sure if she *should* want him nearby. He was a war-worn man with next to no experience around ladies. Though he knew without a doubt that he'd never harm her, he wasn't sure if he'd always be able to hide his attraction to her.

And if he couldn't hide that, then chances were more than good she'd realize sooner or later that he wasn't necessarily the best man to have on her property.

Jackson narrowed his eyes. "Do your siblings know you're here?"

Instead of answering directly, she lifted her chin a tad bit higher. "Bess and Jerome are my stepsiblings, not my true brother and sister. Furthermore, they do know. And what they think is no concern of mine."

Jackson looked momentarily shamefaced. "Of course not. But I'm not sure you know what you're getting yourself into. This man might not be a felon, but he is no gentleman."

Miss Tracey darted another look his way. "Sir, I don't need a gentleman. I need a man willing to work hard and help me with my ranch. I also need him immediately."

It took Thomas everything he had to keep from laughing. She really did have a spark to her.

Judge Orbison seemed as though he was trying not to laugh as well. "I see," he said.

Laurel Tracey fastened her pretty eyes on the judge and said sweetly, "If I hire him, are there any stipulations?"

"You have to keep him on for one year."

She glanced Thomas's way. "And after one year, if he wants to leave or I no longer have a need for his assistance, we can end our contract?"

One of the two ranchers who had been staring at him grunted. "Hey, now," he said. "You can't just give him to her."

Jackson glared at the pair. "Judge Orbison can do whatever he likes."

After a pause Judge Orbison nodded in Miss Tracey's direction. "Yes, miss. That is how it goes."

"I see."

When she met Thomas's gaze again, he was pretty sure he flushed.

Leaving the judge and sheriff, she stepped up the first two steps of the platform. "Sir, do you remember meeting me yesterday?" she asked Thomas.

As if there was any chance that he'd forget. "Yes, miss," he replied, hating that his voice sounded a little hoarse, a little thick from nerves. "But there's no need to call me sir. Best just call me Baker, Miss Tracey. Or by my first."

"And what is that?"

"My full name is Thomas Travis Baker."

She looked about to comment on that when she seemed to notice his bloodstained shirt. She gasped as she walked around the cage to get a better look at his back. "My goodness! That's quite a scar on your neck. And, why, I do believe that is blood seeping through your shirt. What happened to you?"

"It ain't nothing to worry about, miss."

Walking back to the sheriff's side, she glared at him. "Did you do this?"

To Thomas's surprise, instead of telling her such things were none of her concern, the sheriff shook his head. "I did not, Miss Laurel."

"Then how did this happen?"

"There was some miscommunication last night in the jailhouse. It was taken care of."

Now staring at Thomas, she bit her lip.

As Thomas watched those perfect white teeth dig into the soft flesh of one plump bottom lip, he resigned himself to two things. One was that he could no more look away from her than he could get out of this cage on his own.

The second was that it was foolish to get his hopes up. After all, there was every possibility she was going to change her mind.

He didn't know her, but from what he could see, though she had a backbone, she was also a sweet, sheltered woman. She was gentle and she smelled good. She was everything he'd ever imagined a woman should be but hadn't really believed existed.

Time seemed to stand still again.

As she continued to look at him, she no doubt regretted her impulsiveness. He was dirty and smelled bad. He was standing in the middle of a cage and sweat was rolling off him like the tide at sunset.

Then, of course, there was the fact that he'd allowed himself to get whipped at all.

And even though she didn't know him from Adam, she had no reason to completely trust him. Even if she suspected he would never harm a hair on her head, that didn't mean his working at her family's ranch wouldn't have certain dangers all its own. She was liable to lose a good chunk of her reputation, and even he knew a woman could never afford to let that happen.

After staring at him so long that quite a few biddies in the crowd started whispering behind gloved hands, she seemed to come to a decision. "If I want Mr. Baker, can we take him out of there now, Judge Orbison?"

He was going to get hired on. A jolt rose up his spine as he realized his wish was about to come true.

When Miss Tracey met his gaze again, Thomas almost felt tears in his eyes.

She was the prettiest thing he'd ever laid eyes on. As far as he was concerned, heaven did exist, and it was right here in Sweetwater, Texas, in the form of one rather tall, buxom, blond-haired beauty with wide-set brown eyes.

4

As her question rang through the air, a collective sigh tore through the crowd.

Laurel wasn't sure if it was because everyone surrounding them agreed with her assessment or if they were eager to see her regret the consequences of her decision. Chances were good that either might be the case.

It didn't matter much to her either way. She'd ceased to care too much about everyone else's opinions. Verbal chatter didn't help a woman bury her relatives or take care of twenty head of cattle alone in the dead of winter.

As the seconds passed, she steadfastly did her best to look as if she were oblivious to the man in the cage who was staring at her in a bold way. Instead, she focused on the men standing on either side of her who could grant her wish.

Both of them looked a little surprised, but not completely dismayed.

"You sure about this, Miss Laurel?" Sheriff Jackson asked at last.

"I am. Now, it's hot, and I imagine the wounds on Mr. Baker's back are festering. I think it's time he got out of that cage. Don't you?"

Fingering the last of his cheroot, the sheriff said, "I'm talking about you hiring this man. Though he ain't known to be violent, he still isn't one for gentle company."

"I need a man to help me fight those squatters on my property. I need a man to work hard, Will. Not sip tea with me."

Judge Orbison's lips twitched. "Point taken."

Excitement bubbled up inside her. They were taking her seriously, and she was going to get the help she needed. "So may we release him now?"

"Yes. Well, maybe. We're supposed to wait another hour, in case someone else offers for him," the judge said doubtfully. "That's how we've always done things in the past."

It was obviously time to push a little harder. "I could be wrong. After all, I'm only a lone woman used to living on a ranch. But waiting a whole other hour seems kind of hard on everyone, don't you think? Surely you have many more pressing things to do than keep a caged man in the hot sun?"

As she'd hoped, the judge straightened his shoulders. "Indeed, I do."

"Then perhaps you could take care of things right now and move on with your day?"

After glancing over her head at the prisoner, Judge Orbison lowered his voice. "Miss Tracey, I know you need help. But . . . are you sure about this? Once this is done, it's done. Furthermore, I can't help but wonder if your parents would have supported this plan."

It was a legitimate question, one she should be pondering for hours, or at least a whole lot longer than a mere five or six minutes.

But something—something deep in her heart—was telling her to act now and to act quickly. It was as if she no longer had a choice.

Or maybe it was simply that she didn't have a decision to make. She wanted this man out of the cage. "While I agree that my parents wouldn't have necessarily wanted me to hire a prisoner, I don't believe they could have foreseen what my circumstances were going to be like. The truth is that I am sure, sir. In fact, I don't believe I've ever been more sure of anything in my life."

At last the judge inclined his head. "Well then, it looks like you've got a new ranch hand, Miss Tracey." Turning to the sheriff, he said, "Release him, Will. I need to get out of this blasted heat."

Laurel smiled at the judge as the sheriff pulled out a ring of keys. "Thank you, Judge Orbison."

"You're welcome. If it means anything, I'm plumb relieved he's getting out of here."

"I am as well." The moment the words left her mouth, she could practically feel the prisoner's hot gaze settle on her like a hovering bee. It was a tangible thing—so real, Laurel knew she wasn't imagining it.

She supposed she didn't blame Mr. Baker. She was talking about him as if he weren't right there, witnessing her transaction.

She hoped he wasn't scowling at her.

She didn't dare look at him. Not because she feared him. No, it was more that she feared what he'd see if he looked at her.

⚬⚬⚬

Inside his cage, Thomas swallowed hard. He wasn't real sure if he was eager to be a woman's ranch hand, even if that woman was Laurel Tracey. But he was definitely up to the task. He needed to get out of jail like he needed to breathe. Though he had few choices about what to do with his life next, most of them were a far sight worse than helping a woman in need for one full year.

His mother would've been proud of him for doing that. Well, he liked to think that such a thing was possible.

He was drawn out of his thoughts when the hefty judge turned and gently bent over Miss Tracey's hand.

"It's been real good working with you, Miss Laurel." Raising his voice, Judge Orbison said, "Jackson, bring him to my office. I'll prepare the paperwork and then he and Miss Tracey can get on their way."

"Yes, sir," the sheriff said.

Before the judge left, he turned to Thomas. Even though he was a good four inches shorter and was also standing four steps below the platform, the judge somehow managed to sound like he was talking down to Thomas.

"You've just been given the opportunity of a lifetime, Baker," he intoned. "Miss Tracey is a lady and gently bred. You'd best remember to give her the respect she deserves. If not, I don't even want to think about what could happen to you."

"Of course," Thomas said.

"Work hard and keep your head down." Hardening his voice, the judge whispered, "Squatters can be big trouble. Don't lower your guard."

"I won't, sir," he answered in the same tone of voice he used to answer Captain Monroe.

"Good. Hope it works out," the judge said before turning and walking away.

After Judge Orbison disappeared into his offices, Sheriff Jackson ascended the steps and placed his hand on the bars of the cage. Then he turned around and called out, "Alrighty, everyone. It's time to settle down and move on. The show's over. Our prisoner will now be working for Miss Tracey." Then he turned to his guard.

"Ollie, escort Miss Tracey to the judge's office. I'll bring the prisoner along presently."

"Yes, sir," Ollie said. Holding out an elbow, he smiled at her. "Let's go, Miss Tracey."

"Thank you," she whispered. "Please, just give me one moment."

Then, to Thomas's surprise, she walked up the steps to his cage.

Motionless, he stared at her. Her scent—lavender and magnolia and clean, fresh woman—caught hold of him and held him in its grip. It was a mesmerizing thing, and so beautiful he feared she could see its effect on his face.

"I'm glad this worked out, Mr. Baker," she said softly. "I promise that I'll do my best to be a good boss."

How did a man respond to that? Void of words, he nodded.

She smiled before walking back down the steps and taking Ollie's extended arm.

Not wanting to get caught looking after her backside, Thomas deliberately kept his expression empty and his eyes looking straight forward.

As his cage door opened and Sheriff Jackson grabbed his elbow, the sheriff muttered under his breath, "I don't know what you've ever done to be worthy of this opportunity, but you are currently the luckiest dog I know."

Since Thomas reckoned no reply was expected, he concentrated on negotiating the narrow steps with his still sore joints.

Most of the crowd had moved away, giving him and the sheriff a bit more room to walk back to the jailhouse than when they had approached the square.

When they were about halfway there, Sheriff Jackson spoke again. "Miss Laurel is about the sweetest girl I've ever met." Hardening his voice, he said, "Orbison wasn't lying. No one will go easy on you if she comes to any harm in your company."

"And they shouldn't." Afraid he wouldn't get another chance

to ask someone who might know, Thomas asked, "How come she never married?"

When the man inhaled, Thomas called himself ten times the fool. There went his mouth again. He was still in shackles but was asking personal questions about the lady who'd just purchased his freedom?

"Don't know," the sheriff said as he drew in another breath. "I like you, Baker. More than that, I respect the man who telegraphed the judge about your character. If Captain Monroe says you don't belong in a cell, you don't."

Thomas had no idea how Devin Monroe even knew he was in jail, but his reaching out didn't surprise him. "Thank you."

"That said, don't you ever forget something. You hurt one hair on Laurel Tracey's head, you'll get back in here so fast you won't know what hit you. And I'll make sure you don't see the light of day for months."

"Understood."

Thomas had no idea why a woman like her needed to hire on a man like him, why she didn't already have a man in her life. But he did know he'd do everything in his power to make sure she didn't regret her decision.

Besides his freedom from jail, she'd given him something he'd pretty much lost when he was captured and sent up to Johnson's Island prison—his self-worth. His new friends there had helped him see himself in new ways, but being thrown into Sweetwater jail, subjected to the whims of a man like Foster Howell, had set him back.

The return of his self-worth felt awkward and strange. But he was fairly sure it would, over time, fit him like a glove.

5

JUDGE ORBISON'S OFFICE WAS JUST ON THE OTHER SIDE OF the town square. But as Laurel and Ollie walked through the throng of people, it felt like one of the longest walks of her life. She felt weighed down by everyone's judgmental looks.

She also couldn't help but acknowledge that she'd just become part of the town's latest fodder for gossip. Chances were good that in mere hours, her formerly good reputation was going to become tarnished beyond repair.

"You're really going to go through with it, Miss Tracey?" Ollie asked after she'd barely taken four steps.

"I am."

"That man, he ain't what I'd call respectable. Like I told you before, might even be a bit dangerous."

Considering she'd just purchased Mr. Baker from a cage, Laurel figured Ollie's summation was a bit of an understatement. But instead of mentioning that, she kept her silence.

Looking down at his scuffed boots, the guard kicked at the red dirt underfoot. "I know we don't have much to say to each other," he mumbled, "but if you need something, or if you start to worry about your safety, come find me. I'll take care of him."

"I, uh . . . thank you, Ollie."

Just as he finally lifted his chin and smiled at her, another man moved to her other side. "I'll escort her the rest of the way, Burnside," he said.

Laurel inwardly sighed. The very last person she needed to talk to at the moment was Landon Marshall.

Ollie frowned up at him. "I can't let you speak with Miss Tracey right now, Mr. Marshall."

"Sure you can," Landon countered easily. "You know neither Judge Orbison nor Sheriff Jackson is going to have a problem with me escorting Miss Laurel."

"Maybe not. But still—"

"It's all right, Ollie," Laurel interjected quickly. Even though he had failed to recognize the needs of the men on the chain gang on a hot day, he was too kind to have to deal with the ego that was Landon Marshall.

My, how she wished he hadn't become so possessive.

"I'll walk the rest of the way with Mr. Marshall."

Though he didn't look happy about it, Ollie stepped away. "As you wish, Miss Tracey."

The moment Ollie turned away, Landon leaned close and gripped her elbow. "Laurel, tell me I didn't just see you purchase a convict."

"I didn't purchase anyone, Landon. I hired him to help me around the ranch."

"That's basically the same thing."

"Not exactly. Sergeant Baker is going to work for me for one year, then be on his way."

"Sergeant? He isn't a soldier any longer, Laurel. Now he's nothing. Don't forget, the war is over."

"I haven't forgotten." They were all still dealing with the war's effects, though, and likely would for some time. She was also fighting her own personal war to keep her land—and probably cattle too—safe from squatters and determined buyers.

Pulling her away from the judge's quarters, Landon hardened his expression. "I don't know what's gotten into you lately, but it is rather troubling. I'm beginning to worry for your emotional state."

She pulled her elbow out of his grip. "I beg your pardon?"

"You know what I'm talking about. You've been making a slew of poor decisions lately. Decisions that make no sense. This one is surely the worst of them all."

Before the war, she had wondered if she could love Landon one day. Their families were friendly neighbors and spent some time together. She knew some in town assumed they would marry when Landon returned from his service. But four months ago, after giving the possibility of a true relationship a fair chance, she'd told Landon she didn't welcome his suit and that she'd take it as a favor if he stopped calling on her. He hadn't taken her rejection well.

She supposed he had every reason to feel that way. His family was wealthy, and now that his father was deceased, he not only owned a great deal of land but was responsible for his mother and sister. He'd also fought in the war for a whole year. He'd been so brave that she'd heard he'd even been responsible for rescuing a group of unfortunate women from a burning building.

Most everyone said he fought with valor too.

In addition, he was handsome, blessed with golden-blond hair, bright-green eyes, and a strong jaw. He was everything most girls in Sweetwater—or Fort Worth, for that matter—would ever dream about having in a suitor or a husband.

Just not her.

Men like him had never appealed to her. Especially after he returned from the war, he was too confident, too full of himself, and too profuse with his compliments. He also had the unfortunate habit of sharing his viewpoints loudly and with force.

Only his parents' friendship with hers prevented her from severing their friendship.

"I don't believe I'm making a mistake, Landon," she said quietly.

"If you're wrong, you could be dead." Lowering his voice, he added in a dark tone, "That man . . . why, he could murder you in your sleep."

She shivered. "He's not a murderer." Aware that their heated conversation was beginning to garner attention, she said, "Now, I really must be going."

Landon paid her no mind. "Laurel, sweetheart, you are so naïve. Of course he's a murderer. I'm sure he killed during the war."

The fierce thread of disdain in his voice struck her as strange. Eyeing him curiously, she asked, "Didn't you? I thought all men did such things on the battlefield." Noticing he looked increasingly uncomfortable, she added, "I thought you were in several battles. Did you not fight the enemy then?"

"That was different."

"How so?"

"I'm not about to taint your ears with tales from the battlefield," he replied, his voice hard. "All you need to know is that I was a gentleman during the war. I fought with honor."

"But Mr. Baker didn't? How can that be?"

"Obviously this isn't a subject you are ready to discuss rationally. It isn't the right time or place either."

"You are right about that," she said before she could stop herself. Oh, it was certainly discomfiting how she'd started to become so used to speaking her mind. Discomfiting but exciting too. After spending most of her life holding her tongue and letting men tell her what to do, she was learning to be more like her mother had become during the war, to voice her opinion. Even make decisions on her own, like the one she'd made today. It made her feel stronger. She didn't want Landon's help. She didn't need to marry someone she didn't love to save her ranch.

"Now, I really must go, Landon. Judge Orbison is going to wonder where I am."

"I'll come check on you in a few days," he blurted. "That man needs to know you are not alone in the world."

"That is so kind of you," she said in a slightly exaggerated sweet tone before rushing away.

But just as she placed her hand on the judge's office doorknob, Geneva Forte pushed her way through the crowd.

"This is so exciting, Laurel. You buying a man is surely the most exciting thing that's happened in weeks, if not months."

Laurel couldn't help but agree even if Geneva, like Landon, had misunderstood what she'd done. However, unlike Landon's comments, Geneva's prattle was not mean-spirited. Just a tad vacuous. "It's taken me by surprise too."

"Are you nervous about having him on your property?"

She stopped to think about it. By all rights, Laurel knew she should be shaking in her shoes. But instead of feeling nervous, she felt completely at peace with her decision. She needed Mr. Baker's help, and for some reason she trusted him to give it. "No, I'm not nervous at all."

Looking eager, Geneva leaned closer. "Can I meet him one day soon? I promise I'll be everything proper."

"He's coming to work for me, Geneva. He needs to look after cattle and mend fences. You probably won't even see him."

Her blue eyes batted. "But can I?"

Laurel wasn't sure why, but everything in her body was rejecting Geneva's question. She didn't want the woman flirting with the sergeant or gazing at him too long, or even making him uncomfortable. Hadn't he already been through too much?

"I'm sorry, but I'd rather you not visit anytime soon."

"Sure?"

"Maybe you can in a few months." She smiled to ease the rejection. "Now, I need to go," Laurel said as she put her hand on the knob. "But, hey, Genie?"

"Yeah?"

"Help me with Landon, would you, please? Go smile at him or something. The last thing I want to tackle right now is him and his misplaced attempt to protect me."

As Laurel had hoped, her girlfriend looked excited about the task. With a bright smile, she turned toward Landon, who was still lurking nearby, watching Laurel with a cool expression.

When Landon's gaze skittered from Laurel to Geneva, her girlfriend started walking in his direction in a slow glide. It was her trademark move. Impossible for most women to accomplish anywhere but on a ballroom floor, Geneva had mastered effortlessly strolling across any surface by the time she was fourteen.

Finally opening the door, Laurel smiled to herself. Even Landon Marshall would be no match for that.

⚬⚬⚬

An hour later, standing beside the very tall Thomas Baker, Laurel wondered if she had overestimated her gumption.

He was a large man. Taller and more filled out than he'd looked when he was cooped up in a cage or lined up with other men against her fence. It seemed Mr. Baker also had an air about him that she couldn't quite put her finger on. It wasn't aggressive, but she sensed he would never be a passive kind of man either. Instead, he appeared to be tightly wound and watchful. Almost as if he had all kinds of thoughts and ideas floating just under the surface.

This new air about him might also have something to do with his appearance. He was no longer dirty, no longer wearing a bloodstained shirt and ill-fitting trousers.

Instead, he was outfitted in all new clothes, from his leather boots to his snug-fitting denims to his crisp white shirt and tan Stetson.

In short, he looked extremely dashing. So fine and handsome that every woman they passed was going to take a second and third look at him. So fine that Laurel was going to wonder how she'd ever felt sorry for him.

After they both signed the papers Judge Orbison prepared, they had walked silently through town, him carrying a small bag with, she supposed, all his earthly possessions. Eyes seemed to follow them from every window and doorway. She wondered if most everyone understood her reasons for hiring a convict or was simply shocked.

She imagined it was a little of both.

Now they were standing by her buggy and her horse, Velvet, and she wasn't sure what to do. Thomas was capable and powerful. Years ago, her father and brother had looked out for her. They'd taught her to expect all men to treat her with care. But the war had certainly changed things. She'd learned that not all men respected women. She'd also learned not to count on any help, not even from her stepbrother, Jerome. And she didn't want help from Landon.

But she was Thomas Baker's employer. And though he was

certainly dashing, he was no gentleman. Surely that meant she should drive the buggy?

She worried her bottom lip.

Was it even right for her to trust him? What if she gave him the reins, only to be thrown off the buggy so he could be on his way? He had broken the law, after all. She should never forget that.

After no doubt watching her internal debate for a few moments, Mr. Baker cleared his throat. "Miss Tracey?"

She popped up her chin. Looking into his eyes, she realized that was a mistake and shifted her gaze to stare just to the right of him instead. "Uh, yes?"

"I know we're standing on the street and everything, but it occurs to me this might be a good time to clear up a few things."

Forcing herself to look him directly in the eye, she said, "What would you like to clear up?"

Approval sure and solid slid into his expression before he appeared to collect himself. Clasping his hands behind his back, he took a deep breath and looked just to the right of her. "Well, first thing, what would you like me to call you? I heard the judge and sheriff call you Laurel. May I call you Miss Laurel? Or would you prefer Miss Tracey?"

His voice was low and soft. She knew he was speaking gently to her on purpose. "Miss . . ." She shook her head to clear it. Suddenly she didn't want even that barrier between them. "I mean, Laurel would be just fine."

His eyes settled on hers. "I don't think so, miss. Seeing as how I work for you, it wouldn't be right."

She realized he had a point, though she felt a bit disconcerted by the way he was leading the conversation. "Miss Laurel should do as well as anything. Now, should I call you Mr. Baker?"

To her shock, he chuckled. "Definitely not. I've never been

called that in my life and I don't aim to start now. In the army, I was a sergeant, Sergeant Baker. But since I'm not in the military any longer, I reckon either Baker or Thomas will do."

She had noticed something—a note of pride in his voice when he talked about the army. It wasn't the vague, prideful way Landon had talked about his year in the service.

No, Thomas Baker's military career had meant something to him. Meant a lot to him. For some reason, that made her feel good. Everyone needed to have some pride in their life. "I think, if you don't mind, I'll simply call you Sergeant."

Doubt clouded his eyes. "I don't know . . ."

"I do. You were a sergeant, right? I mean, that's not a lie?"

"No, miss. That is not a lie."

"Then Sergeant you will be, at least for now."

His lips twitched, as if he admired her spunk and was caught off guard by it all at the same time. "Yes, miss."

"Are we settled now, Sergeant?"

"Not exactly." Pulling back his shoulders even more, he continued. "I know you don't have any reason to trust a word I say, but I swear to you I will never harm you. Never. I'll even swear it on a stack of Bibles if you want."

She was shocked by his offer, but pleased. "There is no need for that. I believe you."

"You do?"

"I wouldn't have hired you today if I didn't trust you."

Slowly a smile—a rather cocky smile—appeared on his lips. "I'm glad we got that cleared up. Therefore, Miss Laurel, would you be so kind as to allow me to help you into your buggy? Then I will drive you home."

"I trust you actually do know how to handle a carriage?"

"Of course I do."

"Take care with Velvet too. She's a little skittish and requires a tender touch."

"You got me from prison, but I wasn't born there, Miss Laurel," he drawled. "I'll take care with your horse."

She felt herself flush. Realizing it was time to rectify the conversation, she nodded. "Thank you, Sergeant. Having you drive would be helpful."

"Yes, miss." Looking like he was attempting to conceal a smile, he held out a hand. "Miss Laurel?"

Gingerly, she placed her gloved hand in his hand, then started when he carefully placed his other hand on her waist to steady her ascent. But just as quickly, his hand pulled away. She decided to remain facing forward as he got in beside her, took hold of the reins, and flicked them lightly.

Velvet started forward.

After watching him for a bit and realizing he had spoken the truth, that he could control a horse and buggy easily, she exhaled.

He grinned. "Were you worried about my skills?"

"A little," she allowed.

"Only a little?"

"Maybe a bit more than that. I'm glad you didn't lie to me. It's easier to know the truth about things."

"I would have to agree with you about that. The truth always helps, I think." After a minute or so, he added, "I'm grateful you came out today. If it weren't for you, I'd be back behind bars or waiting for one of the men in the crowd to hire me on."

She shivered. "Most of the men who were gathering around you don't have the best of reputations."

One of his brows lifted. "Pointing out the obvious, I don't either."

Laurel knew she should agree, but something about this

man seemed different. She didn't think her intuition was that far off. "You seemed polite enough when you were on the prison workforce."

"Didn't have much choice."

"You might not have had a choice, but I would venture to say you didn't need much incentive to be respectful to me."

"No, miss, I did not," he said with a low drawl. "But I'd be lying now if I didn't point out that there wasn't a man there who didn't appreciate your offer of water."

"It was nothing."

"It was more than that. Prison—and war, for that matter—doesn't give a man much opportunity to feel such kindness. It was a reminder that we are still men and worthy of consideration."

His talk embarrassed her, especially since she had a terrible suspicion that her offer of water had somehow resulted in the lashes he received across his back.

"Sergeant?"

"Yes?"

She opened her mouth to ask about that whipping but chickened out. Instead, she asked a more obvious question. "How did you get your new clothes and boots? Is that customary?"

For the first time since they'd started their conversation, Thomas looked ill at ease. "No. They were a gift."

"From Judge Orbison?"

"Not exactly."

Though it wasn't technically her business, she prodded. "Then from whom?"

Still not looking her way, he said, "As I told you, I served in the Confederacy. I served under a captain and a major I thought the world of. I respected them. I also became friends with them and several others. We're scattered around the state now, but somehow the captain heard I was about to be eligible for release. He arranged for these items to be available. Since I didn't want to be around you looking like I did, I accepted his gift."

She had never heard of such a thing. "Those must be quite some friends."

The lines around his eyes relaxed. "They are."

"Why didn't one of them simply come get you? They could have lied and said you would work for them."

"First of all, I still don't know how the captain knew where I was. I didn't want any of them to know I was in jail. I got in trouble because I was gambling in a high-stakes poker game I couldn't afford. I'm not proud of that." He shrugged. "Then, too, there's the law. They couldn't have gotten me out no matter how hard they tried. And last, I would never allow any of them to pay for my release."

She thought about that. Thought about how hard it must have been for him to wait and have faith that somehow, some way, he would be freed. Visions of him sitting in a dark cell, hurting and alone, struck her hard.

"Sergeant, uh, how is your back?"

"I'll be fine."

"That scar on your neck—"

"That happened a good long time ago. It doesn't hurt."

She noticed he didn't say his back didn't hurt. "When we get to the ranch, I'll tend to your back. I made some ointment that works wonders for burns and cuts. I'll put some of that on it."

He stiffened. "That ain't necessary."

Laurel blinked at his harsh tone. "You might not know this, but we had our fair share of soldiers come through during the war. Some were grievously injured, and I tended quite a few. I promise there is little I have not seen."

"No offense, but I'm not the kind of man who would want his lady boss to be fussing over a couple of bumps and bruises on his bare skin."

She knew the wounds on his back were far worse than mere bumps or bruises. But he was sitting so stoically, she also knew it would be a mistake to push. "If your pain gets worse, will you let me know?"

"I'll let you know," he said shortly, but his voice was clipped. "You didn't bring me on to tend over me, miss. I'm going to work for you."

She nodded. He had a point. She needed to remember that and put the ranch first. Keeping it going was what counted. That was what she needed to care about. Not her loneliness. Not the way this man looked like he needed a friend as much as she did. All that mattered was the land.

Nothing else.

When they arrived at the ranch, Jerome and Bess darted out the door as though they'd been watching for her with bated breath.

Bess was dressed in a pale-pink dress and her hair was arranged in ringlets. She looked like she was about to go to a dance. Jerome was just as dressed up. Why they were outfitted the way they were, Laurel couldn't imagine.

"Laurel, it took you long enough," Jerome called out. "Bess and I have been extremely ill at ease and inconvenienced. In fact—"

Whatever he was about to add vanished as he suddenly realized she wasn't alone.

Bess placed a hand to her lips and coughed delicately. Laurel wasn't sure if she was doing that because she was stunned or intrigued.

Thomas stared at them curiously before pulling on Velvet's

reins and setting the brake in the buggy. Just as Laurel was about to dismount, he placed a hand on her arm. "Wait for me," he said.

She was surprised by his instruction—and rather amused by the way Bess's eyes had widened. She waited.

After Thomas walked around to her side, he held out a hand. Just as she was about to place her hand in his, he reached for her waist and swung her down from the seat.

Unable to help herself, she set her hands on his shoulders and felt a small cluster of butterflies fluttering in her stomach.

"Thank you," she whispered.

"It was my pleasure." His gaze was suspiciously warm.

Embarrassed for imagining something that wasn't there, she turned to Bess and Jerome, who were gaping at Mr. Baker and her as though they were part of a carnival show.

Seeking to quiet her nerves, Laurel gestured to their outfits. "You two look fetching. Where are you off to?"

Bess glared at the man beside Laurel. "We wanted to go into town. Now we're late."

"For what? I'm not aware of any parties going on today."

Jerome glared as well. "I had no idea you were going to be so long."

"It couldn't be helped." They were intently staring at her new employee. Seeing that they were hardly listening, and assuming they were only going to town to spend the bit of money she could spare for them each week, she said, "Bess and Jerome, this is Sergeant Thomas Baker. I just hired him on to work here. Sergeant, these are my stepsiblings, Bess and Jerome Vance."

Jerome stepped in front of his sister as if he was guarding her. "Where did he come from?"

Laurel was curious as to why he asked her. After all, she'd told Bess what she was going to do. Had she kept that information to herself? "Well, Sheriff Jackson sometimes allows men who have served time to be hired on."

Her stepbrother blinked. "Wait a minute. You were here yesterday, weren't you? On the prison detail."

Before Laurel could reply, Mr. Baker stepped forward, almost mirroring Jerome's stance. "I was. Miss Laurel has just hired me for one year."

Ignoring him, Jerome turned to Laurel. "And they told you he would be safe? I'm sure they would say anything to get him off their hands." He scanned her body as if she were a fallen woman. "Furthermore, I am shocked it seems you will do just about anything to ensure that you'll fall into this man's arms."

The sergeant stiffened. Thinking he was about to say something rash, Laurel stepped a little closer to his side. "I'm sure we'll all get along just fine," she declared. "We simply need to give it time."

Feeling panicked at their continuing stares, Laurel continued, "Listen, we need Sergeant Baker's help. He's strong, and smart too. He's not only going to help with the work, but he's going to help watch the squatters. Maybe he'll even be able to help us save the ranch."

"Save the ranch? We need to be done with it." Jerome frowned. "Laurel, you are overstepping yourself."

"You know I'm not."

"I just don't know what to think about this," Bess said. Her eyes looking like a wounded doe's, she lowered her voice in a dramatic way. "We'll be at his mercy."

Jerome nodded. "This is true. Why, this . . . this prisoner could attack Bess in her sleep."

She nodded. "I could be violated."

Laurel flushed in embarrassment. What must Mr. Baker think?

"I will not be attacking anyone, miss," Thomas murmured.

"You might," Bess said. "I've heard men can't always help themselves."

"I will."

"Let's believe him," Laurel said quickly. "It's the Christian thing to do."

"We cannot believe a thing he says. He's going to say whatever he needs to so he can stay here," Jerome sputtered. "While it may be true that you have nothing to worry about, Bess is another story. Everyone in the area knows how attractive Bess is."

Laurel felt like sinking into the dry Texas dirt right then and there.

But after glancing her way, Mr. Baker asked, "Why does she have nothing to worry about?"

"Because of her looks," Bess blurted. "She's . . . well, she's fat."

Then, to Laurel's dismay, the sergeant grinned. His smile lit up his face, and suddenly he didn't look so innocent. "Miss Laurel is a great many things, but fat ain't one of them. Truth is, I've yet to see a prettier female."

"Sergeant," she hissed under her breath. "Your words are not helping."

"Beg your pardon, miss. Though many a time I've said too much at all the wrong times, I don't believe this is one of them. I'm speaking the truth."

Bess gasped. Jerome glared.

And Laurel? Why, she had no idea what to say.

Her new worker seemed to have a true gift for stealing her breath and taking her by surprise.

6

As the sun marched higher in the summer sky, Taylor Orr shifted positions from his spot under the rock overhang.

Dang, but it was hot. He didn't know how these Texans could take this summertime heat. He felt as if the sun were blazing a trail across his face and hands. He surely had the sunburn to prove it.

Now, as he bided his time until dark, he fingered his view-finder. It gave him a good sense of what was happening on the Tracey property.

What he'd just witnessed was unusual and unwelcome.

Soon after he watched Laurel hire on that prisoner, he'd high-tailed it back to his hideout. This rock overhang was a mere half mile from an abandoned barn where he kept his horse.

Now that he'd seen the man escort her onto the property, Taylor was coming to terms with the fact that the situation here had changed. No longer was Laurel Tracey at his mercy or living essentially alone on her property. She'd gone and hired herself a man who looked like he was neither averse to fighting nor averse to shooting anyone in his way.

Taylor would bet good money that the man had served well during the war, too, and hadn't forgotten much in the way of being brave and forthright. From the moment he had helped

Laurel alight from her buggy, he'd been looking around the area as though he was used to ferreting out any number of threats.

And when he wasn't doing that, he was gazing at Laurel. Even through his telescope Taylor could see the man had an interest in her.

If the look he'd seen the man give Laurel was any indication, he wasn't planning to just work his year and then leave the area.

No, Taylor had been in love once, and he remembered feeling that same sense of ownership that had shone in the convict's eyes. There was something between him and Laurel Tracey. This man wasn't going to give up her or her property without a fight.

And that, unfortunately, was a stinkin' shame. He was sick of being on this job. He'd been watching and waiting for weeks now. Waiting for his boss to say it was time to make a move. He was sick of sweating, and really sick of the fire ants that burned when they bit and the spiders that taunted him when they came out at night.

He needed to get back to Chicago. Chicago was cooler and more crowded. He knew how things worked there and didn't have to skulk around like a dang coyote.

The sooner he got this job done, the sooner he could go back and claim the life he'd lost because of his debts. He could go back to courting Dara. If she'd still have him after everything he'd put her through.

Well, she'd take him back if she never found out what he was doing here in the sticks outside of Fort Worth.

Thinking of the way she would no doubt look at him if she knew, Taylor felt a rush of bile scorch the back of his throat. What he was doing was a sin. He'd never been an especially faithful man, but he didn't think a man had to be God-fearing to be ashamed of the things he had done.

Looking at the kerosene he'd given the calf, Taylor shuddered. After the war, he'd never imagined he'd have a weak stomach for much. Killing good and healthy livestock didn't sit well with him.

It made him feel sick inside.

Poisoning cattle was nothing to be proud of. But it had been the only method he could think of that would do the trick. It was his job to do everything he possibly could to encourage Laurel Tracey to sell her land. The man who paid him to do anything and everything to get her to move hadn't been joking. Taylor knew, because he'd seen firsthand how the man dealt with anyone who got in his way.

If Taylor failed, no apology would be necessary. Instead, he'd pay for his mistakes with either a bullet in his head or a noose around his neck.

In his more desperate moments, he'd actually debated which way would be a better, less painful death.

But what was done was done.

As the first cool breeze of the day passed over him, Taylor slapped his hand on his thigh. His boss somehow knew Laurel Tracey planned to raise up her herd, make her ranch profitable. He had his own reasons for fighting that. But Taylor had no good reason to be even thinking about this woman or the people in her life in such a personal way. That would only create sleepless nights, and he already had those in spades. Besides, his boss didn't pay good money for bleeding hearts.

Getting to his feet, Taylor stepped out into the broad sunlight again.

Standing up straight and tall, he raised his face to the burning rays. As he felt them heat his skin, he figured remembering his boss's violent ways was all the encouragement he needed to continue to do what he had to do.

After he hid the kerosene container, he was going to get his horse and go back into town. He would continue to play his role—the not-too-smart greenhorn carpetbagger traveling through Sweetwater—for a couple more days. He'd play poker poorly and not hold his liquor well.

He'd also report to his boss and share what he'd done. And what he was going to do next.

God willing, then he'd hear Miss Tracey was getting desperate. He'd get paid and could go back to Chicago. He didn't need to be in Sweetwater and watch her sell her land to the man who was going to use her misfortune for his gain.

No, he would simply be back in Chicago and Dara's good graces. He could use his ill-gotten money toward paying off the ruthless men he'd borrowed from. And when those debts were resolved, he could return to Dara and she'd be proud of him.

Then he would do his best to be the man she believed him to be. He just hoped he remembered how to be that man. It had been a long time since he'd had much of an occasion to try to make himself into someone worthy.

Scurrying back to the horse, he pretended to think such a thing was even possible.

Pretended to believe a man really could sell his soul to the devil in exchange for mending a few broken dreams.

Pretended to imagine that the man who'd hired him was going to make good on his promises and pay him.

Pretended that he even had a future.

For a moment, a vision flashed in his head. He was sitting on a sofa, his feet propped up on a table, with a dog at his feet. Dara was sitting beside him, chattering about whatever women chattered on about. And his eyes were at half-mast as he pretended to listen.

It was a good dream. Real nice. He'd gotten really good at pretending too. Otherwise, the reality of his life was too harsh to contemplate.

Because no man lived long doing the things he'd done.

It simply wasn't possible.

7

STANDING THERE IN THE HOT SUN NEXT TO A HORSE AND buggy, facing Laurel Tracey's obnoxious stepsiblings, Thomas Baker realized he was a fool.

He was a headstrong idiot who still hadn't learned to keep his mouth shut. Not even when he should be doing nothing but giving thanks that he was standing in the hot sun instead of wasting away in a dark prison cell. One would think his time spent at Johnson's Island would have taught him that at the very least.

Truly, if his captain were standing in the vicinity, he would backhand him upside the head.

It would be no less than he deserved too. Men didn't go around saying such things to gently bred women. They most certainly did not speak of the female form and attributes in mixed company. He hadn't even needed the officers at the camp to teach him that lesson.

Of course, if he was being completely truthful, he didn't deserve all the blame. The problem was partly Miss Laurel's doing. The Lord had been generous with his gifts to her. Actually, she had a whole plethora of attributes that most of the male population would find difficult to ignore.

She was well shaped and soft looking. Beautiful, with golden hair and light-brown eyes that seemed to reveal every emotion.

She was also very sweet. And good. She was . . . Laurel.

All of it was pretty much impossible for a man like him not to notice.

And he would have been ashamed to call himself a man if he hadn't done anything to come to her defense. Why, the moment Thomas saw her flush in embarrassment, he knew he had to put her stepbrother in his place. Well, actually, he'd been tempted to slam Jerome against the door and keep his hand on the man's throat until he promised he would apologize to her.

So he'd been right to help her out. It was just that, well . . . he probably should not have done it quite so heatedly. He'd just made an awkward situation even worse.

As the silence pulled taut between the four of them, he heard Laurel's faint breathing. Glancing at her, he noticed her cheeks were rosy pink. He'd caused that. He'd embarrassed her something awful.

Thomas was about to apologize, to say whatever he could to convince his new boss he was not completely uncivilized when Jerome lifted his chin. "That little speech confirms my worries, Laurel. Obviously this man is not fit for decent company."

"I'm fit for anyone's company," Thomas bit out. Except, perhaps, the company of a good woman like Laurel.

Jerome's eyes flared again. "Laurel, if . . . if this *prisoner* stays, I'll have no choice but to take Bess out of harm's way. She's far too delicate to be near a man of his reputation."

Laurel gasped. "Surely you are overreacting."

"Not in the slightest." Folding his arms across his chest, Jerome continued, "If he stays, we're going."

Thomas forced himself to prepare to be shuttled back into that buggy. It was no less than he deserved. He'd been too bold and brash, and now he was going to be forced to deal with the consequences. No doubt Laurel was seconds away from sending him back to his corner cell in the town jail. Either she'd send her stepsiblings for Sheriff Jackson or she'd take him back there herself.

And he knew he would do whatever she wanted without a fight.

He deserved it. He'd soon have untold hours to contemplate the benefits of holding his tongue.

As the tension in the air heated like the noonday sun, Laurel sighed. "Sergeant Baker can't leave. I made my promise."

"Promises don't count when they're given to someone like him," Bess said. "He doesn't matter."

Thomas stiffened but kept his mouth shut. Bess wasn't completely wrong.

"Of course he matters," Laurel said, her voice full of righteousness. "He is a prisoner no more. He's my employee now. What's done is done."

"You are going to refuse me?" Jerome said.

"There is nothing to refuse. We need the help and Sergeant Baker is a good worker. I already signed a paper that said I'd pay him for the next year."

Bess sputtered, "You're going to spend our money on his wages?"

"Well, of course. He's not a slave."

As her relatives looked at her as though she'd slapped them hard in the face, a transformation came over his boss.

Stepping forward, she reached out to both of them. "Jerome, Bess," she began softly, "I know my bringing Sergeant Baker here isn't what you expected. But please don't do anything so hasty. I feel certain that once you get used to the idea, you'll be glad of the help. We're family, and we've already lost so much. I don't want to lose you too."

"Your parents never should have left you this ranch, and our father should have known better than to go along with it," Bess said. "You are in over your head. You need to sell it. That's plain to see."

"I agree. I am in over my head. Nothing in my life prepared me for this responsibility. But I'll get through it." She looked Thomas's way, and her voice turned hard. "I am not going to change my mind. And I'm not going to leave. And since this is technically my land, I still have that option. If you truly don't think you can abide by my choices, then I wish you both the best with your future travels."

After uttering a small cry, Bess turned around with a sniff and hurried inside. Jerome, on the other hand, continued to glare at his stepsister with something that looked dangerously close to malevolence. "Where am I supposed to live now?"

"I don't believe that's any concern of mine. You've made your choice."

Jerome's eyes narrowed. "Your weak-willed mother may have convinced my father to keep this place, but he did not intend for me to live here."

"Maybe not, but where he did intend for you and Bess to live is gone, and we need to help each other now. We need to try to find a way to live together as a family. You also need to start helping me more."

"I am not going to help you save a ranch that you shouldn't have in the first place."

"Again, it seems you've made your choice then, Jerome. I wish you well."

"You're going to regret this, Laurel. I'm going to make sure of it."

Just as Jerome reached out to grab her shoulder, Thomas

stepped in front of him. "Don't," he warned. "Don't talk to her that way, and don't ever attempt to touch her again."

"Or what?" Jerome scoffed.

"Or you'll regret it."

"How so? You being here is already ruining her reputation."

"It very well might be," Thomas returned. "But she will also be safe."

Looking as if Laurel's well-being only bored him, Jerome stepped to one side, visibly ignoring Thomas, and said, "Since you are casting us out, I'm going to need some money."

While Laurel closed her eyes in an obvious effort to gain patience, Thomas gaped at him.

Didn't that beat all? Her kin were living off of her. Thomas barely refrained from grunting in disdain. He wished he could send her inside and tell this fool what he could do with his proffered hand.

But of course, that wasn't his place. Instead, he stood silently next to her, hoping his very presence would remind her she wasn't alone. Not anymore.

She opened her eyes and, looking as dumbfounded as he assumed he did, stared at Jerome with those big brown eyes. Thomas would swear that a hundred retorts lay on her tongue, every one of them sharper than the next.

After almost a full minute, she spoke quietly. "I don't have any money to give you."

Jerome glared Thomas's way. "Because you spent it all on releasing him from a jail cell."

"No. It's because of everything." Turning to Thomas, she said, "Would you please go take care of Velvet and the buggy? You'll find everything you need in the barn."

This woman had more gumption than most soldiers he'd

witnessed on the field. Tipping his hat gallantly, he drawled, "Yes, miss."

Jerome cleared his throat. "No! Wait. I'm going to need the horse and buggy."

Thomas turned around, giving Jerome enough of a glare to make sure the man didn't consider reaching for her.

But Laurel was holding her own. "Of course you can't take Velvet or the buggy." Her voice full of hurt, she said, "Do you really think I would give them to you?"

"How am I supposed to leave?"

Thomas had had enough of the man's whining and verbal manipulations. "It's only eight miles to town. God gave you two feet. You'll do all right, I reckon."

"You'd cast out Bess and force her to walk?"

Laurel visibly steeled her spine. Then, after another fortifying breath, she said, "If that is the way you see it, then yes. I am casting you out and forcing you to walk to town."

Jerome narrowed his eyes.

Seeing the man's anger looming, Thomas stepped forward. He was prepared to do whatever it took to get the pair out of Laurel's hair, even if it meant using a little bit of force. Actually, he realized he wouldn't mind using his fists for a good reason. He'd even look forward to it.

Though Jerome stiffened, he pointedly ignored Thomas. Instead, he looked directly at Laurel and sent her a look that could only be described as deadly. "You have underestimated me, sister. I promise you will rue this moment."

Though her face remained carefully blank, Laurel's hands trembled before she fisted them.

And though he didn't know beans about being a gentleman, he knew a whole lot about defending someone who was in need.

He couldn't help himself. Stepping forward, he positioned his body so he stood slightly in front of her. "Miss Laurel, why don't you go on inside and rest a spell?" he said in a quiet tone. "I'll take care of your horse in a moment. But first, I think Jerome here and I need to have a talk."

He knew he had just overstepped his bounds by about a mile.

She stared at him, confusion lighting her eyes, before nodding. "All right, Sergeant."

The moment the door was closed, Jerome folded his arms across his chest. "I don't know who you think you are or what you're hoping to get away with, but I'm here to say you had better think again the next time you even consider interfering in my business."

"Is that right?" Thomas found he was almost enjoying this popinjay's dramatics.

"Absolutely. I don't know what kind of man you are, but I'm already counting the days until my sister figures out you are nothing more than a common criminal. Then she'll realize she's made a terrible mistake. There is no way she's going to kick me out and expect nothing to happen."

His temper unleashed, Thomas stepped closer and looked down. "I'll tell you who I am. I'm the man who grew up on the streets and learned to gain respect by the power of my fists. I've forced more people to bend to my will than you can ever imagine."

Jerome inhaled.

"I'm the man who fought on more battlefields than you've even heard of." Stepping even closer, Thomas glared. "I'm the man who held true heroes in my arms while they were dying, and made tougher decisions in a span of fifteen minutes than you've likely ever made in your lifetime."

Jerome's eyes widened. "Hey, now—"

"I'm the man who spent a winter in the middle of a northern lake in prison barracks and has just spent nine months languishing in a jail cell, the last two in the heat of a Texas summer." Thomas lowered his voice but took care to punctuate each syllable so there would be no mistaking what he was saying. "I've hurt and I've maimed. I've killed. I've done just about anything one can imagine to survive, and I'm willing to do it all again for Laurel Tracey."

"Because you are a reprobate."

"No, sir. Not that. It's because I am what I've always been. I'm a man without much to lose."

Jerome's face was pale and his hands were in useless fists at his sides. "I could send you back to jail."

"The only way you could do that is by forcibly taking me there yourself. Is that what you'd like to do? If so, I look forward to you doing your best."

Jerome's eyes nearly bugged out.

At last, feeling as though he was being listened to, Thomas continued. "However, it seems the Lord has decided it's time for a change. Somehow, some way, I did something to deserve getting hired on here. And I ain't leaving. So if I were you, I'd watch real close to any promises or threats you want to dish out to Miss Tracey. Because I'm not going to back down or give up. I'm going to fight you any way I can."

"You're nothing."

Thomas almost laughed. "You're absolutely right. I'm nothing. However, this man with nothing also has a place to sleep tonight, which is more than I believe you have at the moment. I suggest you get on your way and be quick about it. My determination to be here will far outlast any efforts on your part. I promise you that."

He turned then and led the horse and buggy to the barn, unhitched Velvet, and started rubbing her down.

She nudged him with her soft nose, flirting.

He rubbed her again, finding himself relaxing little by little. When she nudged him again, he murmured, "Look at you, pretty girl."

Velvet nodded her head as if she were in complete agreement, pawed the ground with a hoof, then nudged him once more, whickering softly.

Just like that, the memories came back. Of helping his father at the livery. Grooming horses while his dad fitted them with shoes.

It had been years since he'd allowed those sweet memories to take center stage in his head. Years since he'd let himself remember how good his life had been before the raids. Before everyone was gone.

He was so grateful that he leaned into the horse's chest and rested his forehead there. Just like he'd done when he was a boy. Velvet seemed to sense his need to hold her. She stilled and allowed him his moment. Then blew out a breath on his cheek.

As she'd no doubt hoped, he jerked back and wiped his face.

She whinnied, and before he knew it, he was smiling at the fool animal. Loving her affection. Loving the feel of being around a good horse again. It reminded him of serving under Major Ethan Kelly and Captain Monroe. Those men, as strong and stalwart as they were, had also been cavalry officers at heart.

Though he'd worked in a livery for a few years before enlisting, they were the ones who'd taught him to value a good mount, to trust a horse's good sense. The captain himself had taught him to truly care for his horse. His employer at the livery had done only what he could to get by with his customers, and Thomas had also forgotten much of his father's lessons as a way to survive. It had simply hurt too much to remember another life.

But under Captain Monroe's tutelage, Thomas had learned again. He'd first been struck by how individual each horse's personality seemed to be. And how much he'd come to enjoy the calming, solitary tasks of brushing and currying, the rubdowns and oiling of hooves. Other men took shortcuts. And if time was tight, Thomas would too.

But if possible, he would take as much time as he could. Because he'd had too little opportunity to coddle or fuss over anything or anyone. And horses . . . well, horses didn't ask why.

Just as he finished all the chores he could see needed to be done in the barn, the house's front door opened and shut and Laurel's two stepsiblings walked out. Each held a small bag of clothing. Their heads were lifted high and their steps were sure and brisk. Each looked to be wearing shoes far better suited to a cotillion than an eight-mile walk along dusty, rocky soil.

Thomas figured they'd be a sorry, sweaty mess before they'd gone two miles. He was glad Laurel hadn't asked him to take them into town. He'd rather see their backsides from here.

After washing off the worst of his sweat and grime, he turned toward the house.

Now that he could, he took a long look at it. It truly was a thing of beauty, with imposing white columns and a broad, long porch running the entire front. It was a little worn looking, a little tired. But though it had seen better days, it struck him as something special, though he couldn't say why. Hundreds of houses just like it dotted the state. Maybe the reason it looked so sweet was because he now knew he could count it as his home of sorts for the next year.

Counting his blessings again, he sat down on the front steps and waited for his new boss to appear. He didn't mind waiting. In fact, he kind of hoped she'd take her time.

After all, he had claim to the prettiest boss in the whole of the great state of Texas. If his buddies from Johnson's Island could see him now, they'd grin and remark that, against all that was logical, he had beaten the odds again.

Somehow, some way, Thomas Baker had landed back on his feet.

8

As she stood at a window and watched Bess and Jerome walk slowly down the road toward town, each holding a small carpetbag that likely held less than a third of their belongings, Laurel attempted to maintain her composure.

Sitting down, she willed herself not to cry. They'd deserved what had happened to them. They really had. It occurred to her that she could have ordered Sergeant Baker to take them into town, but she was sure he and Jerome only would have provoked each other further.

Jerome and Bess had been twin albatrosses around her neck. They'd moved in just when she was at her weakest, and instead of offering help or support, they took advantage of her home, her savings, and what little bit of charity she had left to give. The whole time she'd kept waiting for them to help. Waiting for them to acknowledge how much she'd done for them.

But instead of doing any of that, they'd taken even more from her. They were part of the reason she'd grown so tired. They were part of the reason she'd been forced to hire a man to save the ranch.

Now, even when they knew their departure meant she'd be living alone on the ranch with a prisoner, they still left. Though

she should have realized that nothing they did would likely surprise her anymore, their leaving this way had shocked her.

Even though she had so much to be upset about concerning
their behavior, she had wanted to give them the benefit of the
doubt. A small part of her had been sure Jerome was merely testing
her. She'd naïvely hoped some part of him would feel responsible
for her welfare.

But instead, he'd waged a war. Bating and badgering her.
Tempting her with callous phrases, doing anything he could to
get her to bend to his will.

She was done doing that.

If she had given in, he would take advantage and claim he was
the head of the household. No doubt he would have then run the
rest of the ranch into the ground—or worse, managed to somehow sell it right out from under her. Then she would be looking
for a place to sleep at night.

But still . . . it was hard.

Of course, she wouldn't have gone back on her word no matter what happened. Not only had both Sheriff Jackson and Judge
Orbison been relieved that a man they trusted was going to
be free at last, but Laurel never could have done such a thing to
Sergeant Baker. For some reason she felt warm inside just thinking
about him.

Indeed, he was Sergeant Thomas Baker. *Thomas* in her private thoughts.

Thomas!

Realizing that she hadn't heard him come into the house, she
felt her mouth go dry. Where was he?

Panic set in as she imagined the possibilities. She really hoped
he hadn't turned her into a liar and taken off while she'd been
sitting inside stewing and trying not to cry.

Getting to her feet, she wiped away the few tears she'd shed and hurried through the foyer to the front door. Perhaps he was sitting in the barn with Velvet, wondering what had happened to her. And he was also probably wondering about his living quarters and a meal. She rushed out the door.

Then, just as abruptly, she drew to a stop.

Thomas was standing on the covered porch facing her, leaning against one of the white columns her mother had begged her father to install years before war had infiltrated their lives.

He was also staring directly at her.

When she parted her lips, trying desperately to think of a reason she had practically flown out the door, something new appeared in those blue eyes of his. Pushing off from the column, he bowed slightly. "Miss."

That courtly gesture—so unexpected—made her flush. "I'm so sorry you've been waiting on me out here. Please forgive me."

He shook his head. "First off, I think we need to remember that you are in charge, Miss Laurel. You don't see to my needs. I see to yours. That means I can and will stand here all day long if that is what you need me to do."

His words might have been true, but it was his lazy drawl and slightly amused look that caught her insides and made her feel as if her world had just shifted to one side.

"I hope I will never treat you so harshly."

"Making me wait for you could never be called a harsh punishment."

There she went again. In spite of her best intentions, she found herself responding to something he said in a way that was completely inappropriate. Goodness! She needed to get back on a firmer, more professional foundation. She needed to get a grip on her emotions as well. Immediately!

"Did you put up Velvet all right?" she asked, hoping she sounded as if she was all business.

"I did. I watered her and gave her a good rubdown."

"You had time to do all that?"

"It wasn't all that much. Just so you know, I also fed her fresh hay and oats and mucked out her stall. And oiled the leathers. I did the same with the other horse too." He raised an eyebrow. "The pretty palomino."

"He's called Yellow."

"Yellow?" His lips twitched.

"I didn't name the gelding. He came with that name, such that it is."

"He is a yellow color. I suppose it makes sense."

"Actually, it kind of doesn't."

When he looked at her curiously, she filled him in. "The story goes that he was a sorry horse in battle. He shied away from the first gunshot."

"I can't say I blame him. The battlefield certainly ain't a pleasant place to be."

"I suppose not."

"For what it's worth, I'm thinking Yellow has the makings of a right fine horse."

"I thought so too. He's real gentle and doesn't seem to mind working long hours. We've been getting along just fine. No doubt he's had some eventful days, given the fact that I didn't know what I was doing when I first started herding cattle with him. But he's been patient with my struggles."

Instead of smiling at her little joke, he turned serious. "If he was being brave, you were too."

She liked the way that sounded. "Maybe so." Holding out her

hands, she said, "I've had my share of aches and pains and blisters. Some days I think it would have been easier to give up."

"But you didn't."

"Not yet," she joked, but it sounded rather pitiful, even to her ears.

But what else could she say? Ever since her father and brother left to fight in the war, and especially after her mother remarried and left to live with her new husband on the property Jerome and Bess later inherited, she'd been bearing the weight of running the ranch. When Jerome and Bess had shown up, their presence had only added more work for her.

She cleared her throat. "You know, I can't remember the last time anyone oiled the tack."

"It was nothing. A man in the cavalry learns real quick that his horse and tack make the difference between life and death."

The easy statement reminded her yet again of all he'd been through. Of what they'd both been through.

As if sensing her unease, he smiled softly. "What would you like me to do now?"

She didn't want to do this. Though she'd freed him from captivity to work, it was now going to be just the two of them on the ranch.

She was going to need to be his boss. A person he respected.

But she didn't want to start their relationship with her constantly giving him a list of chores.

Gesturing to the porch steps, she said, "Maybe we could sit down for a spell and visit?"

"Visit?" He looked a little confused, almost as if he wasn't sure of the term.

"Yes. I mean, if you don't mind. I could bring us some cold cider."

He looked completely taken aback, and she supposed she didn't blame him. "That . . . well, that would be real kind of you."

Feeling relieved, she opened the door again. "I'll be right back."

Laurel walked through the covered opening to the small kitchen, then pulled out two large, speckled stoneware mugs and poured cold cider from the cellar into them.

When she returned, Thomas jumped to his feet. Before she could figure out what to do, he took both mugs from her, set them on the floor of the wooden porch, then held out his hand to help her sit down on the top step. Just like they were in a parlor.

When she felt his touch, she trembled.

He felt it and froze. "Beg pardon, I didn't mean to act so familiar. Please don't be frightened. I would never hurt you."

"No, it wasn't that you scared me. It's just that it's been awhile since I was accustomed to such care." To her chagrin, she blushed again. Blast! She didn't know how to be coy and entertaining. She didn't even remember how to act friendly or relaxed. Obviously she had been keeping company with herself for far too long, though she'd been relieved to convince Landon to stay away.

After handing her one of the mugs, he sat down by her side and took a healthy sip. Pure pleasure lit his expression. "This tastes real good, Miss Laurel. By far the best drink I've partaken of in months. Thank you."

She took a small sip too. "You're welcome. I think it's just the right combination of tart and sweet. I bought it from a woman who was passing through town. She was . . . well, she was desperate for some income. Every time I take a sip, I think it's so much better than I anticipated. The quality of her offering was a welcome surprise."

"The best things are like that, I reckon."

"I've always thought so too." She took another sip of the cold drink, enjoying the way the liquid felt sliding down her throat. "Sergeant, there's a storage room at the back of the barn. There's a window in it, and it hasn't been used for much since the war. I think it might work out as a room for you."

"I'm sure it will suit me just fine."

Though he seemed perfectly at ease with her suggestion, she still felt bad. No matter how shady it was in the barn, it was still dusty and hot, and she had two empty bedrooms in the house now.

But how could she share a house with a man?

"There's no bedding in it yet. I was going to get Jerome to help me move a cot or one of the mattresses out there. But of course he's gone now. I'll help you with it."

"Don't worry about that none. I can sleep on anything you've got tonight, then I'll find a way to get a cot out there."

Looking doubtfully at his back, she said, "I can't imagine your back will thank you."

"Don't you worry about that. I promise it's been through worse."

That reminder made her feel even guiltier. Gathering her courage, she said, "Maybe it would be better for your back if you slept in one of the spare bedrooms upstairs? You would be cooler, and we wouldn't have to go to the trouble of moving a cot to the barn."

He stilled. "You want me to sleep in the house?"

"Yes. I mean, you could have Jerome's bedroom until you heal. It wouldn't be any trouble."

"I'm afraid it would, miss. It would mean a whole lot of trouble for the both of us."

Slumping her shoulders, she said, "I suppose you're right."

"I know I am. Don't spare me another thought. Like I said, I'll be fine out in the barn."

"I'll fetch you some blankets. And a pillow."

His gaze warmed. "That would be real good. Thank you, Miss Laurel."

Her invitation, along with his refusal of it, seemed to change the feeling of camaraderie between them. They sat in silence for a while, neither doing much but looking out at her land.

Laurel was mentally exhausted, thinking about how relieved she was to have hired Thomas, all while worrying about Jerome and Bess . . . and wondering if she was being hopelessly naïve to put so much trust in a man she knew next to nothing about.

After a good half hour had passed, she stood. "I'll, uh, go get your things together. I'll also make a meal." Still feeling frazzled, she brushed a stray strand of hair away from her face. "Is there anything you don't like?"

"A man like me hasn't had much opportunity to be picky. I'll like anything you prepare, miss."

Why did his statement leave her feeling a little breathless? "I have some chicken. And smoked ham."

"Don't put yourself to trouble on my account."

"It's no trouble. I mean, we need to eat, right, Sergeant? No matter what else happens, we need to eat."

"Of course, miss."

His thoughtful expression was a bit disconcerting.

So was his quiet demeanor while he ate every speck of the fried ham, creamed potatoes, and glazed carrots on his plate an hour later.

She'd tried not to let him see that she noticed the way his gaze lingered on her when he thought she wasn't looking. Or the way he insisted on washing both his plate and hers.

Or the way he thanked her for the meal before leaving for a long walk all around her property, and again after their light supper, before he once again went to the barn to care for her animals.

It was only when she climbed into bed and dimmed her lantern that she allowed herself to really think about his actions and words. About the way he seemed so grateful and tentative.

And she began to wonder what his life had been like. She knew he had fought in the war and been imprisoned, that he got into trouble with a gambling debt. But what other events had eventually led him to a jail cell in Sweetwater, Texas, and ultimately to sleeping in her barn?

Before sleep overtook her, she wondered if she really wanted to know.

9

Johnson's Island, Ohio
Confederate States of America Officers POW Camp
Winter 1865

His mouth had gotten him in trouble again.

As Thomas sat on his cot, shivering next to Robert Truax, he could practically feel the animosity rolling off the second lieutenant. Thomas didn't blame him in the slightest.

After all, he was twenty-two years old now. Far too old to be shooting off his mouth the way he had. He'd gotten mad at some new captain from Mississippi over an imagined slight. Before he knew what he was doing, Thomas had called him a few choice names. The captain had taken offense.

That had led, unfortunately, to Thomas punching him in the face with a powerful left hook.

The captain had fallen flat on his face. The man's fellow Mississippians hadn't taken that well and attacked Thomas—which had led, of course, to his own band of friends joining in the fray.

The guards watched the skirmish for a while, then broke up the fight. Soon after, they made sure Thomas's group felt the consequences. They removed their stove.

Since snow covered the ground and their quarters were

essentially hastily erected buildings constructed of green lumber, their usually cold conditions hovered at the freezing mark.

Now everyone was shivering on their cots, irritated with him and nursing various assorted injuries to boot.

Yep, this time the consequences of his inability to keep his mouth shut had been especially miserable. Hating himself, hating the anger that always seemed to be boiling on the surface of his tongue, Thomas swallowed hard and tried not to dissolve even deeper into self-pity. When a lump formed in his throat, he coughed, hoping he wasn't about to do something he was going to be even more ashamed about.

"You ain't about to start crying, are you?" Robert asked.

"Of course not," Thomas replied, his voice thick with emotion.

"Sure?" he asked, his tone now filled with distaste. "'Cause you sound like you're on the verge of tears."

Thomas bit the inside of his cheek and concentrated on that pinch. It was a welcome thing. Far better than coming off as weak. Everyone knew Robert had grown up on the streets of Fort Worth. Rumors abounded about who took care of him. Some said fallen women. Others said old war veterans from 1812.

All Thomas knew was that the man had had a harder life than even Thomas had and still didn't go around hitting captains or picking fights. "I'm, uh, just cold. The wind is blowing pretty bad tonight. It feels like we're sitting in the middle of the lake."

"I wonder why?" Major Kelly called out sarcastically. "Could it be because we have no heat? Thanks to you?"

"That's enough, Ethan," Phillip Markham said. "The boy has already apologized for his actions. Several times."

"Pardon me if I'm not feeling too kindly toward that apology. Words don't mean all that much right now. My feet feel like they might as well be submerged in Lake Erie."

"Just don't kick me with them," Captain Monroe bit out. "If you can help yourself, that is. I've never known a person to toss and turn as much as you do in your sleep."

"You aren't all that great to sleep with either, Devin."

"Yeah, but I'm still better than sleeping alone."

Thomas could practically hear Major Kelly grit his teeth before he exhaled with a bark of laughter. "You may have a point. The only thing worse than sleeping beside any of you would be to sleep alone. I'd have frostbite by morning."

Robert chuckled. "By the end of the night, I reckon all of us will be spooned up like dance hall girls."

"I don't believe spooning is what those girls do," Phillip said, joking.

"Oh, like you would even know," the major said. "You've only been around one woman." He sighed dramatically. "The fair Miranda."

"That is nothing to be ashamed of."

"Indeed it is not. It's a blessing the likes of us have never known," the captain countered. After a pause, he called out, "Do you not have anything to say now, Sergeant?"

Captain Monroe's voice held a definite edge. Feeling rather like a misbehaving child, Thomas cleared his throat. "No, sir."

"Ah, don't be so hard on yourself. If it wasn't you picking a fight with Creighten, something else would have set the lot of us off. We're a group of soldiers used to a lot of physical activity. Sitting around in the middle of a snow and ice storm didn't do us any favors."

"I still regret my actions."

"I regret them too," Major Kelly moaned.

"Oh, stop," Phillip said. "You know as well as I do that Creighten had it coming. That man is an idiot and a blowhard. And a braggart."

"This is true." Amusement entered Major Kelly's tone. "He's a fool. Only a fool would say he could outride the lot of us. Like it even matters at this point in time."

Captain Monroe started laughing. "The man grew up on a farm in southern Mississippi. He was not racing horses; he was planting alfalfa. He certainly never learned to ride like our Thomas Baker can."

For a moment, Thomas let himself luxuriate in the feeling of pride the captain's offhand comment gave him. He could indeed ride well. His father had made sure of that.

"Can you really ride so well, Baker?" Major Kelly called out.

Thomas considered lying, but since there was so little he felt proud of, he couldn't do it. "Well . . . yes, I can."

"How come? You have a natural gift?"

"No. I . . . well, I mean, my father was a blacksmith. He loved horses and made sure I loved them too. He had me riding practically before I could walk. I grew up in the saddle."

"Our sergeant is being too modest. He can ride like the wind. He and the horse move like one," Phillip said. "I've never seen anything like it."

"My brother was better," Thomas blurted.

"Is he gone?" Captain asked.

"Yes, sir."

"What battle?"

"No battle, sir. My brother, Jeremy, died long before the war began." Thomas hesitated, then decided to tell the whole truth. "My family all died when I was eight years old."

"Good Lord," Major Kelly uttered. "What happened? Did they get scarlet fever?"

He didn't want to answer. But he supposed he deserved the pain. "Indian raid. Everyone in my family fought them but me.

Said I was too young," he choked out. "My father made me go to a hiding place and told me not to come out, no matter what." Swallowing, he said, "So I hid while they were attacked and killed."

"And you heard the whole thing," Robert muttered.

"Yeah. I heard everything. Every bit of it."

The silence that met his statement made Thomas want to curl into a ball as a grown man and pretend to be anywhere else. Now they had a whole other reason to look down on him. Only a true coward would admit to hiding while his mother was being tortured by the Comanche, even if he had been a child at the time.

Yet again, his mouth had gotten him into this mess. If he'd held his tongue, they never would have known what he'd done.

At last Captain Monroe cleared his throat. "I'm real sorry that happened, Thomas."

"Yes, sir. Me too."

"What happened after?"

"After? I lived on the streets."

"You didn't go to any relatives' homes?"

"No, sir. I didn't have anywhere to go."

"So you've lived on your own since you were eight."

"I did until I got a job in a livery around the time I was eleven. I slept and worked there until I was seventeen. And then I enlisted."

"And now here you are, living with a bunch of broken men in the middle of a frozen great lake."

"Yes. I mean, no, sir."

"No?"

"I may be living in the middle of a frozen lake, but I'm surely not with a bunch of broken men. You all are some of the best men I've had the honor of knowing."

Major Kelly sighed. "You had to do it, didn't you, Sergeant?"

"Do what?"

"You had to go and prove me wrong. You have shamed me. Made me realize there's quite a bit of you to admire."

"I don't know about that, sir."

"Don't argue with a major, Thomas," Robert said. "Let him win this one."

Thomas smiled in the dark and kept smiling until his eyes got heavy and snoring reverberated around him.

Only then did he start to fall asleep, feeling like he'd finally found a home.

10

DOING THE RIGHT THING WAS DEFINITELY OVERRATED. If he hadn't been so chivalrous, Thomas could very well be sleeping in the comfort of one of Laurel's extra bedrooms.

Instead, he was lying on a pile of blankets in the dusty tack room in her barn. Though it wasn't the most unpleasant bed he'd ever lain upon, it was far from what could have been.

And that loss, the knowledge that for the first time in a very long while he'd had options and had chosen the worst one, was tough to swallow. Was that what doing the right thing felt like? Finding contentment in discomfort?

If so, Thomas realized it was going to take some time to get used to. He moved again on his makeshift bed and tried not to wince. The heat made the wounds on his back fester and itch and ache, which in turn kept him awake.

Realizing he was simply going to have to wait until his body became so exhausted that he fell asleep, Thomas bided his time by chewing on straw and listening to Yellow's and Velvet's breathing. The horses' easy slumber brought back those rare, peaceful memories of being a small boy in his father's blacksmith shop. He used to sit in the back of the shop, near where the horses were stabled, and listen to the familiar clang and sizzle of his father fashioning horseshoes. The horses had seemed to know that his father cared for them, because they always stood easily, eventually lightly dozing.

It was a good memory, one of the few he had. It was also far safer to dwell on than the other matter that occupied his mind—his new boss, Miss Laurel Tracey.

From the time she'd gazed at him with those slightly upturned eyes that seemed to change their hue with every mood, he had been lost.

Added to the mix were her golden tresses, kissable cheeks, and feminine figure. Though he truly felt respect for her, he was only a man. And he'd be lying if he didn't admit to himself that other thoughts had crossed his mind besides distant, cool respect.

Even her personality lured him like no other woman's ever had.

Without doing any one thing in particular, Laurel Tracey was everything he thought a woman should be. And if he was honest, he'd have to admit it was appealing that she needed a protector. Few people in his life had actually needed him, and he loved that she needed him to help with the ranch, to protect her, and to shield her from the cruel remarks of Bess and Jerome.

He still couldn't get over the way those two had belittled her attributes. He found her terribly attractive. He knew he wasn't the only man to notice her beauty either. The judge was certainly smitten with her, and the sheriff too.

From what he could tell, half the population of Sweetwater didn't seem inclined to do much besides covertly stare at Laurel. If he had been her man instead of her new hired hand, he would have stared them all down until they looked away in shame.

What they didn't seem to understand—as far as he could tell, anyway—was that Laurel Tracey's looks weren't what set her apart from most every other woman. No, there was something more about her. Something far less apparent but far more extraordinary.

She was kind and generous. Decent and honest. Tenderhearted and sweet. Almost as if she still believed in goodness in the world, even though she had survived a war, just like the rest of them had.

For the life of him, he couldn't figure her out. She didn't act like any woman he'd ever known. Not that he'd known all that many, of course. But still, she was far too trusting. For heaven's sake, he was a criminal! Surely she knew that meant he didn't always obey laws or do what was right. She should want to keep her distance from him, not invite him into her home.

But that was what she'd done.

He decided right then and there to do everything in his power to look out for her. He didn't know if he could actually help her save her ranch, but he could definitely make sure she came to no harm while he was there.

He was looking forward to it too.

His body relaxed as he imagined her looking at him with gratitude. As if, for a split second, she stared at him with appreciation, like he remembered those officers had in their barracks in prison all those years ago.

As if he was far more than she'd expected.

If that happened, he would count himself fortunate indeed.

He closed his eyes, thinking about her look of wonder. At last, exhausted, he felt himself drifting off to sleep, comforted by the gentle snores of two horses.

∽∞∾

Taylor Orr was a desperate man. He was also running out of time.

That was the only reason he could give himself for sneaking

around Laurel Tracey's house after one in the morning with a dead calf in his arms.

Viewing the calf's suffering and eventual death had brought Taylor no joy. It had only cemented his determination to wrap up this loathsome job as quickly as possible so he could get away.

That was why he ended up carrying the calf on the back of his mount well beyond the house's perimeter, then carried it in his arms all the way to Laurel Tracey's doorstep. He had to be especially quiet with that prisoner sleeping in the barn, but this way there would be no mistake about what had happened. The last thing Taylor wanted was for its owner to mistakenly think the animal died of natural causes if it was found alone. Or worse, not even find it.

After he deposited the animal in front of her door, he quietly darted back into the shadows and headed to his horse. He had no desire to catch sight of the woman to whom he'd been ordered to cause so much pain.

He was going to go to his small room in the boardinghouse tonight and sleep until midmorning. By that time, he should hear word of Laurel Tracey contacting the sheriff in fright.

When that happened, Taylor could let his boss know he was making progress. Surely then he would get another payment.

Mounting his horse, he quietly urged it into a walk, then a canter. Thought about how getting paid so he could pay off his debts and provide for Dara was worth all this.

Some things were so worthwhile that they made even the most evil actions justifiable.

Maybe if he told himself that enough he might actually believe it one day.

11

Laurel couldn't seem to stop crying.

She'd not only slept late, but realized she couldn't be sure Thomas would automatically care for all her animals. Especially the chickens, since she'd cared for them herself yesterday. Knowing Velvet and Yellow would be anxious for their food, and the hens would need their grain before they would willingly give up any eggs, and her dairy cow, Bonnet, would need to be milked, she'd thrown on her oldest worn calico dress and did little more than pull her hair into a makeshift braid before splashing water on her face.

Electing not to even put on shoes since the ground would no doubt be warm already, she scampered down the creaking stairs, threw open the front door, and almost tripped over the dead calf lying just on the other side of the entryway.

The sight of the sweet young thing, with its vacant brown eyes and stiff body, was so horrible, so unexpected, that she hadn't been able to stop herself from screaming. Not once, but twice.

Then, when she realized someone must have placed it on her doorstep in the middle of the night while she was sleeping just up the stairs, she began to sob.

Who could have done such a thing? Had it been Thomas? Was this stranger she'd invited to live by her side evil?

Almost in the next breath, she dismissed the idea. Her new

worker might be a little rough around the edges, but he wasn't the type of man to kill baby animals and leave them at her doorstep. That wasn't who he was.

Ashamed and alarmed at the train of her thoughts, she pressed her palms over her mouth. Anything to help her regain control. Because if Thomas hadn't done such a thing, it was someone else.

Maybe it had been one of those squatters she'd spied a couple of days ago. Everyone knew some of those men were desperate for land, desperate for something to hold on to. Maybe they'd assumed a lone woman, whom they somehow knew was low on assets and money, would be no match for the likes of them.

Maybe it was someone else, someone who knew her well and knew just what would frighten her the most.

Regardless of who had done this, the fact remained that someone had been on her land without permission, killed that calf, and stood right outside her door last night.

All while she'd been in her bed, sound asleep.

Why, she hadn't even locked her doors!

Thinking of how easy it would have been for the trespasser to have entered her home and attacked her, her trembling increased.

"Miss Laurel, what is it?"

Dropping her hands, Laurel turned to see Thomas stride toward her. His hair was sticking up this way and that, his denims hung low on his hips, and his chambray shirt was partly unbuttoned. He was barefoot too.

But what held her gaze the most was the concerned expression he wore. He looked sleepy and unsure and worried. She was no sleuth, but nothing about him indicated he had any inkling of what she'd discovered on her doorstep. It seemed that he, too, had been sleeping while a perpetrator had been lurking about on her land.

Shivering uncontrollably, Laurel curved her arms around herself in another weak effort to gain control of her emotions.

"Miss Laurel?" Thomas called out again.

Running toward the porch steps, he kept his gaze on her. "What's wrong? Did something happen to you?" His tone darkened with obvious worry. "Did you fall? Are you hurt?"

She shook her head. "No. I mean . . . I mean . . . look."

His next words froze as he looked down to where she pointed. Then he drew in a sharp breath. "This was here when you came out this morning?" he asked as he knelt down by its side.

"I almost tripped on it." Not even caring that sloppy tears were still sliding down her face, she continued, "Look at his size. He can't be more than a couple of days old. What do you think happened to him?"

He ran a finger along the calf's side. "God only knows. He feels cold. I reckon he's been dead for a while."

"Someone brought him here while we were sleeping and put him on my doorstep. Who would do such a thing?"

"I couldn't begin to imagine. I've seen a lot of things in my life, but this does beat all."

Staring at Thomas looking at the little calf, Laurel's head spun. She needed to take care of the poor animal. Or at least walk around it so she could talk to Thomas without staring at it. Or even go inside.

But unfortunately, she couldn't seem to make herself do anything but stand frozen.

Thomas took the decision away from her. Stepping around the calf, he wrapped one arm around her shoulders. "Let's get you inside. There's no reason for you to stand out here any longer."

Grateful that he was taking charge, she allowed him to usher her inside.

Once they were in the dim interior of the foyer, Thomas closed the door. The next thing she knew, he was pulling her into a warm hug.

Laurel knew she was not a small person. She was taller than most women. Her body was rather generous too. She usually felt too large, too ungainly when compared to other, more delicately formed women.

In Thomas's arms, however, she felt almost small. Releasing a ragged sigh, she leaned closer to him.

"You go ahead and cry," he murmured, hugging her tight as she laid her cheek over his heart and let the tears fall. He was warm, and to her surprise, his skin was smooth.

Placing both of her hands on his shoulders, she realized that she felt secure. She felt cared for.

Not alone.

How long had it been? Since her stepfather and mother died? Her father and brother? When was the last time anyone had held her while she fell apart? When was the last time she'd actually had someplace to fall?

Far too long ago.

The next thing she knew, she was crying for the loss of her loved ones. And crying because Thomas was there.

"It ain't okay, but I'll make it that way," he murmured, making some kind of sympathetic clicking noise with his tongue while one of his hands began to smooth back her hair. "I'm so sorry."

After giving in to her weakness for another half a minute or so, she straightened and pulled back.

As he stood tall and strong, looking down on her with an intense expression, Laurel knew she should be blushing like a schoolgirl. Her cheek, her face had been nestled against his bare skin. She'd pressed herself against his body.

Not only would her behavior have been inappropriate even if they were friends or sweethearts, but it was especially so because she was his employer! She'd released him from his prison less than twenty-four hours ago and now . . . now she was just wrapped in his arms.

What would he think?

It was going to be up to her to fix this. Two awkward steps backward carried her even farther away from him. "I seem to be forgetting myself. I'm sorry, Sergeant."

He reached out and curved two fingers under her chin. "Why do you feel the need to apologize?" he drawled, his voice rough. "Being upset that some son of a gun placed a dead newborn calf on your doorstep last night? A sight like that would have shaken up most anyone."

She shivered. "I can't believe this happened. It's awful. But I should have handled it better. I shouldn't have . . . leapt into your arms the way I did. It was inappropriate."

But instead of accepting her apology or making one of his own, her sergeant surprised her. "Stop it," he ordered. "We're not going to do this. Not anymore."

Caught off guard by his sudden change in demeanor, she looked at him in confusion.

"We're not going to start apologizing for being human," he said, his voice hard. Before she could question that comment, he added, "Miss Tracey, *Laurel*, you have nothing to be sorry for." When she froze, staring at him in wonder, he continued, his voice sounding more confident. "What you saw, what someone did?" He shook his head. "It's beyond comprehension."

His words, so sure and certain, were able to do something all the voices and doubts in her head hadn't been able to. Feeling far more calm, she breathed in deep. "What should we do now?"

He quirked an eyebrow. "Well, first off, *we* are not going to do anything."

"I don't understand."

Instead of explaining, he curved a hand around her elbow. "Miss Laurel, you need to sit down and rest. While you do that, I'll go take care of that animal. Then we can talk about whether we should ride into town to talk to Sheriff Jackson about it."

Though his words made sense, she dreaded the thought of being on display for the second time in two days. "I'm not sure what I want to do."

"Miss Laurel, I've never been a man with a lot of interest in bringing lawmen into my life, but this might be the exception, don't you think?" Gentling his voice, he said, "Like you said, that little thing didn't get here on its own. And I think we can be sure it came from your own herd."

"I know. It's just that I don't know what anyone else can do. And I'm afraid Sheriff Jackson might even want me to bring back Bess and Jerome so I'm not here alone." Just imagining how difficult it would be to interact with Thomas while her stepsiblings looked on, she shook her head. "I can't have them back here."

"Of course you can't, and I won't let that happen."

"You think he'll listen to you?"

"I know he will, just as I know you don't have to do one single thing you don't want to." Leading her to the sofa, he said, "Now, take a seat and try to relax."

Though she allowed him to guide her, she said, "I can't simply sit here and do nothing, Sergeant. The horses need to be fed and my cow needs to be milked."

"I'll take care of them."

"You will?" she asked in surprise. "The chickens too?"

Looking a little embarrassed, he said, "I never could abide chickens."

There was something about the way he looked when he said "chickens" that made her giggle in spite of the traumatic morning they'd shared. "Are you afraid of a few birds?"

"Yep. And I'm not ashamed of it neither."

"I'll go take care of the hens, then. And I'll make some breakfast too."

"All right. But please rest for a while first, give me time to do those other chores. Then come out to care for the chickens. You can tell me all about them."

"I will. I'm shaken up, but I'm not about to sit and do nothing all morning." Actually, she couldn't think of anything worse than to sit in the house alone and let her mind drift. It would be far better to keep busy.

"We've got a plan, then." Reaching out for her hand, he squeezed it gently. "Don't look out the window, though. I'll take care of the calf. You don't need to look at it again."

Grateful for that, she nodded.

After he closed the front door behind him, she pressed her fingers to her eyes once again. She needed to regain her composure. She needed to stop thinking about what used to be accepted and what was going to cause talk. None of that mattered. She needed to start thinking about herself and her needs.

What was more important than anything else was the future of the ranch. She needed to keep it, needed to get some cattle to market. That, not anything else, was what she needed to concentrate on.

If that was even possible, now that someone seemed to be going to great lengths to threaten everything she held dear. She just had no idea why. Or who.

12

ASSURED LAUREL WAS RESTING IN HER SITTING ROOM AS comfortably as she was able, Thomas wrapped the calf in a worn sheet he'd found at the bottom of her rag basket near the kitchen and carried it to the barn.

The calf was stiff in his arms and so very pitifully small. Probably only a day or two old. His death was such a shame.

When Thomas walked by the horses, both whinnied in alarm. He guessed it didn't take much for them to sense death.

After depositing the calf in an empty stall, he peeled back the sheet and examined it for cuts or any other signs of foul play. But beyond the blank stare and an odd set to the animal's jaw, he couldn't find anything amiss.

Now he was going to have to get other people involved. Definitely the sheriff, and maybe even the doctor if he was willing to take a peek at the animal. Thomas was as sure as the scars on his back that the animal had died of unnatural causes.

If the calf had merely died from a snakebite or from disease and someone had come across it, that person would have knocked on the door in the light of day.

No, someone had gone out of their way to intentionally scare

Laurel. The questions, of course, were who would do something like that, and why?

Though he'd only been around Jerome and Bess for a few minutes, they didn't strike him as the type to do such a thing. It was too much trouble, for one. They both had seemed rather squeamish too. Killing an animal and carting it to Laurel's doorstep in the middle of the night seemed like a lot for a pair like them to take on. Besides, he was sure he would have heard them. No, this was someone who knew how to keep even a former soldier from being aware he was there.

After covering the calf with the sheet again, he hurried to his room. There, he buttoned his shirt, wincing as he realized how exposed he had been in front of a lady, but remembering, too, the soft touch of her cheek on his chest. Shaking his thoughts away, he put on his boots and belt. Then, after caring for the animals, he washed his face and teeth. Feeling more fit for her company, he headed back toward the house to get Laurel.

Whether she saw him walking toward her through the window or the timing had worked out, she exited the door and hurriedly met him on the limestone walkway.

It seemed she, too, had used some of their time apart to put herself together. Her hair was braided more tightly and pinned into a neat bun at the nape of her neck. She had also slipped on stockings and boots, and carried a basket.

He had to admit he was a little disappointed by that. He had loved seeing her bare toes peeking out at him. He'd loved seeing her in a way no one else ever did.

"You put your boots on," he said when she got to his side.

As he'd hoped, her cheeks bloomed into a faint flush. "Oh, yes. I hadn't meant to go out barefoot in the first place."

"I didn't mind."

"I see you've put your boots on too."

He grinned. "A man learns to cover his feet when he's around farm animals."

"A woman learns to do that too."

Looking at her closely, he said, "Are you doing a little better?"

She shrugged. "I can't say that I am. Who do you think could have done such a thing?"

"I was just doing some thinking about that myself." Knowing they would no doubt need to talk about potential enemies soon, he said, "Let's not think about it now, though. Come on and show me how these hens greet you."

She looked at him in a bemused way, but Laurel acted agreeable enough. Leading the way to the henhouse, she said, "I have a dozen hens, ten of which are good layers."

"And the other two?"

She frowned. "They are destined for the stew pot," she whispered as she picked up a scoop of feed and scattered it along the ground.

With a flurry of white feathers, the majority of the hens trotted out and began pecking at the seeds. As they pranced importantly, Laurel went to their nests to gather eggs. She talked quietly to the hens, even going so far as to touch one of the chicken's heads.

Thomas watched with his arms resting on the fence, unexpectedly charmed. He liked that she treated those birds as though they had as much right to be there as she did.

Of course, that made him realize just how heavily that calf's death must be laying on her heart.

When she walked back out, he held out a hand for her basket. "I'll carry your eggs for you."

"I can handle carrying eight eggs."

"No doubt. But I'll feel better giving you a hand."

"Thank you."

He followed her into the house and back toward the kitchen. "Do you want me to wash them for you?"

"If you do that, I'll get right to work on breakfast."

While he primed the pump and washed eggs, she competently made biscuits, then put them in a cast iron pan and into the oven.

"Gravy?"

"Sounds good."

He watched as she sliced off a thick piece of ham, fried it, and then added milk and flour.

While she cooked, he said, "It's kind of surprising to see a lady like you so at home in the kitchen. Did the war teach you to cook?"

"I suppose so, though my mother taught me to cook by her side at a young age. This is a working ranch, you know. Neither of my parents had much patience for men or women who didn't want to pull their own weight."

"I'm guessing, then, that it was fairly hard to stand by and watch Bess and Jerome do next to nothing around here."

After checking on the biscuits, Laurel nodded, her expression pained. "I don't understand their ways, if you want to know the truth. Their father had always been a hard worker, and he always looked pleased about the work I did here."

Thomas was doing his best to keep their conversation general to try to keep her calm. It was a difficult endeavor, however, because all he really wanted to do was swear a blue streak and then go find whoever had done such a thing and make them pay for upsetting her so much.

He was supposed to be beyond all that, however. His moral fiber was stronger, his faith more pronounced. He hoped he'd always be that way. All that time in captivity had to have been good for something.

With all that in mind, he said, "Do you think they might have gotten so mad at you that they would be capable of doing something like what we found this morning?"

"Killing a calf?" She shook her head. "Not at all. To be honest, I don't know of anyone who would do such a thing. Not only would few people be so cruel as to hurt a young calf, but no one around these parts would knowingly put an end to something that could bring in money. Not even if this is one of the men who has been trying to persuade me to sell."

"I wondered about that too." He was tempted to brush a knuckle across her cheek, but he didn't. "How about we do some more thinking about this later?"

"I think that's a good idea, since breakfast is now ready."

He grinned. "Your timing is perfect. I'm starving."

After serving himself, he sat down across from her and stared in wonder at the plate of food in front of him. Just like the meals she'd made the day before, it was more than he'd had at one time in months and was certainly better than anything some jail cook had made. It all smelled wonderful.

He was truly thankful.

"May I lead us in prayer?" he asked.

She blinked, bringing a wave of appreciation into her gaze. "I'd enjoy that, Sergeant. Thank you."

"Dear heavenly Father, please bless this food and the hands that prepared it. Please also be with all creatures on your earth, great and small, and let us not forget to give thanks for even the smallest of blessings, for each day is a gift. Amen."

"Amen," she echoed. When she opened her eyes, she said, "That was a lovely prayer."

"You sound surprised."

"I guess I am. Well, a little bit. I didn't take you for being a praying man. You seem so hard." She blinked. "I meant that in the best way."

"I'll take it in that way. I am hard. But because of that, I've learned to reach out to our Lord. I'm a man who needs all the help he can get."

"I don't know if you're teasing me or not."

"I never joke about my faith," he replied before biting down on a biscuit and tasting heaven.

It was almost impossible to talk after that. Each bite was a revelation. She might have been surprised by his prayer, but he was just as amazed by her expertise in the kitchen.

Beside him, she ate as well, but in a far more desultory fashion.

Realizing he'd probably just inhaled his breakfast with the grace of a feed horse, he said, "I guess it's obvious I haven't had too many opportunities to eat in the company of ladies. Or with anyone who knows how to conduct himself in a proper way. Have my poor table manners taken away your appetite?"

"Not at all. I'm glad you're enjoying your food."

"I am indeed. You are a very fine cook, Miss Laurel."

"Thank you." She motioned to the stove. "I made lots, so go get some more if you're hungry."

Since he couldn't argue with that, he gave himself a second plateful, then took care to eat it far more slowly. When he was done at last, he pushed back from the table and stood up.

"How should we handle things? Do you want to go into town? Do you want me to go in your place? I can do that, you know."

"As much as I'd like you to talk to the sheriff without me, I think I had better go with you. After all, it is my ranch."

Glad that she stood her ground, he nodded.

"We need to do this today, don't we?" Dread filled her every syllable.

"Yes, I think we do." Picking up his plate, he said, "I'll work on the dishes while you get ready to go into town."

"You helped with the dishes last night."

He looked her way as he picked up a bowl. "And?"

"I should have stopped you. Washing dishes is women's work."

"I ate from my plate. I think I can wash it too." When she still hesitated, he smiled. "The faster you get ready, the faster we can get this errand over with."

"This is true. I'll be right back."

When she disappeared up the stairs, he got busy scrubbing pots and washing each dish and fork and spoon with care. He'd just dried the last piece when she appeared again, this time in a light-blue dress with rows of pin tucks across the chest.

On her head was a lovely wide-brimmed straw hat. It was flattering, highlighting her many attributes, and he hadn't thought she needed any help to improve her looks.

"You look real pretty, Miss Laurel."

Twin spots of color appeared in her cheeks. "Thank you, Sergeant. I . . . well, I thought maybe I'm going to need all the help I can get for this errand."

It was on the tip of his tongue to utter that, because she had him now, she wouldn't need to worry about facing the world on her own, at least not anytime soon.

Thank goodness he caught himself in time.

Laurel Tracey had enough to worry about without her new ranch hand making a pest of himself.

13

AFTER THEY FINISHED THEIR ERRAND IN TOWN, LAUREL couldn't wait to depart. Leading the way to the posts where Yellow and Velvet were tied up, she arranged the reins and looked for the block to help her get up into her sidesaddle.

But before she could do anything more than pull the mounting block closer, Thomas was at her side. "Allow me."

Well aware of the many eyes watching them, Laurel slipped her hand in his as he used his other to give her a boost into her saddle. He held her steady while she looped one knee around the horn and arranged her skirts.

Once she was settled, he swung into his own saddle as though he'd been born to it. Then, with barely a nudge, he guided Yellow onto the street.

She and Velvet reached his side, then together they guided their horses the short distance down Sweetwater's dry, dusty main street before heading in her ranch's direction.

After breakfast, Thomas had been prepared to hitch up the buggy again, but Laurel had asked if he'd be willing to ride instead. She liked to ride her horse, and she hated riding in the buggy in the middle of summer. It always felt too stifling and hot.

Thomas had readily agreed. Soon she learned why. Thomas

Baker on the back of a horse was truly a sight to see. He and the horse rode together as one. Whereas everyone else had seemed to need to fight Yellow over every command, Thomas controlled the gelding with ease.

Though she hadn't thought it would be possible, her ranch hand seemed stronger, more confident, and even handsomer in the saddle.

She'd been glad of the distraction the whole way to town, since he'd put the wrapped-up calf across his lap. Laurel's thoughts had alternated between wondering what the sheriff and doctor were going to say and worrying about running into Jerome and Bess.

However, her worries were for naught. After Thomas told the sheriff about discovering the dead calf on Laurel's doorstep, Sheriff Jackson said he'd take the calf to the doc and try to get some answers. As to who might have done this, he, too, had trouble identifying anyone both capable and willing to harm cattle to scare Laurel into selling her land, the most likely motive.

Not even squatters seemed to be likely suspects, though no one really knew how desperate any of them could be.

The sheriff encouraged Thomas and Laurel to head on back home. Doc Barnes was seeing to a mare and likely would not be back for hours. Jerome and Bess were nowhere to be seen.

Now as they rode home, Laurel felt contemplative. She was somewhat surprised to realize that after spending only twenty-four hours with Thomas, she felt as if they were a unit. A team.

"I know I said I didn't think Jerome would ever do such a thing, but do you think it could have been him who carried that calf to the doorstep?" she blurted.

"Like you, I wouldn't have thought so, but it is just under-handed enough to seem like he might have thought it was a good way to scare you into selling the ranch."

"I've started to think about that too. And whoever is doing this, I agree that has to be the reason, to get me to sell. But it's not as if this part of Texas has no other land available. Many a war widow has been forced to sell."

"I know it's hard, but we'll figure it out. You've got the sheriff on it too."

His words soothed her. So much so, it drew her up short. What was happening?

How could she have gone from feeling completely alone to feeling as though she had finally found someone to depend on? It made no sense, especially given the fact that the man she was depending on had just spent several months in jail.

When the house and barn came into view, they slowed their horses. There was a bit of shade now, thanks to a thicket of pecan trees that had been determined to grow and thrive for decades. Since Velvet and Yellow acted pleased to simply meander along in the shade, Laurel relaxed her grip on her horse's reins. All of them needed a few minutes to relax a bit.

She was just about to comment on the weather when Thomas turned to look at her, his blue eyes as striking as ever under the tan rim of his Stetson. "Miss Laurel, I think we should talk about something."

"Yes?"

"I don't like the idea of someone wandering around the ranch at night, especially with you alone in the house. It's not safe."

"I've thought about that a time or two as well," she said with a small smile. Actually, she didn't know how she was ever going to be able to sleep through the night again. Every creak and moan in the house was certain to draw a healthy amount of fear inside her.

Looking as if he'd just solved a difficult problem, he exhaled. "I'm glad to hear you feel the same way. Frankly, the idea of someone bothering you in the house while I'm sound asleep a hundred feet away in the barn scares the heck out of me."

"It scares me too," she admitted after debating for a moment. She didn't want to come across as any weaker than she was, but they were talking about someone killing animals and leaving them for her to find. Not just petty fears.

"Will you allow me to sleep in your house for a spell? I promise I'll sleep on the sofa in the sitting room if you don't want me in a bedroom upstairs. I need to be near in case something happens."

"You're right. But there's no reason for you to sleep on the sofa. I'd like you to take a room."

"If you're sure."

"I'm positive." She would also sleep better knowing he was just down the hall instead of downstairs near the front door.

The lines on the outside of his eyes crinkled in amusement. Then he seemed to gather himself together. "I don't want to worry you, having me so close and all. I promise I'll do my best to only come inside the main house to sleep."

"Sergeant, I don't know why, but I feel safe around you. I think it's also pretty obvious that if you had wanted to harm me, you could have done it by now. I'd rather trust you."

"Thank you, miss," he said as they stopped in front of the barn. Once again, he dismounted easily, then moved to assist her.

When she felt his warm grip on her waist, she didn't dare meet his gaze. She'd worn only a light corset and the minimum of petticoats. Though it was surely only her imagination, she suddenly felt as if she could feel his touch through the layers of her cotton gown.

The moment her feet touched the ground, he let go of her and cleared his throat. "Well, I'd best take care of Velvet now."

"And Yellow?"

"I'm going to let him give me a tour of the ranch. I think it's time I got the lay of the land."

"Would you like me to go with you?" She was tired, but she was willing to sit in a saddle for hours if it would help the ranch.

"Maybe tomorrow. Today I think it's best that I do a little bit of riding and familiarize myself with the area on my own, see what repairs and work need to be done. I think it will probably take me several hours."

Since she'd already told him the boundaries—the creek and the barbed wire to the north and east and the largest pond and wooden fence on the south and west—Laurel knew he wouldn't have any trouble staying on her property.

"Well then, I'll make some food for you to take along and then prepare your room. When you get back, come into the kitchen around six for supper."

"I'll be back on time." He paused. "Miss Laurel, do you have weapons? I had a rifle, but it was confiscated when I was arrested. I think it would be best if we were both armed. I don't want to go out there without protection, and I don't want to leave you here without it."

Agreeing, she took him into the house, where her father's and brother's rifles were safely locked away. After assuring him she knew how to handle a rifle and giving him her father's to load, he left the house to ready Yellow.

She noticed his gait seemed stiff and he seemed intent on keeping his back as ramrod straight as possible. With all the commotion of the calf on her doorstep, she'd forgotten about the lashes he'd received.

As she moved to the kitchen to pack some food, she promised herself to check on his wounds that evening.

14

HE'D BEEN AS GOOD AS HIS WORD.

Thomas had ridden out with Yellow as soon as she'd given him the food she prepared. When she saw him return close to five with a contemplative look on his face, she figured he'd had a good look at her property and now understood why she was willing to do almost anything to keep it.

When he entered the kitchen for supper, his hair was wet and he was wearing a fresh shirt, no doubt another gift from his captain.

She served him chicken stew and some more of the biscuits he'd liked so much. This time she said grace while he bowed his head in prayer.

Then they ate in relative silence.

After he cleared his plate and refused seconds, she finally asked him about his ride.

"Did you find your way around okay?"

"I did. At least, Yellow did." Smiling softly, he said, "That horse could have ridden me around the perimeter without me giving him a lick of guidance."

"Did you see anything?"

"I didn't get to where you say the cattle are today, if that's what you mean. But if you mean anything suspicious, nothing beyond a cleaned-up campground in the north pasture."

"That was from the squatters. Did you see them anywhere?"

"No." He seemed to contemplate the problem as he took a sip of water. Then he shrugged. "Could be they've moved on. That's what most do—stay until they feel they've outlived their welcome."

That explanation felt too pat, but Laurel supposed it had merit. "Maybe that is what happened."

"When we ride together, you can let me know if you spot anything out of the ordinary. Do you know your neighbors well?"

"I do. The Pipps are to the north, and Landon Marshall is on the south."

"Tell me about Landon Marshall. Is he a family man? Did he serve? Is he married?"

"He did serve, though I don't recall the name of his unit. He's about our age. He's unmarried and lives with his mother and sister, Eva. His father is deceased." She wondered whether she should share her recent conversation with Landon, then decided to go ahead and tell Thomas. "He wasn't real pleased to learn I was going to be having you on the ranch."

"Since he doesn't know me, I bet he was worried." He cocked an inquiring eyebrow. "Especially if the two of you are close. Are you?"

"Not exactly."

"That sounds intriguing."

"It's not."

Thomas examined her expression for a moment before nodding. "Perhaps he'll feel better about my presence here when we meet."

"Maybe so. But maybe we could keep the fact that you're going to be in the house at night just between the two of us for now."

The corners of his mouth turned up. "Yeah, I reckon that might not go over real well. Hopefully we'll be able to keep it our secret."

She hoped so too. However, that morning's discovery had served to remind her that there was far more for her to worry about than shocking her neighbors.

"I hope so as well. At this moment, however, I might be too tired to care."

For a moment he was quiet, contemplative.

"I meant what I said yesterday. I might have been in jail, but I certainly am not a man you ever need to fear."

Gathering her courage, she looked him directly in the eye. "I'm not going to start looking for ways to judge you."

"Point taken." After draining the last of his water, he set the glass back on the table, then lifted his chin. "Though I've already said this, it might be worth saying again. I need you to know that I would never hurt a hair on your head. I'd rather cut my own arm off than see you hurt or harmed."

It felt as if they were vowing to do so much more than set the foundation for a work relationship. She wasn't sure if that made her feel better or more nervous. His words, together with the heartfelt, sincere way he was speaking, touched her more than she cared to admit, even to herself.

"I trust you, Sergeant. And I would never send you back to jail any more than I would go there myself."

After staring at her for a moment, he blinked and smiled. "I guess we've made our vows then." Chuckling softly, he said, "I'm thinking what we just promised is more than how most marriages start out."

His statement was so disconcerting, she giggled. "Perhaps so, though I would like to think most marriages start with love."

His gaze softened. "Listen to you."

"What did I say? What is that look for?"

"Your talk of love."

"Goodness. Surely you believe in love."

"I believe it's nice there are still people who want to believe in it," he said lightly. "How about that?"

Feeling both happy to be talking about something as sweet as love and also strangely exposed, she said, "You don't ever think about love?"

He looked down at his empty plate. "Actually . . . no. Not often. What with the war and all, I haven't had much occasion to contemplate love and marriage, Miss Tracey."

She knew she should let the conversation go. Thomas Baker was a man who had fought in many battles and suffered in a Yankee prison. No doubt he had been filled with anger and pain in many moments of his life.

But she'd also spied something in his eyes that was soft and warm. He was not all cold and battle-worn. That tenderness came from somewhere.

"Were your parents in love?" she asked.

And just like that, the pleasant spark that had filled his eyes vanished like the sun in a dust storm. He seemed to be at a loss for words before he quickly regained his composure. "I . . . well, yes, they were."

Her instincts had been right. She never should have prodded. But now that she had brought up the subject, she didn't know how to retract it without making things worse.

"Mine were in love too." She stared at him. "Mine are gone, of course. Do you still have either of them?"

"No. I haven't had them in a very long time."

"That's so sad. Did they get the influenza? Or smallpox?"

"No." Sounding almost as if he were being strangled, he added, "They, uh . . . they were killed when I was a child."

She hadn't expected that. "I'm so sorry. That had to have been horrible."

He rubbed the back of his neck, almost like he was trying to think about that. "I suppose it was."

The cold bluntness of his words made her feel even worse. "I'm sorry for bringing it up."

"There's nothing to be sorry about. I want you to ask me anything you want. Though I am sorry it happened, growing up without parents probably saved my skin in the war."

"How so?"

"After they died, I had no one. Because of that, I could fight with honor. Nothing held me back on the battlefield."

"What did you do after they died?"

"I lived on the streets." Not meeting her gaze, he looked just beyond her. "I learned to fight and scavenge and do whatever it took to survive."

She gasped. "Oh, Thomas."

"It wasn't all bad. I got used to living with next to nothing. I even got used to being uncared for." His chin lifted. "Amazing how a good dose of neglect can serve a man well."

Tears pricked her eyes as she studied him. He was such a handsome man. With his dark hair, truly beautiful blue eyes, and exceptional smile, she imagined he had been a beautiful child. A beautiful child fending for himself. "I'm so sorry."

"Don't be." His voice gentled. "As you can see, I'm just fine."

His words said one thing, but his tone told a different story. As much as he protested, his lack of family did bother him. She took another sip of water and tried not to glance his way.

She wanted to point out the obvious. He had just come out of jail and had welts on his back that still obviously pained him. But if he was going to pretend, she supposed she could too.

She took another sip of water and tried to think of something else to say. But he beat her to it.

"I'm hoping your childhood was much different. You said your parents loved each other?"

She nodded. "They loved each other and were happy with each other too. I had an idyllic childhood. I spent most of it either following my older brother around the ranch or helping my parents. We were happy." She sighed. "You know the rest. The war started, and Anderson and my father rode off to fight."

"Leaving you and your mother to fend for yourselves."

"Yes, but it wasn't so bad, not at first. Like everyone else, my mother was sure the war would be over in a few weeks and then everything could go back to how it used to be. She kept my spirits up."

"I remember thinking that way too. But the war dragged on."

Feeling the dark memories return, she nodded. "First Anderson died, then less than a month later, we got word that my father had too. Mother and I were devastated."

"Of course you were."

Whenever Thomas said things like that, her estimation of him rose. Now that she knew how terrible his childhood had been, she wouldn't have been surprised if he had no compassion for her loss. But instead of making light of it, he looked nothing but compassionate.

After smiling at him softly, she said, "About a year later, Mother met Wayne Vance, who was a truly kind man."

"He was Jerome and Bess's father?"

She nodded. "Wayne had some money. After his wife died, he'd felt unable to care for them well. He sent Jerome and Bess off to a fancy boarding school. They spent most of their lives away from home, learning all sorts of things and being attended to. Neither of them was much touched by the war."

"I didn't know that was possible."

She shrugged. "I feel sorry for them, in some ways. They have little in common with most everyone. They weren't even that close to their father, on account of him sending them off for so long. His death didn't faze them too much."

"Didn't he leave them anything?"

"He did. But not a lot. He left most of his wealth to charity. Then, of course, his Confederate notes became worthless. And I think . . . well, I think his good intentions came back to haunt him. He didn't like how Jerome and Bess turned out. Though he left them property so they would have a place to live, he didn't leave them much for expenses. I believe he thought that would force them to work and become more humble."

"No offense, but I don't think that worked too good."

She chuckled. "It didn't. They sold the house and land he left them and spent their money like water in New Orleans and Mississippi. They arrived here with a whole lot of clothes but little of real worth. They seemed to assume I'd take care of them next."

"Did their father not leave you anything?"

"Not money, no. But he made sure this ranch would go to me. So in that sense he gave me everything."

He thought about the beautiful house, the barn, the land. "I think you might be right."

"If I can get this ranch back on its feet, I believe I will make my mother, father, and even my stepfather proud. I'd like to honor their legacy."

"I'll do my best to help you make that happen."

She smiled. "Thank you. If that does happen, I'll feel like I can breathe again. Maybe actually begin living."

"That's a good goal, then. A woman like you should be living as much as she can."

"A woman like me?"

"Are you fishing for compliments, Miss Laurel? If so, I'll be glad to hand them to you, though they probably won't sound all that good, seeing as they're coming from a criminal."

She laughed. There was no way she was going to focus on her looks again. Not after Jerome's hurtful comments.

Instead, she ached to tease him a bit. To remind him that he was about to do his fair share of living now too. After all, living on a ranch had to be much better than living in jail.

Especially when he was getting whipped there.

"Oh my goodness! I was going to help you with your back."

He stared at her, his expression alarmed. "There's no need for that."

"Oh, yes there is. I noticed you favoring it today. I think I need to check on your wounds."

He stood up, pushed in his chair, and then stood stiffly behind it, almost as if he was hoping the chair and table between them would keep her from him. "Checking my wounds means taking off my shirt."

Surely he didn't think she was that delicate? "I realize that, Sergeant."

His throat worked. "Since we're going to be doing our best to keep some distance from each other, I don't think me taking off my clothes would be the best idea."

She knew he was right. It was going to be scandalous enough with him sleeping in Jerome's room. She didn't need to make matters worse by looking at him when he was half-clothed or touching his bare back. She'd already experienced some of that after her scare with the dead calf.

But it would be even more shameful to leave his wounds untreated.

"Sergeant Baker, I'm not merely trying to be kind. If your wounds fester, you could get blood poisoning. You could die."

"And if I passed on, then you'd be out of both your money and one new worker."

She winced. "Please don't even joke about such things."

"Never, miss."

Yet again, that drawl of his sent a little shiver down her spine. Feeling rattled by the curious response she had to him, Laurel jumped to her feet. "Let's get this over with. Clear off the table and I'll heat up some water to clean your wounds."

He didn't move. "Miss Tracey, I'm still not sure about this."

"You don't have to be. I'm sure," she said as she put the kettle on. "I heated water for supper, so it shouldn't take long to heat up again."

"You know, after we ride out together tomorrow, I plan to start mending some of the fencing I saw today."

"I'll appreciate that. Clear the table, if you please."

He picked up his supper dish. "The reason I'm telling you this is so you understand that whatever good you do on my back might get undone tomorrow. That's a consideration, I think."

Scraping out the remainder of food from a bowl into a compost bin, she raised her eyebrows. "If you fear that you'll undo all my efforts, it's fortunate that we will both be here again tomorrow evening."

Grudgingly, he walked back to the table, retrieved a serving platter, and carried it over to her. "You aren't seeing the point."

"Oh, I see it," she said. "I know accepting a woman's assistance must pain you, but it can't be helped."

"It ain't that. I'm trying to think of what's best for you."

She didn't want to hear another word about what was right and what was wrong. "I know you don't want or need my help, but I think it would be best if you allowed me to assist you. Let's not waste another second on this conversation."

"Yes, miss."

But of course he sounded as skeptical as she did. Actually, he sounded as if he were on his way to another punishment.

As the kettle whistled and she began tearing a clean muslin dishcloth into strips, Laurel said a hasty prayer. Her hands were shaking, her stomach was in knots, and she wasn't at all sure she was going to be able to sound as calm and collected as she needed to be when she was examining his bare skin.

"Help me, Lord," she whispered to herself. "You've been here for me many, many times in my life. Although it might not seem like I need you now, I really and truly do. So help me do my best, would you please?"

It wasn't a good prayer. It was actually kind of frantic and selfish sounding. But still she hoped for an answer.

Half holding her breath, she waited for a response. But no matter how hard she strained her ears, she heard no clatter of thunder or angelic voice.

But she did see Thomas Baker loosening the collar of his shirt. He was going to allow her to help him.

Perhaps that was enough of a sign for anyone.

15

Thomas would be lying if he said he'd never taken his shirt off in front of a woman before. After his family's death, the years he spent on the streets of Fort Worth had taken away most of his innocence and all of his modesty.

But he'd also learned that a person's body was merely a shell that guarded far more important things, at least to him. He now placed far more importance on a person's heart and soul than on one's outward appearance.

Spending what seemed like an eternity in a unit of men only reinforced those feelings. Personal space and privacy became things of the past during the war. He'd gotten used to never being alone. He'd seen other men bleed and cry and hurt while standing or lying beside him. He'd grown to know those men almost as well as he knew himself. Actually, he'd probably learned far too much about the men in his company. They most likely felt the same about him.

His time in the prisoner of war camp had helped him remember that all that really mattered about a person's body was that it worked.

If a man wasn't dying, that was good enough.

Though he'd matured and learned a lot in the army under

Major Kelly's and Captain Monroe's guidance, he'd also spent time with the camp women.

He wasn't proud of that fact, but he didn't dwell on his faults or baser instincts either. The women had been there for a reason, and his upbringing on the streets hadn't exactly prepared him to reject anything offered freely.

He was a man who had never expected to live long. He'd also become selfish enough to yearn for instant gratification. Plans and goals usually meant little to him.

It was only during his months on Johnson's Island that he'd begun to learn the benefits of patience and perseverance. Those attributes paid off when a man yearned to grow into something more than he was.

He'd learned a long time ago to stop feeling guilty about the past and concentrate on looking forward. That was his chief survival skill.

But as he sat down again in Laurel's kitchen, Thomas experienced a new and fairly forgotten sensation. He felt self-conscious.

As he sat and watched her busy herself with heating water and gathering supplies, Thomas realized he'd rarely felt so exposed. For the first time in his twenty-two years, he was going to knowingly allow another person to see his failings. He hated that. He didn't want to ever appear anything other than strong and fit.

He wanted Laurel Tracey to think of him as her protector, as a man who would do whatever it took to guard and take care of her. He wanted her to view him as strong and stalwart. Not weak. Not as someone who needed tending to.

Maybe it was because he didn't have a whole lot of experience in this area, but he was fairly certain if she saw him like this, that memory would be forever burned in her head. Whenever she looked at him in the future, she'd be reminded of a time when he'd sat while she stood, when he rested while she worked.

How could a man of worth ever be all right with something like that?

However, he didn't have much choice. He worked for her. His back also needed help. It was sore and festering. Only because of those reasons did he resign himself to the inevitability of what was about to happen.

"What would you like me to do?" he asked.

She paused at the stove, looked at him carefully, then seemed to take care to hide her true feelings under a guise of steadfastness. "Take off your shirt and sit down. After this water is heated, I'll wash your back and put some ointment on your cuts."

Realizing that she'd see both these new welts as well as a whole mess of older scars, he tried to prepare her. "Miss, my back . . . well, it ain't pretty."

"I should hope not," she teased. "Grown men shouldn't aim for pretty backs."

He swallowed. Thinking of his worst wound, the jagged ridge along his neck, he said, "I meant that I have older scars."

"We've already gone through this. I am not attempting to judge you, only help." Sounding slightly exasperated, she said, "Honestly, Sergeant, I hadn't pegged you to be so timid or shy."

"I'm not shy."

Facing him, her expression one of gentle compassion, she sighed softly. "How about we stop asking questions and giving excuses and just get this over with?"

"Yes, miss." She was right. Turning so he didn't have to face her, he began unfastening the buttons. His hands working the small holes were a little unsteady. Sometimes it took him two and three times to manipulate a button through the fabric.

He told himself it was because, despite sleeping through their nighttime visitor's arrival, he hadn't slept all that much in three days.

But when he slipped the cotton fabric off his shoulders at last and felt the air kiss his back, he felt pure relief. The burst of fresh air felt wonderful. Cleansing. Like a gift.

Until he heard her gasp.

"Oh, Thomas."

Embarrassment made his voice hoarse. "If it's worse than you thought, too much for you, I'm sure I could find a way—"

"Your wounds are terrible. I have no idea how you got through the day without complaining," she interrupted. "I should have tended to you last night."

"I'll be okay."

After a small pause, she ran cool fingers along his neck. "You certainly do have scars."

He tried not to notice how welcoming her fingers felt against his skin. How gentle she was. Each brush was featherlight and made him almost wish she wouldn't stop. So much so, it was almost worth the pain and embarrassment he was feeling.

Seeking to think of more clinical things, he said, "I warned you it looked bad."

"Some look years old, like before the war."

They *had* happened years ago. Well before the war. "Those ain't nothing to be worried about."

As if she'd finally put together a puzzle, she cried out, "Thomas, someone whipped you when you were a boy."

He closed his eyes even though he couldn't see her reaction. "Yeah. A boy sometimes needs persuasion from his boss."

She paused, then said, "I'm sorry to say that cleaning these new wounds might cause you further pain."

Her voice sounded so aggrieved, so thin, he began to get a little worried.

After another endless moment, she gently touched his shoulder. "I'm going to get started. I'll try not to hurt you."

So far, both her voice and her touch had been sweet. He couldn't remember a time when he'd received so much care. "You won't hurt me."

"I might. If I'm too rough, let me know." She added, "It's just that, well, I think I'm going to need to clean them real good. Dirt and who knows what else are embedded in your skin."

Unfortunately, he knew exactly what else he'd been exposed to. The jail cots were infested with all sorts of vermin. "Do your worst, Miss Laurel. Just, well, whatever you do, please get started."

He heard her dip a cloth into the hot water she'd prepared, then felt a sharp sting as she placed it on one of his lash marks.

Unable to help himself, he flinched.

Her voice hardened. "Who did this to you?" She gasped. "Sheriff Jackson said there was some 'miscommunication' at the jailhouse, but who was it? Another prisoner? One of the guards?"

She sounded so incredulous. She was so naïve. Did she really have no idea what cruelties befell men in captivity? Swallowing back a curse as she rubbed hot, soapy water on another cut, he muttered, "You know there ain't no way I'm going to start telling you names."

"Why not?"

"Because it doesn't matter. It's all over with, thanks to you."

"I'm sorry it happened in the first place," she murmured as she washed his wounds with soap.

The abrasive soap stung. He welcomed the feeling. It cleared his head, helped him focus on the present and not the past. When she ventured to a particularly bad spot, he flinched again.

And she apologized.

"Come now, hasn't anyone ever told you regret is for fools? It happened and it's over with. Done."

He was right too. What had been done was done. Fretting and talking weren't going to change the facts. Especially since he aimed to live in relative peace and comfort for the next year.

Sounding resigned, she murmured, "Move sideways, please. You have a few welts I can't quite get to."

Feeling vaguely like a boy again, he moved to the side and then leaned forward. Closed his eyes as she continued her ministrations. Little by little, he realized the pain wasn't so bad if he concentrated on other things.

Like the smell of Laurel's skin, for example. Or the way her soft touch felt on his skin. Or the way he was in her kitchen and was going to be sleeping in a bed just down the hall from her. Not on a pallet in a barn or in a stinking jail cell.

As the minutes went by, Laurel also seemed to relax. She got up once to rinse out her bowl and get more hot water, then continued.

"Whatever man you are protecting never should have harmed you like this," she muttered. "I wish you'd tell me his name."

Still leaning over, he found himself smiling at the thought of her rushing to his aid. "I'm not exactly protecting anyone. Merely saving you from worrying about something you can't change."

She harrumphed. "Didn't he realize you aren't violent?"

She made him sound like a mule for sale. It almost made him smile. "I ain't violent, but I sure am no saint either. I fought in the war, you know."

"That was different. You had no choice. You fought for the Confederacy."

She made that sound like a good thing. If she were anyone else, he'd point out that their side lost. But if he did that, he was liable to hurt her feelings. He'd rather take another lash than do that.

Therefore, he continued to sit silently while she tended to his back. Again and again, he felt the heat of hot water and the sting of soap. Though he tried his best, he was unable to prevent a gasp and a flinch every now and then.

Her hands paused. After hovering over his shoulder, she at last laid a palm on his bare shoulder. "I really am sorry."

Knowing his suffering was almost as painful for her as it was for him, he attempted to think of something good. Something free and sweet. Anything not to focus on the movements of her hand or the sharp pain that surrounded each dab she made.

But the only thing he could seem to think about was her smiling at him when he was on the chain gang and mending her fence. Or the way she looked at him so sure and true when he was in that blasted cage and she told the judge she wanted him.

Or the way she'd said she trusted him.

But, of course, he shouldn't be thinking of such things. He shouldn't be giving in to his feelings toward Laurel Tracey.

He let his mind drift back to the family who had loved him and to the lifelong friendships he'd made in a prisoner of war camp. He had to depend on the good memories he already had when he needed them, not try to make more with a woman who would never be his.

16

THOMAS?" MISS LAUREL REPEATED, HER VOICE TURNING A bit panicked. "Are you all right?"

Blinking, Thomas realized he'd done it again. He'd taken refuge in memories. And in doing so, he'd scared his new employer just a little too much.

She was facing him now, her eyes filled with worry. Her hands were clenched together. The worn cloth she'd been cleansing his wounds with was lying abandoned on the tabletop, bloody and soiled.

He cleared his throat. "Forgive me. Sometime along the way I picked up a bad habit of indulging in daydreams."

Her eyes widened, almost as if she was surprised he would admit such a thing. Then she composed herself again. "Oh. Yes." She straightened, absently ran her hands over her gown. "I must admit to getting lost in thought a time or two myself."

Those brown eyes of hers flooded with concern and compassion, filling him with gratitude. Filling him with a want he didn't dare acknowledge. He tried to force himself to look away. Instead, he examined the rest of her face. Noticed that a tendril of her burnished hair had sprung free from its confines and rested on her temple. It teased him, practically taunting him to reach out and brush it back.

Before he could do such a thing, he turned away. Breathed deep.

And realized that Laurel Tracey was a veritable minefield of distractions he needed to stay away from. She smelled good. Like roses.

It drew him to her. It was the same scent he'd caught when she brought him water that day at the fence. That same scent they'd all caught.

The scent more than one man had talked about in lewd terms late that night in their cells.

He needed space. Distance.

He really needed to get his shirt back on.

Scrambling to his feet, he shoved one arm through a sleeve, then the other.

With a cry, Laurel attempted to halt his movements. Reaching out, she batted at his arm. "Thomas, no! I need to apply the ointment and bandage you."

He most certainly did not need her hands on him again. "Ointment and bandages aren't necessary." Jerking his shirt together, he fumbled with his buttons.

"What is wrong?" Distress filled her eyes. "Did I hurt you that badly?"

She had enough to worry about. The last thing she needed to be thinking about was hurting a convict's back. "I'm fine."

"Then what is wrong? Why are you being so stubborn?"

He exhaled. Thought about fibbing yet again. Then decided it might be best if he was a little more honest. Given the fact that they were going to be living in each other's pockets for the next year, if she had a better idea about his feelings, things might go easier between them in the future.

"Miss Laurel, forgive my bluntness, but the fact is, I'm only a man."

"Yes?"

He waved a hand at her. "I am a man and you . . . well, you are a beautiful woman."

She blinked. "I don't understand."

Of course she didn't. Gritting his teeth, he attempted to maintain his composure and conduct himself in a way that would do the officers who'd become his friends proud. "You see, the thing is . . . I've been in jail, miss."

"I know that."

Lord, have mercy. "At the risk of being blunt, I've got to admit that it's been a real long time since I've, uh, enjoyed any feminine companionship. So while I am sincerely grateful for your ministrations, I think from now on it would be best for both of us if I kept my shirt on around you." And if she didn't touch him again.

"Oh! Yes, well, of course. I see." Looking down, she began to gather the rest of the cloths she'd had out to clean his wounds.

"If you don't mind, I think it would be best for both of us if I went to my room now."

She turned, picked up the bowl and a towel, and walked to the basin. "Of course. It's the one with the folded blankets at the foot of the bed. If you need anything, please let me know. And if you get thirsty or anything, help yourself."

"Thank you. I'll do that."

Then, like the coward he was, he turned and walked up the stairs and started searching for his room.

The scent of beeswax and lemon oil captured his senses. Little by little, his head cleared and his muscles relaxed. Feeling more like himself, he walked down the empty hall. Heard his boots clatter on the wood floor that needed to be sanded and smoothed.

Then, to his misfortune, he looked into her bedroom. And stepped inside. Immediately he was besieged by everything that was Laurel, including that same scent. Saw her bed, covered with two quilts and a great many down pillows. On one side of the room stood a full-length mirror. And on a chair rested a discarded white chemise, the bodice threaded with a pale-blue ribbon.

Startled, he turned away, but it was too late.

The memory of seeing something he shouldn't have, of entering her bedroom, would now be burned brightly in his mind. He'd had no business there. He should have turned around the moment he'd realized this was her personal space, not staying for even a second.

Hardly aware of what he was doing again, he darted into one of the other bedrooms, saw the blankets she mentioned, and shut the door behind him.

He pulled off his boots and pulled off the shirt already sticking to his back. Then, clad only in his denims, he climbed onto the bed, curved his arms around a down pillow that smelled like sunshine, and stretched out on his stomach.

He'd just embarrassed himself, but he'd done worse things. Therefore, it didn't really matter.

What mattered was that he was in a room all by himself. He was holding a real pillow, and soft sheets and blankets and fresh, sweet-smelling air surrounded him. His wounds were clean.

More important, he wasn't running anymore. Not from his mistakes and not from his past. In short, he was in a better place than he'd been in a very long time.

With great care, he shifted, pulled over one of the light blankets Laurel had set out for him. As the soft fabric swooshed around his lower body, he enjoyed the clean scent that wafted upward and held him close.

It smelled like a faint memory, like a time before he'd learned to be afraid.

Feeling better and more content than he could remember being in years, Thomas gave thanks and counted his blessings. He had many. Even better than enjoying physical comforts, he knew where he was going to be sleeping tonight. He had a great many things to be thankful for indeed.

Only then did he allow his eyes to close and his mind to drift.

17

ONE FULL HOUR HAD PASSED SINCE THOMAS HAD PRACTI-
cally run from the kitchen. He'd cited exhaustion. Laurel had
been concerned that she'd done more harm than good to his back
and that he was suffering from her best efforts.

After going out to the barn to care for the animals, she
returned to the kitchen, poured a glass of cool cider, and worked
on mending. As she threaded her needle and repaired the torn
hem of a dress, she listened for Thomas to descend the stairs.

But as another hour passed, she realized he had retired for
the night.

She didn't blame him.

And she was used to being alone. She'd spent most of her days
and nights after her mother remarried alone. Even when Jerome
and Bess were living with her, they didn't spend time together.
She should have been used to her own company. She'd thought
she was.

But even after just a couple of days, Thomas Baker had
altered everything. She'd begun to look forward to his company,
even if so far it had been filled with more worry and stress than
anything else.

After putting away her mending, she sat on her sofa in the

sitting room and tried to come to terms with all that had transpired since she'd stood at the window to watch Thomas work with the other convicts. She'd freed him, Jerome and Bess had left, and a calf had died. Then they'd returned to town together. She'd become part of a team. Half of a partnership that was built out of necessity but seemed on the verge of turning into something else too.

She didn't know how to stop the way she was starting to feel about Thomas. Didn't know if she was capable of stopping.

And if she didn't?

Well, the consequences would alter her life, and that was almost too much to take in. Maybe far too much to take in.

❧

Laurel woke on the sofa with a start the next morning when she heard Thomas open and shut the front door. Embarrassed that he'd seen her asleep, she ran upstairs, changed her dress, and washed her face. Next she went to the kitchen, made coffee and flapjacks, and waited for Thomas to return to the house.

When he did, he was pleasant yet distant.

"I fed the animals and milked Bonnet," he said as he set her egg basket next to her. "I even gathered these. Everything looks to be in good order."

"Thank you." Pointing to the serving plate next to her range, she said, "I made flapjacks."

"These look real good." He grabbed a plate and placed three on it.

"Go ahead and eat. I'll fry you a couple of eggs too."

"Thank you."

She washed two eggs, then cracked them into a hot pan, all

while casting furtive looks his way. He was eating methodically, his attention solely focused on his flapjacks.

When she placed the eggs on his plate, he thanked her again but said nothing more.

Her stomach began to feel like it was in knots. "Would you like anything else to eat?"

"No, Miss Tracey. This is more than enough."

"Are you sure?"

"You always give me more food than I got in a day in jail, miss. It's plenty for me."

"Ah." Placing one flapjack on her plate, she sat down and nibbled a bit of it. It tasted like sawdust.

Pushing it away, she said, "Is your back hurting you this morning?"

"My back is mending," he said quickly. "You won't need to bathe it again."

Though she realized he was trying to ease her worries, she still felt a little hurt. "I didn't mind helping you."

Thomas set down his fork. "I'm here to work for you. Not be tended to."

Feeling like there was nothing she could say to erase the unease that was festering between them, she got up again and washed her dish.

A couple of minutes later, Thomas set his dish on the counter next to her. "Thank you for breakfast. I'm going to go back out to the barn now. I have something I'd like to do before we head out on our ride."

"All right, Sergeant."

When she heard the kitchen door close, she felt more alone than ever. Not for the first time, she wished she'd been blessed with sisters or cousins. An aunt. Some woman who was smarter than she was in the ways of the world, who would freely give advice and offer suggestions. Like what to do about Thomas.

But what would this mystery woman say or counsel her to do? Laurel was fairly sure there was no correct protocol to follow when it came to developing a relationship with a scarred and secretive former prisoner.

Tired of waiting and stewing, she picked up her broom, went out to the front porch, and pretended to sweep off some of the debris and dust that had gathered there overnight. It was a rather silly task, and a poor use of her time. She had far too many other things to do besides pretending to sweep while actually spying on her worker.

But she couldn't help herself.

Soon she realized Thomas was cleaning out the barn. Velvet was tethered to a hitching post and Bonnet was bawling mournfully in one of the holding pens her father had built a year or two before the war. Scattered in front of the structure were saddles and blankets, jars and buckets, and a hundred other tools and implements men had stored in its depths over the years.

She went out there and offered to help him, but he brushed off her offer like it was a painful thing.

Now she was back on the porch, reduced to spying on him again.

She was just thinking about taking him some water when she noticed two riders approaching.

Resting a hand on her forehead, she tried to see who it was, but all she could see was an appaloosa and a paint. Both horses were stepping lively. The faces of the men astride them were hidden by dark Stetsons.

Glad she was at least wearing a clean calico, she stood motionless and watched the riders come closer.

Seconds later, Thomas exited the barn and walked to her side. "Who's here?"

"I'm not sure."

He nodded, his expression intent as he watched the riders' progress. Minutes later, he sighed. "One of the men is Sheriff Jackson."

"Maybe he has some news about the calf."

"I hope so. I hope it's that and not the twenty-five other real good reasons he has to be here."

Realizing Thomas was referencing the amount of money she'd paid for him to be set free, Laurel looked at him dubiously. "The transaction has already taken place, and Will knows I'm happy with how things have turned out. Everyone should." Herself, for one.

Thomas snorted. "People don't care about feelings, Miss Laurel. They're going to revel in the fact that you made a mistake."

"But I didn't."

"Even if you think you didn't, they won't care. Their minds were made up about me the moment they saw me in prison rags."

"They might have been wary of you, but they'll change their minds."

"Not necessarily."

"They will. After all, lots of people saw how helpful you were yesterday when you helped me take the calf to town."

"For some people, what they saw will mean nothing. They'll only care about what I am."

She wasn't sure what more she could say to Thomas to ease his mind—or their relationship. Since it was doubtful that he was going to be of a mind to listen to anything she said, Laurel decided to focus on the approaching visitors. Now that they were fairly close, she recognized the man by Sheriff Jackson's side. "The other man is Landon Marshall."

"Your neighbor and friend, right?"

She nodded. Remembering the way Landon had spoken to her in town, and how vaguely she had described her relationship with him to Thomas, she said, "We've, uh, recently drifted apart."

Thomas studied her. "Usually a person is a friend or he isn't," he drawled.

"Our relationship isn't that easy to define." Kind of like another relationship she was in.

"Huh."

She thought that sentiment said it all. The man's appearance was certainly unexpected. After she'd refused his suit, he had stopped visiting her. Then, of course, there was what had happened in town. He hadn't liked her standing up to him at all.

When they were a mere hundred or so yards away, Sheriff Jackson raised a hand.

She raised a hand in return, taking note of their solemn expressions.

Thomas must have taken notice of their serious looks, too, because his expression turned less combative and far more protective. He stepped a bit in front of her, almost like he was attempting to shield her from whatever was about to take place.

Though she knew she probably shouldn't, she allowed herself to relax. Maybe the tension between them was about to ease.

When the men drew their horses to a stop and dismounted, Laurel moved around Thomas to greet them. "Hello, Sheriff Jackson, Landon."

"Good day, Laurel. Baker," Sheriff Jackson said.

"Miss Tracey," Landon said, tipping his hat as his gaze strayed toward Thomas, who was looming behind her. She didn't need to see him to know he was staring at Landon.

She turned awkwardly and tried to smile at each of them. "Landon, this is Sergeant Thomas Baker. My new hand."

"I've been concerned about you. I hope you are faring all right." Landon didn't so much as even glance in Thomas's direction.

Thomas stiffened by her side but didn't say anything.

Eager to get to the point of their visit and then send them on their way, Laurel said, "Did you discover what happened to the calf, Will?"

The sheriff shook his head. "I'm afraid not. Doc promised to look at the little thing, but he hasn't had a chance yet. It might have simply died of natural causes."

"And it decided to die while on her doorstep?" Thomas asked, doubt thick in his voice. "I find that hard to believe. Someone is attempting to frighten Miss Tracey."

"We don't know that for sure," Landon said. "After all, a good Samaritan could have brought it over."

Thomas blinked. "Really? Like who? You?"

"Of course it wasn't me. But that doesn't mean it wasn't another of Laurel's friends." Looking at him derisively, Landon added, "Here in Sweetwater, we look out for each other. We're a close-knit community made up of good people. You're probably not familiar with such relationships."

Thomas lifted his chin. "Even if a friend did leave the calf, I'm not real fond of the idea of someone dropping off dead animals on Miss Tracey's doorstep in the middle of the night, Marshall."

"You almost sound as if you *are* insinuating that I brought her the animal."

"I'm guessing you had as much opportunity as anyone."

"I wouldn't have done such a thing. I want the future of this ranch to be as profitable as anyone, and killing any of its cattle would hardly make sense." Crossing his arms over his chest, he added, "I'm also not fond of convicts living in such close proximity to my neighbor."

"Who would you rather see here? You?"

"Of course me. At least I would not be attempting to take advantage of her."

"And how would I be doing that?"

"Don't act so innocent," Landon drawled, disdain lacing his tone. "You probably don't know the first thing about being around decent women. But if you harm one hair on her head, you will definitely regret it."

Thomas stepped forward. "Are you threatening me?"

Before Landon could reply, Laurel raised her hands. "Gentlemen, please stop! I can speak for myself."

"You shouldn't have to, Laurel," Landon said. "You need a real man to speak for you."

Realizing that Thomas was barely holding on to his temper, Laurel ignored Landon and turned to the sheriff, who had been noticeably silent. "Thank you for coming out all this way to check on me. It was real kind of you to go to so much trouble."

Sheriff Jackson's expression turned pensive. "I hate to tell you this, but we didn't ride over here to check on you or talk about the dead calf." Rubbing the back of his neck, he said, "You see, something else has come up."

Before she even realized she was doing it, she stepped closer to Thomas. "What's happened now?" Thinking quickly, she asked, "Does it have to do with Sergeant Baker's freedom?"

"No. That's done, much to your stepsiblings' dismay, I should add." Smiling a bit wryly, he said, "They were in quite a state when old Alan Corntree picked them up in his wagon two days ago."

She almost grinned back at him. Mr. Corntree was a peddler who drove a donkey cart around the area in the summer.

She doubted Bess or Jerome had ever deigned to give that man a second look, much less speak to him. And now they had been reduced to accepting a ride in his wagon. She had a feeling that set their high horses back a notch or two.

"Now that you've had time to think about it some more, Sheriff, do you think there's any chance one of them could have harmed that calf?" Thomas asked. "They've been after Laurel to sell. I'm not sure how they would have managed it, but maybe they resorted to trying to scare her into it."

Sheriff Jackson's expression hardened. "Their involvement is doubtful, but I haven't ruled it out yet. They have rooms at a boardinghouse, and I mean to keep my eye on them." He cleared his throat. "But we came to talk to you about something else that happened. Last night."

"Yes?" Laurel asked.

"One of my outlying storage buildings was ransacked," Landon said. "It was completely cleaned out."

Sheriff Jackson added, "Several items of note were taken. Some extra equipment, grain, and a trunk with some ammunition in it."

Thomas raised his eyebrows. "You stored ammunition in an outlying building?"

"I had my reasons for keeping it there," Landon said.

"Which were?" Thomas asked as he stepped closer to Landon.

Landon glared. "The point is that the ammunition is now gone."

"We suspect it might have been the squatters you've been worried about who've been coming onto your property from time to time," Sheriff Jackson interjected smoothly. "Any chance you saw them yesterday, Laurel?"

"No, Sheriff. I haven't seen anyone for days."

"I rode much of the ranch yesterday," Thomas said. "I found evidence of someone being in the north pasture, but nothing else."

"Interesting that this theft happened after you arrived," Landon said.

"What is your point?"

"I don't have a point. I'm merely making an observation."

Thomas looked at the sheriff. "Did you come out here to accuse me of raiding this man's shed?"

"Not at all," Sheriff Jackson said. "We just wanted to let you know what happened so you could keep your eyes open."

"I'll do that. If I see something amiss, I'll be sure to let you know."

Landon coughed. "I can't see how we can start relying on a man like you."

"Like me?"

"Don't pretend to act so surprised. You must have known your reputation would be in tatters after you went and got yourself arrested."

"I didn't go and get myself anything."

Sheriff Jackson sighed. "Gentlemen, this is beyond enough."

Landon stepped closer to Laurel. "This is exactly the kind of thing I was worried about when we talked in town. You are at far too many people's mercies, living alone like this. You need someone looking after you. You're just a woman, you know."

"Landon—"

He smiled as he cupped her cheek. "You know I'm right."

"I have help now."

"You wouldn't have needed to hire a convict if you'd simply let me help you in the first place," he murmured. "Let me help you, honey."

She felt the hard stare of Thomas's appraising eyes on them as she stepped back from Landon's touch.

"Watch yourself, Mr. Marshall," Thomas growled.

But Landon ignored Thomas's warning as if he weren't there. He ran his fingers down her arm. "Are you afraid of me? Don't be afraid. You know I don't want to do anything besides make you happy."

"I'm not afraid of you." However, though she wasn't afraid, she wasn't completely sure her happiness was the main thing on his mind. Stepping a little farther out of his reach, she eyed him carefully. "We've known each other for a good long while, Landon. Let's keep things the way they are."

"I'd love to do that. And since we're still such good friends, let me have you over one night soon. Eva will make us supper."

"Thank you for the invitation. Maybe I'll take you up on it one day soon."

"How about tomorrow?"

"Tomorrow?"

"I'll come fetch you, say, around five?"

Before she could accept, Thomas interrupted. "There's no need to pick her up. I'll drive her wherever she needs to go."

They all three looked at him in surprise.

"I don't want to burden you, Sergeant," she protested. Plus, though it made no sense, she felt a little apprehensive about involving him in her invitation.

He shook his head slowly as his gaze warmed. "Now, Miss Laurel, don't you be forgetting what we talked about," he drawled, his voice suddenly sounding a bit like honey. "I'm your hired hand. You're supposed to burden me."

"I don't believe driving me around is what either of us intended for you to be doing when I hired you."

"That don't matter. I'd be happy to drive you wherever you need to go. Always."

His offer was so sweetly worded, she couldn't resist smiling.

However, Landon didn't look all that enchanted by the idea. "There is no need for you to drive Laurel anywhere. I'll fetch her tomorrow evening."

Before Laurel could comment, Thomas spoke again. "No, sir. With squatters and so forth creating disturbances, I'd feel better if I was looking out for Miss Tracey as much as possible."

Before either Laurel or Landon could respond, Sheriff Jackson clapped his hands. "Well, that's settled. Turns out this little visit has been productive in more ways than one," he said brightly. "We got out our news and Mr. Marshall got his wish." He tipped his hat with a smirk. "We'll be on our way. We've got two more ranches to visit. And, Laurel, when I hear something about your calf, I'll let you know."

"Thank you, Will."

Landon didn't look nearly as pleased but tipped his hat as well. "Until tomorrow, then."

"Until then. Thank you both for coming out."

"I wanted to," Landon said, "even if I'd had no theft. You know how worried I've been, thinking about you living here like this."

Thomas stayed still and intent until they mounted their horses and took off. Only when their images were blurred in the distance did he speak again. "Does that happen often?"

"Does what happen? Does the sheriff come out often to pay me a house call? No."

Still staring off into the distance, he shook his head. "I'm talking about you getting asked out by your neighbor."

"No." She felt her cheeks heat even though she knew she had

no cause for embarrassment. "Mr. Marshall has asked me for a drive before, but never invited me to supper."

"I wonder why he's asking you now."

Laurel looked at him curiously. Thomas's posture hadn't eased. He was still standing alert in his shiny new boots and dark denims. The new, stiff cowboy clothes should have made him seem awkward. Maybe weak. Perhaps like a greenhorn. Instead, his clothing emphasized his toughness. She was starting to see that, unlike with most men, clothes did not affect him in the slightest. He looked just as dangerous and aloof dressed in a new chambray and denims as he had in his prison garb.

She swallowed. "To tell you the truth, I think he was always afraid to ask me to supper because of Bess and Jerome."

"He wasn't a big fan of theirs?"

"He was not. I think he was afraid they'd join me," she said. "They were truly insufferable." Before Thomas started asking more questions about Landon, she gestured toward the barn. "I know you've been doing some cleaning, but I think we should saddle up the horses now. I want us to check on the cattle. We can be back in time for our noon meal. I'll go put on a better bonnet and meet you in the barn."

Just as she was about to turn away, he called out, "Miss Tracey?"

"Yes?"

"Are you in the market for a man?"

She wasn't sure if she was or not. But because she was all too aware of the way Thomas was looking at her, as though she was something to be sought after, she stated uneasily, "I don't believe that's any of your business."

"I reckon it isn't. But it would be good to know."

His words made her feel flustered. Maybe a little warm. "That is something you won't have to worry about, Sergeant. I'm simply a woman trying to hang on to my family's ranch."

"Do you really believe that's all you are?"

"I believe I'd rather not discuss my personal life anymore," she said. She didn't like the idea of making choices about her future marital status that weren't based on love. She really didn't like the idea of thinking about making a future with a man who was nothing like the man she was walking beside.

"You might aim to pretend you're ordinary, but nothing could be further from the truth."

His words were soft. Kind. Still altogether too personal.

She ignored that familiar flutter of awareness as she ran inside and switched bonnets.

Later, when Thomas easily lifted her onto Velvet's saddle, she did her best to appear unaffected by his touch.

But instead of easing the tension between them, it seemed to increase it.

After assuring himself she was situated comfortably, he took hold of her father's rifle and mounted the gelding.

"Lead on, miss. Wherever you want to go, I'll follow."

Laurel motioned Velvet forward, trying all the while not to think about how his statement made her feel.

18

THOMAS HAD BEEN AN EXCELLENT HORSEMAN AND A PAR-
ticularly good soldier. He'd ridden across half of Tennessee and
Kentucky during the war without complaint.

He'd charged into battles, sure the whole time he wouldn't survive. He'd also been sent on scouting missions, walking through
swamps and woods and enemy lines to obtain information. Once
he even pretended to be a Yankee lieutenant to procure vital coor-
dinates for Major Kelly.

He'd ridden beside officers without a hint of uneasiness or
self-consciousness. Even when he served under Captain Monroe,
he felt fairly sure of his abilities. He attacked each task with the
intention of doing his best and hoping it would be good enough.
That said, he had many faults—that couldn't be denied.

He was impatient and could be emotional. He was barely lit-
erate and shamefully ungentlemanly. He was definitely not a good
choice to be any woman's suitor.

But now, as he accompanied Laurel Tracey across her ranch,
Thomas was starting to wonder if he knew himself at all. For the
first time in forever, he felt like a weak-kneed greenhorn. He was
antsy and uneasy. A sixth sense told him something was about to
happen. He just didn't know what it could be.

Because of that, he kept gazing around their perimeter as though they were on a dangerous mission.

No, he felt as if he were a rattler, ready to spring at a moment's notice. Or a skittish colt, wary of everything in sight. It was disturbing, and more than a little unsettling . . . until he realized he wasn't worried about them being ambushed.

No, he was dwelling on the woman beside him. It was she who occupied his mind and kept him on his toes. The problem was, of course, that he was too conscious of Laurel Tracey.

He doubted she could brush a strand of hair away from her face without his notice.

Though his infatuation was his fault, he perversely wanted to put the blame firmly on her shoulders. It was Laurel's fault he was so smitten. She was too pretty, too kind, too delicate. Too everything.

He was running out of ideas about how to treat her too. When she'd purchased his release, he intended to push aside his attraction to her and simply treat her with the respect she deserved. Keep it as a business arrangement.

But last night everything had changed.

The feel of her hands on his back had ignited a need he'd forgotten he'd ever possessed. Her tenderness and care had washed over his heart the way the warm water had soothed his skin.

And those feelings had encouraged him to think about all the wishes and dreams he buried when his parents and brother died so long ago. Then, just when he had a handle on himself, he had gone and accidentally spied her bedroom. That hadn't helped matters one bit. He hadn't been able to get out of there fast enough.

A night of fitful sleep, as all along he assumed she was down the hall from him, had only sent the rest of his body on alert. He'd lain in bed on his stomach, wishing it had been his sore, aching back that occupied his mind. But instead of reviewing his injuries, Thomas spent hours remembering the conversations he and Laurel had shared.

By the time he got up with the sun, he'd almost convinced himself he had the two of them firmly back in place in his mind. She was the owner of the ranch. He was her hired hand. For one year he would do his best to help her keep the ranch afloat. In three hundred sixty-five days, he would leave and never see her again.

That was what was supposed to happen. Somehow, over time, he was sure he was going to accept that and be fine with it.

After finding her asleep on the sofa, he vowed to continue this plan. It almost felt as though it was possible.

But then Sheriff Jackson and Landon Marshall arrived, and he saw the way Marshall gazed at Laurel.

Then and there, Thomas had realized there was no way he was going to be able to sit by and watch another man court her. It had come on suddenly, but the possessiveness he'd felt had been so strong he didn't even attempt to tamp it down. Some emotions couldn't be hidden.

That was why, when Marshall asked Laurel to come to his home for supper tomorrow, his first instinct had been to step completely in front of her and refuse the man's proposal.

He'd had to make do with gritting his teeth while Marshall cajoled and Sheriff Jackson looked on like a doting father. The only bright spot was that he'd made sure he was the one who was going to take her back and forth. At least then she would be under his protection.

Watching Marshall put his hand on Laurel had been the last straw, but somehow he managed not to shove him away from her, letting her manage him herself.

Still, when the men left, Laurel hadn't been happy with him. He didn't care. He aimed to see her safe. Unfortunately for her, the only place he could be sure she was completely safe was by his side.

All the time.

Now, as they rode, Laurel pointed out various landmarks he might have missed on the ride he'd taken alone. Thomas pretended to be attentive, but all he really did was attempt to figure out a way for her to accept him as a suitor one day.

It was likely only another one of his daydreams, but he couldn't resist imagining such a thing actually happening.

"As you can see, the creek isn't wide, but it stays filled most of the year," Laurel called, bringing him back to the present.

"Most?" He raised his eyebrows. Now that she'd caught his attention, he wasn't real pleased with the news she was giving him.

"We have dry spells from time to time, but that's rare."

He glanced to his right and left but didn't see anything other than more of the same rolling hills. "Where do you run the cattle when that happens?"

"There's a good-sized pond on our southwest. The family that owns it is fair and doesn't object if other ranchers use it from time to time. My father and brother used to take the herd there when needed."

"That's generous of them."

"Indeed. They're good people, but older. They wouldn't be a lot of help if I had to lead my herd to their property. Thank the Lord, I haven't had to do that yet."

He hated the thought of her having to do so much on her own. To cover up his unease, he teased, "Are you thanking the Lord because you don't like the terrain or don't like moving cows?"

She grinned. "Both, I suppose. I have no problem with managing one or two or three cows at a time. When they are in a large group? I can't explain it, but they still intimidate me."

"That's not so surprising. Rounding up cattle can be arduous for the most experienced cowboy."

"Thank you for not saying it's difficult *for a woman*."

"I would be lying if I didn't admit to feeling concerned about a little thing like you taking on so much. You could get hurt."

Even in the broad sunlight, he could tell her cheeks flushed. "Only you would say I'm little."

Before he could reassure her, Laurel fanned her face. "Forgive me. I'm not usually so eager to fish for compliments."

"I never thought you were. And you weren't fishing. You were just being your usual modest self."

Smiling, she tucked her head. He let her take the lead again, happy to lazily scan the area while she told him more of the land's history.

About twenty minutes later, they rounded the top of a hill. "Here they are," she said as they looked down on the small herd of cattle, their brown-and-white hides standing out against the pale-green grass like Easter eggs.

"Good-looking cattle," he said.

"They're in good health. Some of them must be farther up the creek, but their numbers are increasing. Altogether we have twenty now." She blanched. "Would have been twenty-one."

"Don't think of that," he said quickly. "It does no good to dwell on the past."

She swallowed. "You're right. Well, tomorrow or the next day we'll need to guide all of them to another pasture." She turned to him. "I just realized herding cattle might be a new experience for you. I hope cattle don't intimidate you too."

"Not yet, miss. Those cows and I should get along just fine."

"You sound as if you've worked with your fair share of cattle."

"Some." Eyeing a mother heifer nudging her calf, he continued, "My father was a blacksmith. I was used to being around animals at a young age, and I worked in a livery before I went into the army, where I also worked with horses. And when I first got out, I did some odd jobs, one on a ranch."

"You've always been a hard worker, haven't you?"

"Learning quickly helped garner me extra nights on a cot. I've never been a fan of sleeping on the ground."

All traces of humor vanished from her expression. "I'm so sorry, Sergeant. You've had such a difficult time of it. Even after the war you were jailed."

"That was my fault. I was attempting to make some money in the wrong way and lost in a poker game to a pair of powerful men. I deserved what I got."

"You certainly didn't deserve to be beaten."

"Maybe not. However, it's all over now." He smiled her way. "Thanks to you."

"Don't thank me too much. You're going to be working hard for me over the next year."

"I'm planning on it. The hard work will do me good."

Their conversation turned easy as they continued on, riding along the filled creek bed. Eventually they slowed their pace to a walk. The sun was bright overhead and sent the temperatures skyrocketing. The shade from trees by the creek was a welcome relief.

Velvet whickered, showing her appreciation. Yellow, on the other hand, pranced a bit, illustrating his displeasure with the slower pace.

Thomas had been about to suggest they dismount and allow

the horses to drink, but he quickly discarded that idea. Until Yellow got over whatever was making him so skittish, he would likely be difficult to control.

Since Laurel didn't mention a need to stop, Thomas stayed quiet and concentrated on examining the area, looking for traces of squatters. He was so focused on tracking he only half listened as Laurel continued talking about the history of her family's land ownership.

"Oh!" she called out, interrupting herself.

"What?"

"Oh no!" she whispered as she motioned Velvet into a canter.

"Miss Laurel, what is it? Please slow down and—" He stopped talking as he caught sight of what had her in its grip.

At least six cows were lying on the ground in front of them. From the position of their bodies and the flies buzzing about them, it was obvious they were dead—and that they hadn't died of natural causes.

"Stay here," he barked as he dismounted, then hurriedly tied his reins to a nearby tree.

She ignored him.

More quickly than he had thought a woman could move in long skirts, Laurel leapt off Velvet and hurried to his side without bothering to tether her horse.

Thomas didn't know whether to order her to see to her mare or reach for her hand. Ultimately, he decided to do neither. He needed to focus on the poor cows and attempt to discern what had happened. As he approached, he noticed a pungent smell first. It wasn't death as such; it had more of a copper tint to it.

It was the scent of blood, the scent he would know anywhere, thanks to three years of standing in the middle of bloody battlefields.

Instinctively, he turned to the horses. If he'd been riding his old mount, Settler would have been dancing awkwardly and breathing hard. Thomas was having a difficult time not reacting to the scent of blood himself, even after all this time.

It was impossible to breathe in the scent and not be reminded of death and danger. However, neither mount looked ready to bolt. Their nostrils were flared and their ears were standing up, alert. But beyond that they seemed calm enough.

Stepping closer, he resolutely pushed the scent from his mind and scanned the ground for the evidence he was looking for. Eventually he did find blood, but it wasn't from either a bullet or a blade. Instead, it looked as if the steers were bleeding from their mouths.

It looked to him like they'd been poisoned.

The hairs on the back of his neck stood up. As Laurel said before, killing cattle made no sense. Especially in war-torn times like these, cattle were a valuable asset. No man he'd ever come into contact with, no matter what issues he might have with his enemies, would seek vengeance by killing five head. That was a waste of good money and a squandering of thousands of future dollars.

"This is terrible. No, it's worse than that. It's . . . it's a tragedy," Laurel whispered. "I don't understand how someone could do something like this."

"I was thinking the same thing."

"What happened to them?" she whispered.

"My guess is they were poisoned."

She looked around. "Thomas, over there. What's that?"

A paper had been nailed to a tree next to the creek. Thomas opened it.

"It's a note. It says, 'Next time the kerosene will go in the creek.'"

Just as Laurel gasped, they heard a rustling in the distance, followed by a loud crack.

Unfortunately, Thomas was as familiar with that noise as he was with the scent of blood. Grabbing her arm, he forced her to the ground and covered her body with his own.

"Thomas!" she called out. "I can hardly breathe. I'm lying facedown in the dirt."

"Settle," he ordered as he braced his hands on either side of her, lifting his chest and shoulders so he could scan the distance.

But instead of serving to calm her, she fought him with a cry. Her efforts were futile. He was far bigger and heavier.

"Laurel, calm yourself. Someone fired a weapon," he said in a low voice.

To his surprise, she stopped thrashing. "Do you think someone is hunting?"

"Maybe." He shifted slightly, giving her a bit more space. "Could be one of those squatters you mentioned you saw."

She shivered.

Though he longed to hold her close and comfort her, military training kicked in. He concentrated on their surroundings, attempted to find a place where Laurel could remain safe and out of danger.

A minute passed. Another two.

Just when he was about to exhale, he heard another rustling, followed by another sharp crack. As Laurel's shoulders began to shake, he bit the inside of his cheek so he wouldn't let out a stream of the vilest curse words he could think of.

Whoever was out there was coming closer.

19

SOMEONE WAS SHOOTING AT THEM. RATHER THAN ANYONE
hunting, it was likely whoever had poisoned six of her cows, and
they had now set their sights on her and Thomas.

Well, Laurel thought so. It was hard to know for sure, seeing
that she was currently pinned underneath her hired hand. He
had his elbows propped up on the hard earth, his rifle clutched in
his hands. From what she could tell—and she couldn't ascertain
much from her position—his focus was on whoever was firing
shots.

She, on the other hand, couldn't seem to concentrate on
anything other than the fact that she was lying on the ground
underneath a very large man.

She was sweating profusely. It was making her hair stick to
her neck and her durable riding dress feel like it weighed two hundred pounds. A smattering of gravel and rocks was digging into
her palms and cheek. What little bit of air she could inhale was
infused with dust and grime.

She should be in pain. She should be terribly uncomfortable.

Instead, as each second passed, all Laurel could seem to think
about was how Thomas's skin smelled of soap and leather. How

he was holding his body firm and still, seemingly from sheer force of will.

She realized then that he'd probably participated in many such battles. His body was conditioned to respond to danger.

After several minutes passed in silence, she whispered, "Are they still out there?"

"I can't tell," he muttered under his breath as he shifted again, obviously attempting to cover her even more completely.

There was no way she was going to let Thomas get shot while trying to protect her. They both needed to move to safety. "Thomas, I need to get up."

"Stop squirming."

Feeling certain that she would rather face whatever was about to happen head-on than continue to lie underneath him, Laurel pushed against his torso with her shoulders.

He groaned. "Laurel—"

"No, this won't do," she protested. Though the way she was half squashed on the ground, there was no doubt her words came out garbled.

"I'm trying to keep you safe, woman."

"I understand that, but you are also stifling me. I'm finding it difficult to breathe."

He shifted, somehow managing to cover her body even more. "If you are alive, that's all I care about."

Though she appreciated his gallantry, she knew she wouldn't be able to live with herself if he died shielding her. Thinking of the only thing that might encourage him to ease up a bit, she hissed, "I'm not going to be alive if I suffocate. Please. Allow me some space to breathe."

At last he moved, but it was with obvious reluctance.

"There," he said when he shifted a few inches to his right. Now he was only covering a portion of her body. "Inhale."

The fresh, clean air felt like a gift to her lungs. She breathed in deep. "Can you see who's out there?"

"No. This old rifle is better than nothing, but it doesn't have the scope my old Winchester did." Ruefully, he said, "I'd give a whole lot to have it in my hand right about now."

She was wishing she'd brought her brother's rifle. She wasn't a sure shot, but she could certainly handle a weapon well enough to feel safer with one in her hand.

Glad that he hadn't yet pushed her back down, she kept herself close to the ground as she took several more fortifying breaths. She also scanned the horizon, silently hoping the people who'd already done so much harm had already left.

Beside her, Thomas was looking intently to the west, his eyes squinting in the sun. "Down," he commanded.

She pressed herself flat again, but not before she saw a sparkle of metal in reflection off the creek. Seconds after, she heard another crack of a gun.

"Whoever it is, he's closer," Thomas said. "We need to get you out of here."

"We both need to get out of here, Sergeant."

"I thought we'd moved to calling each other by our first names."

She didn't want to waste time verbally sparring. Instead, she stayed silent, hoping and praying she would be able to follow whatever instruction he was about to give her.

After another minute passed, he tilted his head toward Velvet and Yellow, who for some reason hadn't run off. "How well can you ride?"

"As well as you need me to."

"Good." After looking in the direction from where the shots

were fired, he said, "On my mark, we're going to rush to our horses, mount them quickly, and race to the house."

"I can do that."

"Laurel, when you're on that horse, you keep your body low and ride fast. As fast as you've ever ridden in your life," he continued, his voice rough with worry. "You understand?"

She was getting nervous now. Doubting her abilities. But she couldn't let him know that. "I understand."

He looked at her again. "If I fall behind for some reason, you continue without me. Don't wait."

No, that didn't sound good. "Thomas—"

"I'm real glad you're calling me by name now, darlin', but what I need to hear is your promise."

"I can't promise you that. If you're hurt—"

"You can. You must. Promise me." He paused, obviously waiting.

"What kind of woman would I be to leave you?"

His tone became more emphatic. "I'm trying to keep you alive, Laurel." Before she could protest again, he glared at her. "On three, move," he bit out. "Promise me you'll do it."

"I promise."

"Thank you." His blue eyes scanned her face, softening for the briefest of moments, then he spoke. "One."

She tensed, pressing her palms against the rough terrain. The corner of a sharp rock dug into her skin.

"Two."

Her mouth went dry as she moved to a crouch.

"Three."

Not daring to focus on anything but her promise, she sprang to her feet, turned with a stumble, then rushed toward Velvet.

As she ran over the rough earth, dust and gravel lifting into a cloud around her, she concentrated on making it to her mare.

She felt Thomas's presence behind her. Still shielding her. Still urging her forward.

The horse was skittish, looking at her with one wary eye, pawing the ground with one hoof.

"Velvet," she whispered.

As she reached out a hand for the reins, another crack filled the air. Closer to the horses than before. Velvet whinnied, then reared in fright. Laurel scrambled backward, ducking to avoid being inadvertently struck.

When Laurel straightened, reaching out a hand to try to calm the mare, the horse whinnied again, then tore off into the distance.

When Yellow cried out, then stumbled, Laurel cried out, too, as Thomas attempted to calm the spooked horse. But just as he got the reins loosened, the intruder fired again, this time even closer.

Kicking his hooves, Yellow let loose a sharp cry. Thomas jumped back, barely preventing himself from getting kicked.

"Thomas!" Laurel called out.

"I'm okay," he said around his panting as Yellow reared and snorted, then darted to their right. Seconds later, the horse raced away, a cloud of dust rising around his hooves.

Though Laurel ached to be tough, it was disheartening to see their mounts disappear like birds in flight.

They had nothing now.

Hooves pounded the ground, the vibration feeling like a train was approaching. Their attackers were much closer now. At least two riders by the sound of it.

Thomas reached for her, pulling her back to his side as they took shelter next to the creek's bank.

Fearing the worst, afraid as those who seemed to enjoy preying on them drew near, Laurel closed her eyes and silently cried out to the only One who could help them.

Why, God? she asked. *Why would you take away my parents, my brother, my future, my cattle, but then bring me a helper in Thomas . . . only to take even that away?*

What was she going to do? The situation felt so hopeless. She'd never felt so alone. Tears flooded her eyes and began to trickle down her cheeks.

"Don't, Laurel," Thomas said roughly.

Confused by his words, she turned, only to realize he was now crouched and pulling her against him as he guided her next to the deceptive safety of a pair of mesquite trees.

"Don't you start crying," he ordered.

"I'm trying not to."

"Good. I need you tough now. Don't you dare give up on me."

"I won't." After a few endless minutes passed, she realized she could no longer hear the riders.

"I think they're gone," he said, affirming her thoughts.

His voice was flat. She imagined that he, too, was realizing that not only could their attackers come back, but they were in the middle of her ranch in heat that had now risen to at least a hundred degrees.

"It'll be okay."

"You sound so certain."

"I've been in worse situations. I'm not worried."

His words were so welcome, so needed, that she allowed herself to lean against him, taking refuge in his solid form, even though her head reminded her there was little he could do to ensure their protection or propel them to safety.

"Breathe, Laurel."

Dutifully, she did as he bid. But even the intake of oxygen did no good. The air was so hot it felt like it was burning a path down her insides each time she inhaled.

After a few seconds, Thomas shifted and wrapped one strong arm around her shoulders. She felt the hard muscles of his arms and chest against her curves. His scent surrounded her once more. Leather and man.

Against her will, she found comfort in it. Even though it was all too much. Too intimate for two people who really didn't know each other all that well.

Nonetheless, she leaned into the comfort and took refuge in it. "I'm scared," she admitted. "I'm trying to be brave, but I fear I'm all out of bravery. I'm sorry."

"Don't be sorry." Rubbing her shoulder and arm, he said quietly, "Matter of fact, I'd be real concerned if you weren't scared."

Something in his voice caught her in its grip. Was it the thread of doubt? The thin wavering of his confidence? "Are you?"

"Scared? A little bit."

Laurel twisted to examine his expression. When she realized he was being completely serious, she blurted, "I'm scared we won't get home. Is—is that what you are afraid of too?"

"I'm afraid someone is going to try to hurt you again and I won't be able to prevent it. I'm afraid my best efforts won't be enough."

They heard another thundering of hooves, sending them both back to high alert. But to Laurel's surprise, the two riders were moving away from them. "They're not circling back toward us," she said after a moment.

"It seems so."

"Why would they do that? Now that we're here without horses, it would be so easy to finish the job."

"I couldn't say why they're leaving," he said after a pause. "Perhaps they only wanted to scare us, and then scare the horses as well to strand us."

"That makes sense." Poisoning cattle was bad enough. But horses, of course, were even more valuable than cattle. No one shot at horses, unless their intention was to run them off.

He tilted his head back so he could see her whole expression. "You doing all right now?"

"Yes. I think so."

"Good." Carefully, he removed his arm and stood up. "You're right about all this not making a lick of sense. It certainly doesn't. But I don't suppose it really matters. What is a concern is that we're currently at least three miles from your homestead in this heat."

Leaning down, he offered his hand to assist her to her feet. "We need to get you home as soon as possible. Or at the very least, out of the sun. That means we had better get started."

"Yes." She looked back at the dead cattle. "I also need to inform Sheriff Jackson about all that's happened."

"We both will. After we get back to safety."

"Walking will take us hours." She sighed. "Bess and Jerome aren't even on the ranch anymore to miss us. Too bad Landon didn't ask me to supper for tonight. He would no doubt come over when I didn't show up at his house. Maybe he'd even send out a search party," she added.

"Though it pains me to say it, I would hope he'd come quickly." He smiled then, showing his beautiful teeth. The effect was no doubt what he intended—blinding.

She barely refrained from rolling her eyes as they started walking. He truly was too much. "You have attitude in abundance, sir."

"I've been told that once or twice before."

"When you were a boy, did your mother despair of you?"

The muscles in his cheek twitched. "She did. She, uh, thought I was incorrigible. She said I would never be the scholar my brother was destined to be."

"And were you ever like him?" she teased.

"No."

She looked at him in surprise. "Why not? You didn't care to be?"

"I was too hotheaded, I'm afraid." He held out an arm as they climbed over a small thicket of large prickly bushes. "Careful. These thorns can hurt."

She held on to his hand as she maneuvered her way around the thicket. Once she was satisfied her calico wasn't stuck in the thorns, she smiled up at him. "What did you do that was so wrong?"

But he didn't smile back. If anything, he looked more pained. "Nothing I would care to talk about."

Realizing she'd struck a nerve, she refrained from pushing anymore. After all, she had just as many people in her life who were long gone and memories she didn't care to talk about.

After another twenty minutes, she wiped at the trickle of sweat dripping down her forehead. "Do you think we've gone a mile yet?"

"Maybe half. No farther."

She pulled at the collar of her dress. "You sound so sure."

"You're talking to a man who spent the majority of his days in the war marching across miles of fields and roads. My feet have a good idea of what walking a mile feels like."

Staring forward, she said, "Maybe Velvet will be waiting along the vista."

"I hope so."

"We should have taken a sip of water from the creek."

"It's good we did not, Miss Laurel," he said, his voice rough. "We can't be sure that note told the truth." He paused. "Though the cattle looked like they had been dead long enough for the other cattle to have been poisoned by the creek, too, if there was something in the water. After all, they were positioned downstream, but they looked fine when we saw them. I'll find out what happened. I promise."

Thomas looked so certain, his expression so determined, she began to fear what he was going to do when he did discover what happened. "And then . . . and then you'll tell the sheriff?"

"No. And then they'll pay."

His voice was so cold, his words so dark and filled with terrible promises, she stumbled again.

Automatically, he took hold of her elbow. "Careful now. You almost hurt yourself."

"I'm fine."

He didn't release her. "I see that. But still, slow down now. We've got time and it's hot."

That was where he was wrong. She needed to do something. She needed to do anything she could to make things better! Shaking her head, she said, "No, Sergeant. We need to hurry. We've got to inform the sheriff about what happened. And the men . . ."

Instead of moving away, he held her closer. "And the men are long gone," he finished, his voice gravelly in her ear. "That means we don't need to get overheated. We need to pace ourselves. Everything will happen when the time is right, Laurel. I promise, the Lord takes care of his children. Somehow, some way, he's gonna make sure we get back to your place okay."

"You . . . you really believe that, don't you?"

"I used to not believe. But now I know better. I still make mistakes, do things my own way too much. But I haven't forgotten what I learned from the men who became my friends on Johnson's Island. They knew that no matter what, God was in control. And they lived accordingly." Gradually, he released his hold on her. "Okay?"

As his words permeated at last, she realized everything he'd been saying made sense. They needed to trust in the Lord. They needed to bide their time and be cautious. Only then would they survive.

She drew in a ragged breath. "Okay."

He flashed her one of his perfect smiles. "Good girl."

She nodded. Thinking about his advice, about everything he'd done for her in the last twenty-four hours, she said, "Thomas, have I thanked you enough?"

He pulled back his hat so she could see his bright-blue eyes. "You shouldn't be thanking me for anything, Laurel."

"How can you say that?"

"Easily. You're in my care but walking miles in the heat after being shot at."

"You know what just happened was not your fault. There were only two of them, but they had the advantage. We were no match for them, especially with only one rifle." She frowned. "And since I cried out and hid, I don't think I even count."

"I should have been able to handle them. Two against one ain't much of an obstacle."

"Surely you don't mean that."

"I mean everything I'm saying. I know better. I know I didn't respond to any of what's happened like I should." His voice was harsh.

"Even though I hate to admit it, if you weren't here, I would be hopelessly lost."

"You're not giving yourself enough credit. I have no doubt that you'd find your way home without a problem." He winked. "You'd do your horse proud, for sure."

Her horse. Even after everything that happened, he could still manage to make her smile.

"That's quite a compliment, Thomas."

"You watch out, Miss Tracey. Before my year with you is over, I'm liable to say all kinds of sweet things to you. You might even become used to it."

"I'll try to prepare myself."

When he laughed, the sound echoed around them. Caught her heart and made her wonder what she was ever going to do when he left her.

The thought was almost enough to make her start crying all over again.

20

Johnson's Island, Ohio
Confederate States of America Officers POW Camp

THOMAS HAD JUST FINISHED EATING HIS SUPPER OF BEANS and a couple of ripe tomatoes and cucumbers from their makeshift garden when he noticed the other members of his group looking at him funny.

He dropped his spoon with a clatter. "What?" he asked, feeling suddenly self-conscious. No matter how hard he tried, he could never remember the "right" way to eat everything. It was a constant source of amusement for the other men. It seemed half of them had learned the right way to hold knives and forks by the time they'd learned to walk.

When no one jumped at the chance to point out his mistake, he began to get irritated. Why couldn't one of them just spit it out so they could laugh at him, and then he could go back to eating? It wasn't like they got many opportunities to eat fresh vegetables.

Just as he was about to say something about how each of them should mind their own business, he noticed their expressions looked different than usual. Especially the major's. He looked almost pleased about something.

"What is it now, Major?" Thomas finally blurted. "How did I hold my tomato wrong? *Whom* have I offended? I could have sworn I've been doing real good tamping down my temper."

Phillip Markham leaned back his head and laughed. "You know what? I think you have been calmer than usual. It's been impressive."

If his manners and behavior had been so much better, Thomas really didn't understand why Phillip was laughing. Or why the lot of them had been eyeing him in such a funny way.

Looking from Phillip to Robert Truax to Major Kelly to Captain Monroe, he searched for answers. "Is that it? You wanted to tell me I've been doing better?"

The captain sat down on the bench next to him. "Settle down, Sergeant. No one is trying to make you uncomfortable."

"Well, I am. You'd be uncomfortable, too, if four men were staring at you like your pants were unbuttoned."

Captain Monroe's blue eyes sparkled. "I didn't look, but I think your trousers are securely fastened, Thomas."

"Y'all are just staring at me for the heck of it, then?"

"No. It's that we just discovered something new about you."

This wasn't good news. Thomas had taken great care to try to keep his worst traits and the worst parts of his past concealed. "What did you find out?"

"Something of note," Major Kelly said with a grin. He was sitting across from him on the ground. His legs were stretched out before him and he was bearing the rest of his weight on his hands. "See, when Monroe and I went over to greet the newest arrivals, one of them happened to see you from a distance."

"So?"

Sharing a smile with the captain, Major Kelly continued. "The long and short of it is that the man was in awe."

The major had lost him. "In awe of what?"

"Of you, you idiot," Robert said.

"What are you talking about?" he asked.

Robert slapped him on the back. "Thomas, only you would take something good and turn it on its ear. The major and captain are talking about how you've been holding out on us."

Thomas stared at the captain and silently begged him to get to the point.

Thankfully, Captain Monroe did. "The gentleman we talked to happened to be a lieutenant colonel with a unit out of the Carolinas."

"Lieutenant Colonel Isaac?"

"Uh-huh." The captain's eyes brightened. "Ring a bell?"

"Yes, sir." Thomas nodded. "I met him down in Kentucky."

Lieutenant Markham folded his arms across his chest. "He told us how you fought off no less than five Yankees by yourself to save a young lady and her daughter."

"And that you were bleeding from numerous cuts and gashes but still spent the majority of one afternoon helping them get packed up, then took them to their nearest relative's house," Captain Monroe continued. "Five miles away."

"All while bleeding and sporting any number of cuts and bruises," the major added softly.

Thomas swallowed. He had been in a heap of pain that day, but his pain had paled compared to the things the woman had endured. "It was nothing more than any of you might have done. I can't believe Colonel Isaac remembered me."

"It's more than that, Thomas. He said he'd never forget you as long as he lived," Major Kelly said. "The colonel remembered you because that woman was his eldest son's wife. You saved her. You saved his granddaughter too."

The lady's name had been Helena. She'd been a sweet thing.

So scared, though. He vaguely recalled hoping she would be one of the few women who got to welcome her husband home. "Do you know what happened to her man? Is he still alive?"

Captain Monroe nodded, a big smile on his face. "He is, and after incurring a nasty wound, he got to go home. When he heard what you did, he swore he'd pray for you every night for the rest of his life."

Thomas reckoned no one besides himself had ever prayed for him before. It made him feel good, almost like he was worth more than he'd thought. "That's something."

"That's more than that, son," Phillip Markham said. "The old man said you've got quite the reputation among his men."

He was embarrassed now. "I sure hope not."

"Thomas, you're their hero," Captain Monroe said.

Thomas looked at each of the men, the men he respected more than most anyone in the world. They'd all put themselves in harm's way and had saved countless soldiers. "That happened almost a year ago. I'm not sure why you all care."

"Because you never told us, you nitwit," Robert said. "We had no idea you hide a heart of gold underneath all your cagey ways."

Putting his plate down at last, Thomas cleared his throat. "I appreciate you letting me know Helena and her daughter survived. Thank you for that."

Robert Truax blinked. "That's it?" he asked, dismay thick in his voice. "That's all you're going to say?"

Thomas got to his feet. "It was one afternoon. I'm pleased they're faring well, and will also admit to being gratified to know they remembered me. But I don't understand why you all think it's worth getting into such a fuss about."

Major Kelly shook his head. "You *don't* get it, do you?"

There it was again. Another reminder that he didn't catch on to things quick enough. "Don't get what?"

"I knew you were brave. I knew you were sent behind enemy lines, and I knew you could ride like the wind. I knew you had a bad temper, and I knew you had an excellent right fist. But this . . . well, this proves you have heart too." Looking him up and down, Major Kelly smirked. "The truth is, I'm kind of smitten."

"Smitten?"

"Indeed, soldier. If I were a girl, why, I'd likely be in love." While the other men chuckled, Major Kelly winked. "You are destined for great things, Thomas Baker."

"Because I was able to help a woman and her child?"

"No, Sergeant. It's not because you were able. It's because you did," he said before walking away.

As Thomas stared at the major, Captain Monroe gripped his arm. "We're right proud of you, son." He smiled then. "I'm tickled that man has been telling your tale to everyone for months. You deserve all the recognition. You are a good man. One of the best."

Thomas nodded as he felt his face flame.

Only when he was going to sleep that night did he dare allow himself to feel that euphoric bubble of worth lift inside him.

He wasn't smart. He had no money. He didn't have any family. But he had friends who valued him, and he also had done something worthwhile.

He realized then and there that even if he died in his sleep tonight, he had already become the kind of man he could be proud of. A faithful man. A Christian.

July 1867

TAYLOR HAD BEEN DREADING THE MEETING FROM THE MO-
ment a boy knocked on his door at the boardinghouse and deliv-
ered his boss's missive. But he had no choice but to send him word
about what had just been reported to him.

Nothing good happened when a man didn't follow through
on his directives. With weighted feet, he'd wandered to the edge
of Clearwater. Earlier, he'd threatened to tan their hides if they
weren't cleaned up and ready when he got there.

Luckily, they'd taken him seriously. They'd been a quiet trio
when they walked the half mile to meet their boss.

Now the four of them were standing in the middle of a field
full of overgrown prairie grass and littered with prairie dog holes.

"I knew y'all weren't smart, but I didn't take you for complete
idiots," Landon Marshall said once he'd gotten a good look at them
all. "What were you thinking, shooting at Laurel Tracey that way?"

Taylor looked at George Irwin and Foster Howell, the two
men he'd persuaded to work by his side. They, like him, had been
in dire need of some quick money. Unfortunately, they were more
unreliable than Taylor had ever imagined. He should have known
better. Not only had Irwin deserted his unit during the war, but
he'd since made his living cheating at cards. He was as lazy as all
get-out.

And Foster Howell? Well, he'd always had a bone to pick with
anyone in authority. But now he was eager to put both Thomas
Baker and Laurel Tracey in their place. For some reason, Howell
was sure the woman had been the force behind Jackson's firing
him. Not that that theory made any sense. Howell had been fired
before the woman showed up on the square that day and wouldn't
have known about Baker's beating before that.

Taylor was beginning to wonder why Sweetwater's sheriff had hired him in the first place. That man couldn't follow instructions if they were painted on rocks and placed in front of his feet.

"They weren't thinking," he muttered as he glared at the two men standing sullenly by his side. "I told them to poison more cattle, not shoot at people. But when they went to make sure the cattle were dead and saw the woman and her man, they got all riled up."

Howell spit a good amount of tobacco juice on the ground. "Seeing Laurel Tracey there was a surprise. I'll admit that we shouldn't have scared her so bad."

Marshall gritted his teeth. "You shouldn't have scared her at all."

Howell shrugged. "Yeah, all right. But I don't know why you care about what happened to Baker. A man like Thomas Baker is nothing but a waste of space." Waving a stained hand in the air, he said, "He was a prisoner. A prisoner in my jail."

Taylor rolled his eyes. "It wasn't your jail. You only worked there . . . until you got fired."

"Like I said, he's nothing. I still can't believe Sheriff Jackson got in such a tizzy. Why, if I had gotten my way, Baker would already be dead."

"However, he is not," Marshall said with a sneer. "Plus, didn't you say Baker has friends who matter?"

"Yeah." Howell looked away.

"Who are they?" Taylor asked.

"Some former captain of the Confederacy, the one who sent that telegram to the judge. Though he's of no consequence, on account of us losing the war and all."

Marshall tapped his foot. "The judge thought otherwise."

"Judge Orbison is easily impressed. Don't worry about any friends of Thomas Baker's."

Marshall seemed convinced. Looking a bit calmer, he eyed Taylor. "Let's pull back for a while. A third of her cattle are dead, and thanks to these two, she no doubt now fears for her own life. And I convinced the sheriff someone is also lurking about stealing supplies. Laurel doesn't know what's going on. But I'm going to pressure her to accept my suit one more time. I'm hoping she realizes she has no choice but to marry me. Then I'll get what I want."

"Are you sure you don't want me to scare her myself?" Taylor asked. "I can do some damage to her house in the middle of the night. Maybe even scare Baker away, if today's gunfire didn't do the trick."

"Like I said, hold off. I'll send word when I'm ready for more."

"All right." When he'd first seen his boss's irate expression, he'd been worried that the man was going to take out his frustration on him. Now he could spend the rest of the day in the saloon.

Just as Marshall turned away, Irwin whined, "What about my payment? You promised me ten dollars."

Marshall turned back around and said softly, "You want to be paid for almost killing my future bride?"

"Well, yeah." Irwin folded his arms over his thin, lanky frame and nodded toward Howell. "Orr hired me to ride with him. I did that. It weren't my fault he got all trigger happy."

"It wasn't your fault," Marshall repeated slowly.

Irwin raised his eyebrows. "You heard me. Now give me my money."

"Or?"

"Or else you're going to regret it."

Marshall lifted his Colt and shot Irwin between the eyes.

The man died instantly and fell, his expression forever looking surprised.

Taylor stared down at the man with a sinking heart. When he lifted his head, he saw that Marshall directed a chilling stare toward him and Howell.

Taylor swallowed and tried to stop his hands from shaking like leaves.

Marshall lifted his gun again. "Do you two reckon you need your payment right now too?"

"No, Mr. Marshall," Howell bit out.

"I can wait too, sir," Taylor said.

Looking pleased, Marshall lowered his gun. "I was hoping you would say that. Now, deal with this."

After Marshall left, Howell groaned. "What are we gonna do with Irwin? He weighs a ton."

This was why Taylor had been brought down from Chicago. Foster Howell was as dumb as a box of rocks. "All we have to do is put him in a shallow grave over there by the thicket of brush and the creek. I'm certainly not about to cart his body anywhere."

"Let's find something to start digging with then. At least Marshall got him in the face. Belly wounds make more of a mess. We have that to be thankful for."

This is what's wrong with Howell, Taylor thought as he looked around for a stick or something else to dig with. *A man is killed in cold blood by his side and he only thinks about how easily he can get rid of the body.*

As he lifted Irwin under his arms and began dragging him toward the thicket of bushes, Taylor realized he was hopelessly failing in his efforts to become a better man for Dara.

Actually, at this rate, it was unlikely she'd even recognize him when he returned. If he ever returned.

21

THEY'D MADE IT HOME. AT LONG LAST, HER HOUSE WAS IN sight. Laurel felt like both raising her arms in triumph and falling on the ground in thankful tears.

But instead of doing either, she settled for stating the obvious. "Thomas, we're almost there. We did it!"

When he smiled at her, the lines around his eyes crinkled. "Yes, ma'am. And I must admit that no building has ever looked more welcome to me than this one does right now."

His voice was raspy, no doubt because he was so parched. And hungry.

She was too. They were covered in sweat and grime, and the sun had burned so brightly her face was likely blistered, despite any shade from her bonnet. "The moment we get inside, I'm going to drink seven glasses of water."

"I hope you will," he said, his gaze turning soft. "You must be parched."

"You know I am. We both are." They had been walking so long. At least four hours, though she'd stopped guessing after they'd walked two or so. She'd soon learned that attempting to figure out how far they'd gone or how far they had to go did neither of them any good. All it had done was make each footstep heavier.

"I'll be drinking my fair share of water too," he said after they'd gone another fifty or so steps. "However, I'm looking even more forward to taking a cool bath. I feel like I'm wearing half of your ranch on my skin."

"I'm certain it's only half, because I know I'm wearing the other half on mine," she said. Fingering her dress's fabric, she grimaced. "I think my dress is a new shade of brown."

"I think I have a buffalo nickel somewhere. We can flip it to see who gets to bathe first." He smiled then, letting his perfect teeth flash.

Laurel smiled back at him because they both knew he was joking. Thomas had proven to be an especially attentive companion. There was no way he would ever bathe before she did. He wouldn't do anything before making sure she was taken care of first.

"I think I'll let you bathe first, Sergeant," she said. "Even more bothersome than the dirt and grime on my body is the condition of my feet."

He looked at her in confusion. "Are they paining you?"

"I'm afraid so. I have blisters on top of blisters."

He frowned. "But I haven't noticed you limping."

Somewhat proudly, she lifted her chin. "I've been taking care not to limp. I didn't want to worry you."

But instead of looking proud of her, he looked even more agitated. "You should have told me you were in pain."

"There was nothing you could do, Thomas." Realizing he was blaming himself all over again, she ordered softly, "Stop, now."

"Stop what?"

"You know what. Stop taking on my burdens. I wouldn't have mentioned it if I thought you would be upset."

"After we get cleaned up, I'll take a look at them." When she was about to protest, he gave her a hard look. "And don't go getting all delicate on me. I've seen bare feet before. Even yours."

"I remember." Could it have been just yesterday when he'd found her barefoot and screaming about the calf on the front porch? It felt like years ago.

"So you'll let me tend to you?"

She simply nodded.

"Thank you. Now let's get you to the house so you can have those glasses of water."

The house's proximity seemed to blur now. It teased her eyesight. Every time she was sure they'd reach it within a few minutes, it seemed to bounce farther backward. "These last few yards feel the longest, don't they?"

"They always seem to," he said.

She figured truer words had never been said.

They walked quietly side by side until they reached the bend and saw that both horses had returned and were standing near the front of the barn. Velvet was watching Laurel intently, almost as though she'd never seen her owner walking down the lane.

"Thomas, I can't believe Velvet and Yellow are here. I never imagined they would have both come home."

"They are smart horses, to be sure." When they got near the house, Yellow turned his head and whickered in their direction. Thomas grinned. "That horse is quite full of himself. I do believe he's looking at us in confusion. As if he's wondering what took us so long!"

Laurel found herself giggling. "I'm sure you're right." Now that they'd reached the front porch, she said, "Let's go get some water before you do anything with the horses."

"No. First, you wait out here a minute."

"Why?"

"I want to walk through the house to make sure it's safe."

She was exhausted. She was dirty. She also wanted to take a much-needed break from the stress and danger they'd been under in the last few hours.

But she had obviously been terribly naïve. She hadn't even imagined they could still be in danger. A shiver ran up her spine. "Surely you don't think those men are lying in wait for us."

"I hope not, but we can't know what they're capable of or predict what they'll do." His expression was cold and hard, illustrating just how upset he was about the day's events—and how serious he was about staying vigilant. "Stay here while I go inside, Laurel."

She hadn't been afraid, but now she didn't want to be alone. Suddenly every outbuilding and corner of the house looked like an ideal place for someone to be hiding. "I want to go inside with you."

"Honey, if there's trouble, I'd rather not worry about guarding you."

"If there could be trouble inside, it could be lurking around here as well. Thomas, I don't want to face it alone."

After studying her for a long moment, he held out a hand, his rifle in the other. "Come along, then."

Slipping her fingers into his clasp felt right.

When they walked in, she steeled herself to see overturned furniture or damage, or worse, bandits sitting on her settee and calmly waiting for them.

But everything looked exactly how they'd left it all those hours ago. As they walked down the hall and up the stairs, Laurel found herself peeking tentatively around corners and keeping a death grip on Thomas's calloused hand.

"Do you think they've been here?"

"It doesn't look like it." His voice sounded noncommittal as he guided her into Bess's old room, her mother's old sewing room, and then his bedroom.

She hadn't been inside since he'd taken it over. She was surrounded by his usual scent and a plethora of discarded items on one of the dressers. Otherwise, his bed was neatly made and his clothes were hanging on pegs on the far wall.

"Does everything seem like you left it?"

"I reckon so." He walked her down the hall to her bedroom. After pausing at her doorway, he let loose of her hand and walked around the room. "Was this your parents' room?"

"Yes. I moved into it when Bess and Jerome came. Otherwise they would have taken it over."

"It's a pretty room. I'm glad you're sleeping here."

"Thank you." She noticed he was examining every nook and cranny the same way she'd looked in his room. In a way that had little to do with looking for signs of trouble and everything to do with looking for signs of her.

She thought he was imagining her in it.

A new tension festered as she realized that such a thing wouldn't bother her.

Eager to dispel it, she cleared her throat and tried to focus on their safety, not the curious feelings sparking inside her. "Maybe they don't know where I live?"

"There's no telling what they know."

When he walked out of her bedroom, then headed down the stairs, she followed on his heels. She was starting to get the feeling that he knew far more than he was letting on. She hoped he'd share.

He stopped outside the bathing room at the back of the main house. "I think everything is as tight and secure as we can hope for."

"Thank you for checking on everything. It's very kind of you."

"Not kind, Miss Tracey. This is why you have me working here for you."

She felt a little deflated, though she knew what Thomas was doing. He was reminding both himself and her of their roles and relationship.

She realized he needed that line drawn once again as much as she probably did. Therefore, she didn't argue the point but merely nodded.

He looked relieved. "I think it's safe for you to take your bath now."

"Did you forget? I need to have my seven glasses of water first. And you need some too," she teased.

To her relief, he smiled. "I can hardly wait."

She was thankful he didn't protest. Instead, he followed her to the kitchen, stood by one of the rows of cabinets as she retrieved two heavy stoneware mugs, then accepted his mug gratefully after she poured some water she'd kept in the ice chest.

Oh, but that first sip felt and tasted like heaven! Laurel drained her mug in record time. Just as she was about to pick up the pitcher, Thomas took it from her hands and refilled their mugs. Again they quickly drained them.

After the third round, he set his mug on the counter. "Thank you. That helped a lot."

"Are you done already? You can have as much as you want."

His gaze settled on her before he turned with a jerk. "I'll get some water from the spigot in the barn. I need to see to the horses."

"But—"

"And you need to see to yourself," he said lightly, his blue eyes lingering on what had to be her sunburned face. "You need to take your bath and rest your feet."

"You'll come back inside after you see to the horses?"

His expression was almost tender when he replied, "Of course I will. Don't worry. I'll let you know when I've returned."

After she heard the kitchen door open and shut, she carefully pulled off her boots, then walked as best she could upstairs on her sore, blistered feet.

When she got to her room, she gathered some clean clothes, then hobbled back to the bathing room. She was looking forward to this bath like she hadn't looked forward to one in years. Almost like it was going to be a life-changing experience!

Or maybe it was? This bath was going to remove all the dirt and grime from their horrifying journey. And serve to remind her that she had survived it, and grown stronger too.

Returning to the kitchen, Laurel turned on the spigot, then set about heating water, all while drinking as much cold water as she could. When at last the tub was filled with enough warm water to be both practical and relaxing, she sighed, feeling as if she'd just accomplished a great feat.

Sitting on the side of the tub, she winced at the condition of her feet. She hadn't been wrong. She had some terrible, broken blisters on her toes, heels, and the pad of one of her feet. For some reason they began to sting more when the fresh air came in contact with them.

Gingerly, she stepped into her tub and allowed the warm water to soothe her sore feet for a couple of minutes. And then she went about the process of becoming as clean as she possibly could, focusing on dirt and sores instead of what they'd just overcome. If she dwelled on how close they'd come to dying or being seriously hurt, Laurel knew she wouldn't be able to think about anything else.

She'd just finished slipping on a fresh dress and combing out her hair when she heard Thomas calling.

"You decent?" he teased.

"Of course." Striding from the main house into the kitchen, she said, "I'll heat you up some water, Thomas. You start gathering a towel and your things."

After he had everything he needed, he closed the bathing room door behind him. Then, in the kitchen, though Laurel knew she needed to concentrate on making something for them to eat, she couldn't seem to do anything other than imagine him getting undressed, filling the tub with cool water, then adding the hot water little by little to make it more comfortable. He would test the temperature, running his hands through the water again and again.

Finally, at last, he would lean back against the metal side and wash his skin.

Her face and neck heated.

She pressed her hands to her cheeks, attempting to clear her head. There was no reason to dwell on his ablutions. After all, he was doing nothing that she hadn't just done herself.

It just seemed different somehow.

Because, she realized, she was different. And her feelings for him were different too. This realization was as much a surprise as anything else that had happened to them today.

Suddenly, she knew. She was falling in love with Thomas Baker.

22

THOMAS MIGHT HAVE BEEN TWENTY-TWO YEARS OLD, BUT he wasn't too old to appreciate the soothing comfort of a warm bath. From his time on the streets to the war to this very moment, he hadn't had all that many opportunities to luxuriate as much as he was in this private room while resting in a half-filled tub of water.

Picking up the bar of soap Laurel left him, he noticed that it smelled good, like lavender. It felt good on his skin too. It didn't burn or sting.

It was a woman's soap. Laurel's.

Closing his eyes, he allowed himself a moment to think about her, to think about how close he'd come to losing her. It had scared him half to death. It would have been a tragedy if he'd lost her. If the world lost someone so precious.

His heart pounded like a dozen horses' hooves every time he recalled hearing the gunshots and forcing her onto the ground. He'd always been a praying man. But in those precious few moments, he'd felt as if he couldn't pray enough or hard enough for the Lord to be with them at that moment.

He'd been willing to do anything to keep her safe.

His objectives hadn't changed after they began their long walk home. He'd kept a vigilant eye about them, ready to shoot who-ever or whatever attempted to disrupt their journey.

After the first couple of hours, when his breathing had slowed and he no longer felt as though he were standing in the eye of a hurricane, he'd begun to watch her even more closely.

He was aware of each tentative step of hers, each pained expression. He noticed when she stumbled, when she swatted at a hornet, when her lips had turned chapped. He noticed it all.

The only thing he hadn't seemed to notice was that she'd injured her feet.

He was torn about what to do about his attraction to her. Part of him didn't exactly blame himself. He was a man who'd been given precious few sweet things in life.

Most of the time he'd been given only the leftovers, what no one else wanted. His only exception had been his relationships with the other men in Captain Monroe's unit.

Those were the best men he'd ever met, and he'd felt as if the Lord had given him those men's regard as a gift for all that he'd endured in his lifetime.

He'd certainly never had the opportunity to be around a woman like Laurel.

As he rested in his bath and imagined what she was doing in the kitchen, Thomas knew he didn't deserve a woman like her. But he didn't care.

The fact of the matter was that he needed Laurel. He needed her, and he wasn't ready to give her up. Not now.

Maybe not ever.

It might even be for her own good. If the rest of the men in Sweetwater were anything like that arrogant Landon Marshall, he doubted any of them could treat her as well or care for her as completely as he could. It might have been his pride showing, but he knew no other man around those parts was any better for her than he was.

It seemed God had given him a gift in Laurel. And though he was far from perfect, she needed him, just like he needed her. To turn his back on her at this moment, when she needed him the most, would be like turning his back on one of the best presents he'd ever received.

"Thomas?" she called out. "I mean, Sergeant?"

He smiled to himself. No matter how hard her heart told her otherwise, Laurel was still attempting to keep their relationship businesslike. When she remembered.

He decided to answer her in kind. "Miss?" he called right back, smiling as he rested naked as the day he was born, leaning against the back of the tub.

"Would you mind if we had eggs and spoon bread for supper? I know it's not much."

"It's everything. It's perfect."

"I'll get to work on it when you get done. But take your time," she said hurriedly.

"I will. Thank you."

When he heard her move away from the door, he smiled again. Then gave in to temptation and closed his eyes. Tried to come to grips with all that had happened to the two of them. He'd almost lost her today.

He had almost lost himself too.

And he wasn't convinced those men had intended only to scare off Yellow and Velvet either. Perhaps it was only thanks to the horses' good sense to run off as quickly as they did that the gunmen hadn't shot and killed Laurel's two fine mounts.

But why was anyone doing all this?

The squatters seemed to be gone, so who were these men?

Did they really want Laurel to die, and him along with her? Or did they just want her to give up the ranch, thinking she'd be too beaten down and frightened to stay if they killed her cattle and threatened her life? Either way, he imagined Bess and Jerome were the only ones who could benefit from her death, and he doubted Laurel would give them any proceeds from the sale of the place. But he still couldn't see them as the culprits.

Then there was Landon Marshall, someone Thomas was sure he couldn't trust. Was he trying to destroy Laurel's future on the ranch so she would marry him? But why not just bide his time? Or was he doing this because Thomas was now a threat to getting his way?

But Laurel had known him a long time, and she didn't seem afraid of the man, only annoyed. So maybe he would never turn to this kind of violence. Besides, he was rich. Why would he need Laurel's land anyway? And someone had stolen his supplies in that outbuilding, too, assuming that was the truth.

What if all the ranches in the area were under some kind of attack?

He was in over his head.

Sinking down into the soothing water, he took a deep breath, then let his neck and head submerge. Little by little, his muscles relaxed. He only lifted his head when he couldn't hold his breath any longer.

He figured that action was a fitting metaphor for all that had been happening to him. He was close to drowning, and it was only by sheer force of will that he hadn't yet drowned either himself or Laurel.

He needed to face facts. There was too much against him and what he had at stake. If he didn't open his eyes and reach out to others, he could put everything—Laurel, her ranch, her future, and maybe her life—in jeopardy.

He needed to do whatever it took and whatever he had to do to improve her situation.

And that meant he had to come to terms with the fact that he couldn't continue to try to handle all this on his own. Laurel had someone poisoning her livestock and shooting at her. Both were heinous crimes. Who knew what was next?

While he felt like he was keeping her safer by sleeping just down the hall, it wasn't much of a help. Maybe if he could sleep with her in his arms he might ensure her safety for the time being.

But obviously that was not a possibility. And if trouble came stealthily when he was asleep, it wouldn't matter where he laid his head. Yet he couldn't stay awake all the time.

It was also painfully apparent that he couldn't keep Laurel safe and watch her livestock at the same time. He certainly couldn't do either of those and hunt down the men who had dared to take aim at her.

Instinctively, he knew the men in town weren't the ones he needed to help him. While he might trust the sheriff, he didn't trust him enough to put Laurel's life in his hands.

Therefore, there was only one thing left to do. He would send a telegram to Captain Monroe and ask for help.

Just as he often called on the Lord to help him find the strength he needed, Thomas realized there was no shame in reaching out to the best men he knew to ask for the same thing.

Actually, it was comforting and made him feel as though he had finally matured enough to be the man a woman like Laurel needed him to be. It took a strong man to know it wasn't a sign of weakness to reach out to others.

Perhaps, at long last, he'd finally become the kind of man he'd always wanted to be. Yes, he'd regained some self-worth in the army, he'd become a man he could be proud of, but he'd never fully become everything he could be.

Feeling better about himself and his goals, Thomas pulled himself out of the tub, drained it, then hurriedly got dressed. He was eager to tell Laurel about his plans. He was also eager to put her fears to rights. He didn't want her to worry that he couldn't take care of her.

When he entered the kitchen, Laurel was sitting at the table with her feet propped on a chair. Her eyes were at half-mast.

"Laurel?" he whispered.

Hearing his voice, she sat up abruptly. "Sorry. I was just taking a rest."

"I'm glad you were." Reminded of how she'd complained about her feet, he took the chair next to where they were resting and studied them.

They were certainly in a bad way. Her toes looked red and swollen, and there were already scabs and some bleeding. Gently, he picked up one foot and set it on his thigh.

Her eyes widened as she attempted to free her foot. "There's no reason to do that, Thomas. My feet are fine."

"I beg to disagree." Lifting one slender foot in his hand, he noticed there was a sizable blister on her heel and another on the pad of her foot. "Laurel Tracey, what kind of boots were you wearing? Could they have fit you any worse?"

"They were old ones of Bess's."

"Why were you wearing them? Surely you have boots of your own."

"I do, but they're worn out." Blushing a bit, she said, "Hers were so pretty."

"You wanted to wear pretty boots?" He was beginning to wonder if he'd ever understand the complexities of the female mind.

"Yes."

"Laurel, you're smarter than that."

"In my defense, I hadn't imagined that I'd be walking several miles in them."

He chuckled. "You have a point there." Knowing she was still embarrassed, he said, "I'm a little surprised she left anything here of worth."

"Based on the condition of my feet, maybe she knew something about those boots I did not," she quipped.

"Indeed." After resting her foot more comfortably in his lap, he brought the other one up and inspected it.

"Thomas—"

"I'm not doing anything untoward. Merely looking at your toes." Carefully, he placed her feet back on the chair.

She sighed. "I hope Bess and Jerome are doing all right."

"If they didn't get shot at today, I'd say they're doing a far sight better than we are."

"This is true."

"Don't worry about them. They weren't helping you, only wearing you out."

"Jerome was the culprit, I think. Maybe I should have tried to speak to Bess alone."

Thomas didn't think Bess would have listened to anything Laurel would have said. "I can't help you there. I don't have much experience talking to women."

Luckily, instead of feeling awkward, Laurel seemed to find his statement amusing. "You didn't learn how to manage women when you were riding in the cavalry?"

"I did not. Our conversations revolved around guns and horses, I'm afraid."

"That's too bad. I could use some good advice."

"I have none to offer. Even though I learned a lot from the officers on Johnson's Island, we never covered that topic," he said lightly. He leaned back slightly, stretching his legs.

She opened an eye again. "I can't help but notice that you don't talk about your time in the prisoner of war camp as being especially horrible."

"It was bad at times. Sometimes worse than that." Remembering the cold and the boredom and the ever-present hunger, as well as the feeling of hopelessness, he said, "Don't get me wrong. The men who guarded us reveled in their power. They didn't make it easy on us, especially as the atrocities came out about Andersonville and such."

"But you choose not to think about it that way?"

"It ain't that." He swallowed. "It's more a case of me choosing to remember the friendships I made there. The men I was with were some of the best men I'd ever met." Meeting her gaze, he said, "Actually, I can't imagine that I'll ever meet another group of men I admire more. I felt privileged to be thought of as their friend."

"Based on what I know of you, I'm sure they felt the same way."

Thinking of the day they'd brought up his bravery, he murmured, "Sometimes I think they did."

"I'm sure it was more than sometimes, Thomas. I've never met a braver man."

Her sweet honesty was so kind. Far kinder than he deserved, given the fact that her life hadn't been any easier since he'd entered it, and in some ways it was much harder. "You see, the thing of it is, I wasn't supposed to be there in the first place. I was enlisted, and most times enlisted soldiers didn't mix with the officers."

"Not even in a prison?"

"No." When she shifted and moved her feet back to the floor, he shifted as well and stared across the room, once again reliving those moments as though they had just happened. "But I had done a lot of missions for Captain Monroe. Capturing him was quite a coup for the Yankees because he even had a good reputation among them. He demanded that everyone in his unit who'd been captured go with him to the POW camp."

"I'm surprised they listened to him."

"If you met the captain, you wouldn't be surprised. He's a formidable man." He sighed. "In any case, I'm glad they did listen to him and transfer me. You see, before we were imprisoned, I hadn't really known him. I merely did what I was told."

"You followed orders."

"I did." Smiling at himself, he added, "It might be hard to believe, but I was an excellent soldier. I followed my directives without question. It was only when I had spare time that my temper and my mouth got the best of me."

She smiled then. "Forgive me, Sergeant, but I do find that hard to believe. I would have liked to have seen you be biddable."

"You would have been impressed." He grinned back at her, thankful that he'd found a way to make her smile after such a horrific day.

"Speaking of being impressed, I think we should eat the meal I made," she said, getting to her feet and walking awkwardly to the stove. "I scrambled some eggs and baked them with some bread and cream and ham. I think it should be ready by now."

When she picked up a towel to get her pan out of the oven, he took it from her and did the honors himself. "You sit down. I'll do the serving today."

"Thomas, that isn't necessary."

"Your feet are hurt and I don't mind. Let me do this."

"All right. Thank you."

After filling two plates, he brought them to where she was

sitting and returned to her side. Then, as they were now in a habit of doing, they prayed together.

Thomas led the prayer. "Heavenly Father, we give you thanks for this meal. Thank you for providing for us with water to drink and enough food to allay our hunger. Thank you for the hands that made the meal and even for the chickens that provided it. Thank you for looking out for us today and for helping us arrive back here safely. Now please watch over us tonight so that we might both rest. Amen."

Her lips twitched. "I know you like to eat eggs, but you're giving thanks for the chickens? I'm impressed."

"You should be, given how much I don't care for poultry."

She giggled before taking her first bite. Thomas followed suit, enjoying the warm goodness of the simple fare after missing their noon meal, enjoying even more the company and the fact that somehow they'd been able to arrive home with nothing more than a couple of sore feet and some rattled nerves.

When he cleaned his plate, he decided he was going to have to tell Laurel about his decision right away. Tomorrow he was going to send the wire. Time was of the essence.

"Laurel, I'm glad we talked about the men of my unit tonight, because I think I need to contact Captain Monroe."

"You want to fill him in on what we've been going through?"

"No. I need his help," he said, correcting her. "We both need his and my other friends' help."

She wrinkled her nose. "They'll be strangers here. They won't know me or the land. Do you think they'll truly be of use?"

"They are smart men, and we vowed to be there for each other, always. I think we both know I can't protect you and your cattle while tracking the men who fired at us. It's an impossibility, even for a good soldier like me."

"If you think we need more hands, then you don't need to send a wire to Captain Monroe. All you have to do is contact Sheriff Jackson. He's a good man."

He might be a good man, but as far as Thomas was concerned, the sheriff hadn't been doing anything at all to help Laurel. "I think we need more help than what Jackson is able to provide. After all, he has a town to run. And it's possible the theft of Marshall's property was the work of squatters. He'll have to stay on that."

But instead of looking reassured, worry and disappointment clouded her eyes. "I'd rather you didn't ask your friends for help."

He was surprised, and not a little bit dismayed. "Why not? I promise they are better men than me. You wouldn't have to fear them or worry that they would behave inappropriately or that you would be in danger. They would even sleep in the barn if you wanted them to."

"While I appreciate that, and believe you, that isn't what gives me pause."

"Then what is it, Laurel? I don't understand."

Regret filled her pretty eyes. "Everything happening to me isn't your concern, Thomas," she said quietly. "And the men who shot at us are dangerous. Violent. I don't want you bringing your friends into a harmful situation. I don't want them to get hurt."

This girl was too much. She didn't seem to understand how much she meant to him.

Taking a deep breath, he said slowly, "Laurel, first of all, they didn't just shoot at you, they shot at me too. That has made it my problem as much as yours. No man is going to attempt to kill me without me taking it personally." Only all his years of practice enabled him to keep a handle on his temper. "I didn't survive a war only to die by a coward's bullet in the middle of your field."

She bit her lip. "Maybe it would be best if you just left."

"If I left what?"

"My employ."

"And return to Sweetwater's jail cell? Thank you, but no."

"I'm not speaking of going back to jail," she said, hesitant.

"What are you speaking of, then? Sheriff Jackson didn't leave me any other options that I recall."

"Actually," she said, "I wasn't thinking of following the sheriff's directives." Before Thomas could protest, she said, "You could leave in the middle of the night. I wouldn't tell anyone you were gone."

She was offering him the opportunity to slip off in the middle of the night. But not only was the thought of leaving her in the lurch repugnant, he also had nowhere else to go. "Miss Tracey," he said, "I would never do that to you."

"I promise I won't tell—"

"I am not that man. I am not the kind of man who abandons women when they are in need. And frankly, I'm a little offended you think I would."

Now she was the one who looked hurt. "I am not questioning your honor, Sergeant."

"I hope not. Because you need to understand something. You are stuck with me." When her eyes widened like saucers, he continued, "Let me be clear. When you offered me water, I became intrigued by you. When you freed me from that cage in the square, I became enraptured." He lowered his voice. "And when you took the time to see to my wounds, to attempt to heal me when I had done nothing to deserve it?" He inhaled. How did he bare his heart without becoming vulnerable?

"Yes?"

He met her gaze again. And realized that maybe being vulnerable wasn't necessarily a bad thing.

"Well, I began to care for you," he said at last.

Her eyes widened and she swallowed. "You care for me?"

He held up a hand to stop her from protesting. "I don't say any of this to scare you."

She swallowed. "I'm not scared."

"I don't even expect you to return my feelings. I don't expect you to ever feel obligated to me either. Even if you were to fall in love with someone else, I wouldn't begrudge that of you. Because I want the best for you."

Surprise filled her gaze before she tucked her chin and fiddled with a fold in her dress. "You want the best for me because you are under my employ for the next year."

"No, because, well . . . actually . . . I more than care for you, Laurel. The truth is that I have fallen in love with you."

"You've fallen in love. With me." She sounded rather stunned. And who could blame her?

Yet again, he was saying too much. Far too much. But since it was too late to take it back, he added in a lighter tone, "Now perhaps you will understand why I want you to be as happy and cared for as is possible for this year."

When she raised her head again, he saw that her eyes were clouded with worry. He wondered if it was a reaction to his profession of love or if it was because he set the deadline for one year. "I want you to be happy, too, Thomas."

"If you do, then you're going to have to accompany me tomorrow in the buggy so I can send off that wire."

"I could stay here alone."

"That isn't possible. Until I know for certain that you're safe, I never intend to let you be alone again."

"You mean for this year," she said, correcting him this time.

Blast it all. She sounded hurt and sad like he'd just kicked her in the shin. Why had he said so much?

More important, why, if he'd been so intent on telling her his feelings, did he not go ahead and be completely honest?

"I mean I'll be here with you for as long as you need me. Even if it is longer than a year."

Something new lit her eyes. Getting to her feet, she said, "In that case, I suggest we wash these dishes and get some rest. We have another full day tomorrow."

As he followed her, Thomas couldn't resist smiling. He felt like he'd just achieved a small victory.

No conquest had ever felt so sweet.

23

SITTING BY THOMAS'S SIDE, DRESSED IN HER SUNDAY FIN-
est, Laurel felt almost pretty. Maybe it was the way Thomas had
stared at her when she walked out to join him in the barn. He'd
been hitching up the buggy to Velvet but had stilled when he saw
her approach. She'd felt his gaze pass over her. It lingered, as if he
was almost reluctant to look away.

As she came closer, he straightened and his eyes filled with
appreciation.

"Miss Laurel, you look very fine today."

Instead of reacting in a cool and composed way, she'd nervously fussed with her skirts and blushed. "Thank you."

"I'm almost ready," he said. "Velvet seemed to enjoy the ride
out to Landon Marshall's property this morning, but she needed a
bit of coaxing to get hitched to the buggy."

"She's not a great fan of leading my buggy, I'm afraid."

"I don't blame her. However, we all have to do things we'd
rather not do."

She wasn't sure if he was making conversation or making
a veiled comment about seeing Landon. When she'd asked if
Landon had been upset that she'd changed her mind about having supper with him, Thomas had only said the conversation had
gone well enough.

Because she'd been relieved the visit was no longer looming, she didn't ask him to explain. Now the silence seemed to suit them both. She simply stood to one side and watched him situate Velvet. When he was ready, she took Thomas's hand when he held it out to help her into the conveyance.

When they approached the town's square, she felt everyone's eyes on them. She didn't fault their curiosity. But instead of demurely averting her eyes, she took care to sit proud and tall by Thomas's side. No matter what everyone else thought, she knew he was a man of honor. He was honest and true. He was also brave. He'd not only saved her life yesterday; he'd saved her soul. She'd needed someone to believe in her, to believe in her future.

Thomas certainly did.

The goal they'd chosen was honorable too. It was time to fight whoever was intent on hurting her animals and threatening them.

After Thomas parked the buggy near the mercantile, he walked around, tied Velvet's tethers, then at last helped her down.

"Let's go to the bank first, Miss Tracey," he said, his formal manners out for show. "I can send a wire from there."

"Then we can get some supplies."

"Whatever you want," he said as he held out an arm.

She placed her hand on his arm and walked into the bank.

It might have been her imagination, but it felt like the room went silent as they walked to the line to wait their turn for the teller. Nervously, Laurel looked around.

A few women nodded her way, but most seemed intent on pretending they didn't know her. No doubt they assumed her relationship with Thomas was far more intimate than it was.

She tried not to let their cool reception bother her. After all, it wasn't as if anyone had come to offer her help over the last year. Though she might have had a better reputation, she had still been essentially alone.

When Mr. Cassidy called them over, he smiled at Laurel. "What can I do for you today, miss?"

"Our errand is actually for Sergeant Baker here."

Mr. Cassidy's smile faltered. "Oh? What may I do for you, sir?"

"I need to send a wire."

Mr. Cassidy pulled out a small sheet of paper. "I'll be glad to handle it, sir."

"It needs to be sent immediately." Thomas stared at the teller with some suspicion in his eyes. "You will do that?"

"Of course."

"Very well, then. Please send the following missive to Captain Devin Monroe of the Tremont Hotel, Galveston, Texas."

Mr. Cassidy scribbled his notes and then looked up expectantly. "Message?"

"Attempt on my life. STOP. Help needed. STOP. Red Roan Ranch. Sweetwater."

Mr. Cassidy's pen slowed. He began to write each word with extreme care. After he finished writing the last of it, he stared up at Thomas with a new respect in his eyes. "Is that all, sir?"

Thomas nodded. "After it's transmitted, I'll pay."

"I'll get to it momentarily."

"Please, Mr. Cassidy," Laurel said. "If you could do as we ask, it would be most appreciated."

Looking far more intent, he turned, walked a few steps to a long table with a wireless machine, put on some headphones, and began tapping out the message.

Laurel noticed that Thomas visibly relaxed once the teller began to send the wire.

"Things will be better for you now," he said, looking far more at ease.

She wanted to believe him, but how could one friend's arrival make such a difference? "How long do you think it will take for him to get here?"

Mr. Cassidy returned, and Thomas asked, "What is the time?"

"It is nine in the morning."

Ignoring the teller's curious expression, Thomas replied to her comment. "Someone will be here by nightfall."

"That soon? You're that sure?"

"Very sure. The captain will not let me down."

"That'll be three bits, sir."

Pulling out the correct amount, Thomas nodded his thanks before holding out his elbow again. Laurel had been prepared to pay for the wire, but Thomas said the captain sent a little money to go along with the new clothes.

Laurel waited until they exited the building before commenting. But once they were standing on the hot sidewalk, she stared at him in wonder.

"Inside, when you talked about how quickly help would come . . ."

"Yes?"

"Were you making a jest, or were you serious?"

"I'm always serious about Captain Monroe."

"But if he's in Galveston . . . plus he's got to ride all the way here. And make preparations."

"He will leave within the hour once he receives my message. He'll also take the time to contact the other three men in our unit. They'll come as well, and some of them are no doubt closer."

Thomas's expression was sure. His voice was sure. She saw

no doubt in his face. He actually believed these other men would rush to his side.

She couldn't imagine such a response.

Besides her parents, had anyone ever dropped everything to help her?

With a start, she realized someone already had. Thomas had placed his body over hers. He'd been willing to be hurt or killed to keep her safe. Now he'd even swallowed his pride and asked for help.

"I'm beginning to think this band of brothers of yours is an impressive group."

He laughed as they walked back toward the mercantile. "You will see for yourself when you meet them."

Opening the door to the mercantile, he said, "Get what you need to feed four or five men."

Laurel didn't question his request. She was beginning to think that whatever Thomas wanted to happen would.

As she mentally reviewed her own kitchen's supply of dry goods, she opted to purchase coffee, some dried black-eyed peas, and cornmeal. She had enough flour, beans, leavening, and sugar to make most anything else the men might need.

After telling the clerk what she wanted, she went to check on Thomas, who was looking at a box of ammunition and a very fine-looking Colt.

Just as she approached him, he looked over her shoulder and narrowed his eyes.

Quickly, she turned.

There was Foster Howell, one of the guards who had come to the ranch with the prisoners. He was eyeing Thomas with a look of suspicion and glanced at her with a small smile.

She felt uncomfortable but decided to brazen it out. "Hello, Mr. Howell."

"Miss Tracey. Good morning." His gaze swept over her, making her feel strangely exposed. Then he smiled. "I see you are out with your man."

She didn't like anything about his greeting. She didn't like how he was making her feel or how he was acting as if Thomas weren't worthy enough to be standing by her side.

Just as she was debating whether to tell Howell off, Thomas leaned closer. Placing a hand on the small of her back, he whispered into her ear, "Don't say a word. He ain't worth a bit of your time."

Unfortunately, the former guard heard his comment. "I'd watch who you're calling unworthy."

Thomas stared at Howell with a look that could only be described as loathing. "Did you need something? If so, you need to direct your questions to me."

"To you?"

Thomas seemed to let the man's scorn roll off his shoulders. Standing up straight and tall, at least a full three inches taller than his former guard, Thomas said, "There isn't a reason in the world for Miss Tracey to ever have to converse with you again."

Howell's gaze darted from Thomas to Laurel and back again. Laurel felt a trickle of perspiration slide down her spine. Was this how it was going to be for the next year? Everyone coming into her path and feeling free to judge her?

Howell rocked back on the heels of his boots. "I was only checking to see how Miss Tracey is doing, living in sin with the likes of you." He smirked. "How are you, miss? Is he treating you good?"

Thomas stepped closer to her when she flinched.

"Her welfare is no concern of yours," he said. "This is the last time I'll warn you. Don't speak to her again."

Howell backed up but didn't look completely cowed. "I can't wait to see you get your comeuppance, Baker. And you will, I promise."

"Do you know something I don't know?" Thomas asked.

"I know a lot you don't know. But I'm thinking most people do." Before Thomas could respond, he smirked again. "I'll be going on my way now." He stepped backward, then paused before turning around. "Miss Tracey, if this one lays a hand on you, you be sure and let me know. It would give me pleasure to get him back in line."

Though her brain was telling her to say something and stand up for herself, Laurel couldn't seem to make either her feet or her mouth comply. Therefore, she simply stood frozen and wished she was bolder.

Feeling the other customers' curious stares, she drew in a ragged sigh. "We're causing a scene. It's time we left."

But instead of dropping his hand and stepping away, Thomas bent his head a little so she could see his eyes. "We haven't done a single thing wrong," he said quietly. "We're simply shopping in the mercantile. There ain't a thing irregular about that."

"People think differently."

"It doesn't matter. Don't dwell on it."

"I hate that Howell looked at you the way he did, as if you are less than him."

"Honey, trust me when I say his scowl didn't bother me none. I've had far worse directed my way."

She smiled, though she knew her effort was likely more than a little wobbly. "I don't know how you managed to make me feel better, but you did."

Stepping to her side, he held out his arm. "That's because I'm a charmer, Miss Tracey."

His irreverent comment sparked one of her own. "You are incorrigible."

"Yes, I am." Pressing a hand to the middle of her back again, he murmured, "Come now, let's go inform Sheriff Jackson of the latest developments, then head back home."

Since she, too, was ready to end their visit to town, she followed him to the counter to buy her supplies.

Thomas seemed to be making a purchase as well.

24

By four in the afternoon, Thomas knew his nerves were shot. He couldn't count the number of times he'd gazed out toward the horizon, hoping to see a cloud of dust signifying that his friends were on the way.

He only hoped Laurel was handling the wait better than he was.

After they'd finished their shopping at the mercantile, Thomas loaded everything into the buggy, then got Laurel right home. Though he'd tried to pretend otherwise, the townspeople's curious, intrusive stares had bothered him. He also despised having to stand still and watch Howell leer at Laurel.

But what he hated even more was that he was the cause of all that. If Laurel hadn't taken a chance and gotten him out of that cage, he'd still be in jail. And though a better man might be thinking only about how such a kind woman felt, he had hated seeing the man who'd beat him so badly look at him with disdain.

After they returned, he took care of the buggy and Velvet, then saddled Yellow and rode around the house's perimeter. Laurel was still too shaken up for him to feel comfortable leaving her to check out the far areas of her property. To be honest, he didn't feel all that good about being out of sight either. Someone was watching her, watching them, and he wasn't going to stop until he got what he wanted.

Just as he directed Yellow to head back home, Thomas saw some hoofprints on the ground and what looked like a skid from either a foot or a knapsack.

Climbing off the saddle, he knelt down and inspected the area. Rocks were disturbed.

Someone had definitely been here recently, and they'd taken care to keep their appearance a secret. Had it been those squatters and they simply wanted a piece of Laurel's land? Picking up one of the rocks, he saw a dark stain. Or had his shot yesterday met its mark? He hoped so.

While he was debating whether to circle back around or go back and stay closer to Laurel, Yellow raised his head and pricked his ears forward.

"What is it, boy?" Thomas murmured as he got to his feet.

Yellow pawed the ground with a hoof. He looked uneasy but was waiting for Thomas to give direction.

As he ran a hand down the horse's flank, Thomas shook his head. Whoever named the horse hadn't known a thing about him. This gelding was exactly what every soldier needed—steady and responsive. A partner.

Grasping the reins, he listened harder.

And then he heard it. The faint rumbling of hooves. Had one of his comrades arrived? Or was it the men who'd shot at them yesterday?

Directing the horse around, Thomas felt behind him for the Winchester that had belonged to Laurel's father. He wasn't eager to start pointing a rifle at approaching riders on Laurel's property, but he was far from a greenhorn. There was no way he was going to allow himself to ever be at risk again. Clicking softly, he nudged Yellow forward with his knees.

Yellow seemed to sense his suspicion, because the horse slowly stepped out into the clearing, each hoof moving delicately and silently. It was as if he'd had as much experience dodging the enemy as Thomas had when he'd been asked to spy on enemy troops in the area.

Squinting against the hot glare of the sun, which had barely begun its descent in the west, Thomas found what he was looking for.

Two riders.

From force of habit more than a real awareness of what he was doing, Thomas grabbed the rifle and laid it across his lap.

Yellow continued to patiently step forward, each step slow and measured. They were in a clearing of sorts. It was obvious that he was as visible to the men riding forward as they were to him. And they weren't shooting.

Now, if he could only figure out who was approaching. Old memories of riding along with his friends slammed into his brain but dissipated with almost as much force. The problem, he knew, was those memories of the men on horseback had faded. Most of Thomas's memories of Major Kelly, Captain Monroe, and the other two men rested firmly on the soil of Johnson's Island. He could recognize their voices and even how they rolled a cheroot or held a tin cup better than the way they were seated on a horse.

Drawing Yellow to a stop, he watched the riders come closer. Unlike him, they were moving across the open field at an easy clip. Then one raised his hand, and Thomas saw a hint of a sparkle on the man's cuff.

Unable to hide his relief, he laughed. Enemies weren't approaching. His friends had arrived.

He reckoned there was only one man in the state of Texas who would ride into a potential battle zone with gold cuff links on his wrists, and that would be Major Ethan Kelly. The man came from money, and had never been particularly shy about it either.

He wasn't sure who the other fellow was, but it didn't matter. If Kelly was here, Thomas knew everything had just made a turn for the better.

Nudging Yellow forward to a brisk trot, he rode out to greet them, a smile on his face.

When he was about a hundred yards out, he called, "Welcome!"

Major Kelly pulled his dark-gray Stetson from the top of his head and held it out in greeting. "Baker, after the things we heard about you in town, the last thing I expected to see was you riding along on a fine-looking palomino like you were out for a Sunday stroll."

"There's a story there, I bet," the major's companion said, who Thomas now realized was Robert Truax.

When they drew to a stop in front of each other, Yellow's nostrils blowing air out impatiently as he tried to get a sense of the other horses, Thomas held out a hand. "Robert, Ethan, you two are a sight for sore eyes."

The major clasped his hand, his brown eyes lighting on him as though he was inspecting every new wrinkle and scar on his face. "I can't wait to hear what's been going on."

"From what Monroe said, it sounds like you should have called for us a whole lot sooner," Robert said, his voice lightly chiding. "Were you really locked up in this town's jail?"

"I was."

Robert frowned. "Someone told me you'd been whipped too. Was that a lie?"

"It was not."

Robert looked toward the sky, like he was asking the Almighty for patience. "It pains me to hear that. You really should have reached out to us earlier, Sergeant."

"I had my reasons for not contacting you."

"I would certainly like to hear them!"

"At a later date, perhaps."

"Well, why did you contact us?" Robert asked impatiently.

Thomas opened his mouth to try to describe Laurel's problems in a nutshell, but the words stuck in his throat. How could he attempt to convey Laurel's situation without the men guessing how much she meant to him?

Looking for help, he turned to face the house. Laurel was standing on the front porch watching them. Her hands were clasped in front of her. "I'll tell you more when we get to the house."

Both men turned to stare at the large home with its Southern grace and five majestic white columns. Major Kelly whistled low. "Ah, now I understand," he said. Smiling softly, he said, "Robert, I do believe I'm beginning to see what, exactly, is at stake."

"Indeed," Robert said, his voice thick with humor.

Noticing their looks of appreciation, Thomas hardened his voice. "No matter what you might think of me, you gentlemen need to be respectful. Miss Laurel Tracey is a lady through and through."

Major Kelly adjusted his Stetson, his gold cuff links glinting. Turning to Thomas, his expression filled with respect, he said, "Of course she is, Baker. Forgive me if I gave you the impression I thought otherwise. Now, lead on."

Just as he turned toward the house, Thomas asked the question that had been on his mind. "Is Captain Monroe coming too?"

"He is," Robert said. "I happened to be in Waco when he got your wire in Galveston. I fully expect him by nightfall. I believe he was going to take the train partway. He pulled some favors and got a compartment on the first one out."

"I am obliged."

"You call and we come," Ethan Kelly said as he encouraged his mount to a trot.

"Though I had expected as much, I have to admit that it's nice to realize that my hopes were not vanquished."

"Never fear. Some promises will never be forgotten."

The major had never said anything truer. He was exactly right. Some promises would always be fulfilled, no matter what the cost. Come hell or high water.

"Thank you, sir. Thanks to both of you."

"Don't mention it again," Robert said. "It's an honor to help a friend in need."

And with that, the three of them headed to the woman who was waiting for them.

To the place Thomas now considered home.

25

Johnson's Island, Ohio
Confederate States of America Officers POW Camp

JOHNSON'S ISLAND HAD ONE THING THOMAS WAS FOND OF, and that was lightning bugs. From the moment they made their first appearances on the Lake Erie shore at the end of May, the bugs had become a source of fascination for Thomas. He spent a great many hours watching their flickering lights dance across the camp and light up over the calm waters as though they were stars falling from the sky.

Their dancing and darting had become a source of hope for him. Thomas liked to think their appearance in his life was a sign from God, a reminder that good could be found anywhere and at any time. One just needed to have his eyes open and be watchful.

"Looking at the fireflies again?" Major Kelly asked as he sat down on the ground beside him.

Though he was a bit self-conscious about it, Thomas nodded. "Yeah." Thinking he needed to share some kind of explanation for his infatuation, he added, "I ain't never seen them before here."

Kelly smiled softly as he watched the insects flicker and flutter across the field next to him. "I hadn't seen them before I signed up. Don't know why they aren't in Texas, but I guess we can't have everything."

"Just fire ants and hornets."

"And roaches the size of men's hands." Grimacing dramatically, he said, "I'd be happy to trade the roaches of San Antonio for these little things."

Thomas grinned, liking the easy conversation. In many ways, he was closest to the major, though they sure didn't have much in common. Major Kelly was from a well-to-do family outside of San Antonio. He'd gone to the military academy and was book smart. He had money and was rather eloquent. Rumor had it that he was also the son of a well-respected man who was serving with Lee himself. The major never spoke of his father, though.

In short, he was rich, educated, and well connected. Thomas Baker was none of those things.

However, something about Ethan Kelly was a little flawed, which made him—by Thomas's estimation, at least—far easier to relate to than Captain Monroe. Their captain was the best man he'd ever met. Thomas looked up to him like none other. But the major, though he was higher in rank, hadn't garnered quite so sterling a reputation. He had to be told things, often hesitated when he needed to charge forward, and was sometimes a bit indolent.

If the world was fair, then Captain Monroe should have outranked Major Kelly. Actually, the captain should have been a colonel or a general, someone really important.

But the world wasn't fair, and neither was the military.

However, the reason no one begrudged the major his rank or his authority was that he was just so darn likable. He often blurted out loud what the enlisted men were thinking but were too afraid of facing discipline to say.

Major Kelly also had a habit of doubting rumors, questioning orders, and overthinking strategies. It drove Lieutenant Markham crazy. However, when Kelly made his decision, he charged ahead, fighting with great valor and tenacity.

Thomas admired the man for that.

Kelly could also, as he was doing at the moment, sit in silence for long periods at a time. Bracing his elbows on his knees, he said, "Mail came today."

"I saw." Thomas never got any mail. Thinking that maybe the major wanted to talk about something in particular, he said, "Did you receive anything good, sir?"

"A letter from each of my sisters and one from an aunt, who seems to have a strange fascination with some of the bawdy girls in a saloon down the way from her house."

Thomas grinned. "Shame, that."

Kelly chuckled. "Indeed. I need to find a way to tell her to guard her reputation." After a pause, he added, "I also received a letter from Faye."

"Four letters from four women," Thomas teased. "An impressive mail call, I'd say."

"Not hardly. All this correspondence can become rather taxing." Looking him over, he said, "I ought to tell them to start taking pity on a certain sergeant. Then you can write to them every week."

Thomas could barely read and write. No matter how many times Ethan or some of the other men had tried to work with him, Thomas couldn't seem to grasp it. For some reason, every time he tried to read the words, letters got all jumbled up and turned around.

He didn't know why God decided he needed to be so stupid, but he must have had his reasons. "I don't think they'd be wanting to hear from a lowly sergeant, sir. Women like the officers' uniforms."

Major Kelly's teeth flashed in the dim light. "You are right, Thomas. Some women like my uniform very much."

Searching his brain for something of worth, Thomas said, "Your Faye certainly does, I believe."

"That she does. Well, she used to."

"Used to?"

"Yes. She . . . well, she wrote to tell me that she no longer favors my uniform."

Thomas sat up. "Sir?"

"Faye has regretfully ended our relationship. It seems she has been making friends with a certain lieutenant who was severely injured and is recuperating in the hospital."

"He must be quite the man for her to turn you over for a lieutenant." Realizing how that sounded, Thomas blurted, "No offense, sir."

To his relief, Major Kelly laughed. "None taken. It seems that a lieutenant with a broken and beat-up leg bests a healthy major locked in a prisoner of war camp."

"She's a fool, then. Injured lieutenants are as plentiful as . . . well, as fireflies on Johnson's Island. You are one of the best men I've ever met."

Major Kelly stilled as he turned to stare at him. "You mean that, don't you?"

"Yes. I mean, you are a good man, sir. And you have everything. Money and family. Education. She should be waiting for you. Not letting you go while you're here."

Slowly Major Kelly smiled. "Thank you for saying that. To be honest, I've been too embarrassed to tell Devin or any of the other officers that I've been discarded. I was afraid they'd act like they knew something about me that Faye did as well. Or simply look at me with pity."

"Oh, I'll look at you with pity, sir. What she did ain't right. She never should have broken things off while you're behind prison bars."

"I did find that rather heartless."

"If it's any consolation, I don't imagine too many women are like Lieutenant Markham's Miranda."

Major Kelly chuckled low. "I think you're right about that. Miranda Markham is the epitome of womanhood."

Thomas wasn't exactly sure what that meant. "She's real pretty too."

"Yes, she is. Phillip is blessed to have found a woman sweet in both appearance and heart." After a pause, he asked, "Have you ever had a sweetheart, Thomas?"

"No."

"Probably just as well. If you did, you would be doing what I was doing, trying to keep a relationship going through letters. That doesn't warm a woman's heart or body."

"I don't think I'll ever be the kind of man ladies write to, sir."

"Why not?"

Thomas saw no need to hedge. "I'm too rough. Too big. I'm not smart, and I get in fights all the time too. None of those things are what women want."

"You may be right, you may not. But I will tell you something every man in our unit knew, Sergeant. If there was something that needed to be done, we all knew who should take care of it. You."

Those words sounded so good Thomas was tempted to ask him to repeat it. But of course he didn't dare. Instead, he simply pointed to the woods. "It looks like someone lit a hundred candles out there, don't it?"

"It does. Those fireflies aren't much in the daytime. But at night, they sure do shine."

"Yes, sir," Thomas murmured, realizing that most things were like that. When one was by himself in the clear light of day, he didn't look all that special. But then, at just the right moment, his light could certainly shine.

26

TWO OF THOMAS'S FRIENDS HAD ARRIVED.

As Laurel watched the men ride closer, each one sitting so tall and straight in the saddle, she felt her stomach twist into knots as her memories from the war slid into place. She'd stood on the porch countless times, watching groups of soldiers approach, never knowing how they were going to treat her.

Though she didn't think she had anything to fear, she could tell even from a distance that they were a formidable band of three. Each man looked almost as large as Thomas, which was quite a feat in itself. In addition, they rode with a confident air, the way only someone who had spent a great amount of time on a horse could.

She noticed that even after such a long time apart, they weren't talking a lot. Instead, their eyes were constantly searching. Each also had a rifle resting across his lap as if he was prepared to take on any sort of trouble at a moment's notice.

What kind of men were they? What kind of men dropped everything and rode miles and miles on the basis of one telegram?

Men unlike any she'd ever known.

Continuing to watch them, Laurel decided that, together, they looked like an unmovable force. Now she was able to see their facial expressions. Like Thomas, their faces looked tanned and their mouths were set in thin lines. They looked hard.

Another flicker of unease coursed through her. What would the men be like? Thomas had said he knew them from the war, from being in the prisoner of war camp. But what did that even mean? Were they good men who had been at the mercy of an enemy? Had they just happened to have been captured and were victims?

Or was there something else about them that had set them apart from other soldiers on the battlefield?

Did they, too, have dark pasts that had marked them like Thomas's did? Or were they everything she'd grown up to believe gentlemen and officers of the Confederacy should be?

Everything she'd been brought up to believe was so blurred in her mind now.

To her surprise, Thomas didn't bring them right to the hitching posts at the front of the house near where she was standing. Instead, the three of them rode toward the barn. At first, she was a little hurt and confused. Wasn't he eager to introduce them to her?

Then it all began to make sense. Of course. The horses would need to be watered and taken care of. The men had likely ridden for hours in the hot Texas sun. No doubt the animals were exhausted.

No doubt the men were too. Should she go right in and prepare for them or wait until Thomas gave her some direction?

After debating a moment about the right course of action, she walked to the barn to greet them. She would say hello, then let them take care of their mounts while she prepared a simple meal. That seemed to be the most polite way to act.

All three of the men stopped what they were doing when she approached. She hesitantly smiled back at them.

Then, to her bemusement, Thomas walked out to meet her halfway. When he reached her side, he presented his elbow for her to take.

She clasped it as he led her to the other men, liking how she now had Thomas to hold on to.

"Miss Tracey, may I present Major Ethan Kelly and Second Lieutenant Robert Truax?" He took a breath, then continued in a firmer, more authoritative tone. "Ethan, Robert, may I present Miss Laurel Tracey, owner of the Red Roan Ranch?"

Both of the newcomers bowed slightly at the waist.

"Miss," Robert murmured.

"Miss Tracey, it's an honor to make your acquaintance," Ethan said with a kind-looking smile.

Though it had been awhile since she'd done so, Laurel moved her right foot back and executed a curtsy. "Gentlemen, welcome. Thank you for coming to our aid."

"The pleasure is ours, I assure you," the major said with another smile. "Plus, it gave us a reason to see each other, which is always a blessing."

"A blessing," she murmured.

Thomas groaned a little bit under his breath. "Don't mind Major Kelly, Miss Tracey. He can't seem to help but be charming. It's a character flaw."

In spite of the gravity of the situation, Laurel felt her pulse race a bit. The major really was extraordinarily handsome. Blessed with an impressive height, wide shoulders, slim hips, and chestnut-colored hair, he no doubt had set many a woman's heart aflutter. Especially when dressed in his officer's uniform of gray and gold.

Beside him, Robert Truax appeared far less refined. He had piercing dark eyes, almost black hair, and pronounced cheekbones.

He looked as if he could take anyone on in a back alley and come up the winner.

Realizing she'd been staring, she turned to Thomas. "Sergeant, please do bring your friends into the house after you get your horses settled. Their rooms are ready, and I'll set out a light meal."

A pair of lines formed between Robert's brows. "There's no need for you to go to any trouble on our account, miss. We can bed down here in the barn and help ourselves in the kitchen."

"Of course you'll do no such thing! Just come in the house when you're ready." Turning to Thomas, she said, "I'm counting on you to make sure they listen to me."

"Yes, Miss Tracey," Thomas said with a hint of a smile.

Major Kelly chuckled. "Thomas, you've just answered the question every officer has ever asked after they met you."

"And what was that?"

"If it was ever going to be possible for you to settle into your skin."

"And what was your answer?"

"Get you a woman to order you around, obviously!" Robert finished with a laugh. "Miss Tracey, I would have paid good money to have you at my side when I gave Thomas orders during the war. Your presence would have saved us from many hours watching him pace and fidget."

As the major's grin broadened, Thomas scowled. "Don't you pay them any mind. I wasn't ever that bad."

Enjoying the light bantering, Laurel couldn't resist joining in. "Somehow I can't help but think they might not be exaggerating too much."

"We are not," Ethan Kelly said. "He was as difficult to supervise as he was a skilled tracker and horseman."

"It sounds as if you are a man of many talents, Sergeant."

Cheeks red, Thomas said, "My former officers enjoy bringing up my flaws a bit too much. I'm sorry for their clumsy conversation. They are usually as polite as preachers on a Sunday morning."

"I think I'd rather have them like this. Take your time, gentlemen. I'll see you inside."

Laurel couldn't help but smile when she turned her back. Something told her she was just about to learn a whole lot more about Thomas, thanks to these friends of his.

Though she regretted the reason for their visit, she was certainly looking forward to getting to know more about Thomas. From the moment she'd first seen him, he'd intrigued her more than any man she'd ever met.

❧

It was almost a full hour later when the men entered the house. She'd expected them some time earlier and had even heated up water so they could bathe before supper.

But a quick glance told her that wasn't going to be necessary. Each of their faces looked freshly scrubbed. The edges of their hair were damp too.

"Please tell me y'all did not bathe outside. I've been heating up some water for you to bathe in the bathing room," she blurted before realizing it was rather unseemly to talk about such things.

"That's right kind of you, but my mother would've had my hide if I'd come inside your home smelling of dirt and sweat."

"Well, my mother would have been ashamed of my poor manners, allowing you to bathe in the barn."

"I'm not sure what my mother would have said," Robert said. "But I do think she would have cautioned me not to worry about such things when one was among friends."

Thomas, who was standing to one side with his hands clasped behind his back, looked a bit aggrieved by his friends' gentle flirting. "Miss Laurel, would you care to serve supper now, or wait a bit longer?"

"Everything is ready and warm in the oven. If you would follow me?"

She led them to the dining room, then brought in bowls of bean salad, fried chicken, and mashed potatoes. She also set out some pickled cucumbers and peppers she'd been saving for the right occasion. This had seemed as good as any.

The men stared at the table as if in wonder.

Robert cleared his throat. "Thomas led me to believe you didn't have any help in the kitchen."

"I don't. I made it all myself."

"Just now?"

She shrugged. "It's never too much trouble to fry up chicken and boil potatoes."

"It looks wonderful," Robert said. "I'm obliged."

Thomas led her to her seat and held her chair for her. She smiled up at him, feeling as if the situation was becoming more awkward by the second. Sure that the newcomers wouldn't enjoy a blessing, she said, "Gentlemen, I hope you will enjoy your meal."

"I'll lead us in prayer," Thomas said easily.

After they bent their heads, Thomas spoke. "Dear heavenly Father, thank you for this food we are about to receive. Bless the hands that made it. Be with our captain as he makes his way here. Let him feel your protecting arms as he makes his way across the state to come to the aid of friends. Amen."

"Amen," Robert and Ethan murmured. Laurel followed suit.

Moments later, after all the serving dishes had been passed around and the first tentative bites of her meal had been taken,

Robert sighed in appreciation. "Only you would be taken prisoner, be beaten, then land in a spot as fine as this, Thomas. You really do always land on your feet."

"One could say the same of you." Looking pointedly at the man's gold ring on his finger, he said, "I didn't know you had gotten hitched."

"It's a recent development. It only just happened. Two weeks ago."

"There's a story there too," Major Kelly said with a ghost of a smile. "He married Markham's widow."

Thomas set down his fork. "You married Miranda?"

"The one and only," Robert said.

"I can't wait to hear how that came about."

"It's quite a story, I'll tell you that."

"Major, were you there to witness the nuptials?"

"I was there when Robert sent word that he needed help. Monroe and I did what we could."

Thomas looked hurt. "I didn't receive such a missive."

"It all happened just weeks ago. The captain told us you were unable to join us, but I know now how you were otherwise occupied. In, uh, your jail cell."

"Indeed, I was." Looking back at Laurel, he said, "I'd still be there if Miss Tracey hadn't seen fit to release me."

"I'm glad I did, though I fear the sergeant has probably spent more than one evening wishing I'd left him where he was," Laurel said.

Thomas grinned before turning solemn. "I wish I could tell you this"—he gestured toward the table—"is all I've been doing since I arrived, but that certainly hasn't been the case. Miss Tracey has had to endure one loss and fight one problem after another since the war began. However, her troubles have escalated as of late."

"Care to tell us about it now?" the major asked.

Not hungry, Laurel spoke. "I'll do it. The first morning after the sergeant arrived here, just two days ago, I discovered someone had left a dead calf at my doorstep."

"Strange calling card."

Thomas nodded. "Feeling sure that it hadn't died of natural causes, I took it into town to the sheriff and to get looked at by the doctor."

"What did he discover?"

"As far as I can tell, nothing yet. No one has been out here to tell us."

"Then, one day after that, yesterday, we were out riding. We not only discovered six more cattle dead, but someone shot at us."

Robert turned to face them. "Say again?"

"One moment we were reading a note left by whoever had poisoned the cattle, and the next I had pushed her to the ground and was trying to get in a shot," Thomas said.

"Do you know who did such a thing?" the major asked.

"I wish we could tell you, but we never saw them close enough to know," Laurel said. Unsuccessfully fighting a shiver, she added, "It was frightening."

Laurel noticed that all three men exchanged concerned looks.

"Forgive my sad manners," Robert said. "Thomas might have told you that I had to learn about comporting myself in social situations. Apparently I still have to learn. We'll discuss this at another time. Most especially when we are not enjoying your delicious meal."

"Indeed," Major Kelly said.

But Laurel wasn't about to let them decide her future without her input. She had come too far to pretend she didn't need to be completely involved.

Though she was nervous, she raised her chin and spoke with

complete sincerity and not a little bit of force. "Forgive my bluntness, gentlemen, but I think we are far beyond such social niceties. Lately I've been inundated with squatters taking advantage of my lone state, been approached by multiple men offering to purchase my beloved ranch, been browbeaten by my stepsiblings to sell, and now someone is killing cattle and attempting to kill me."

She sighed. "Please don't treat me as though I don't count."

"You count," Thomas said, his voice firm and sure. While she gazed at him, struck by the depth of emotion she saw in his blue eyes—and how his words made her feel—he softened his tone. "Of course you need to be part of this conversation, Miss Laurel. However, I would rather not start making suggestions or bantering about ideas until Captain Monroe arrives. When he arrives, we'll just have to go over everything again."

She didn't need to look around to realize the two other men at the table were listening to their exchange with interest. No doubt they were imagining something was going on between them too.

Laurel was sure her face was probably bright red. "Oh. Yes. Please just forget what I said."

"Never that." Getting to his feet, Thomas said, "Gentlemen, if you have had enough to eat, would you mind making yourself at home while I help Miss Laurel with the dishes?"

"I'll do one better," Lieutenant Truax said. "I'll help with them too."

Laurel was just about to assure him that was not necessary when someone knocked at the front door.

She stood up eagerly. "Sergeant, perhaps your captain has arrived?"

"Maybe so," Thomas murmured, though his expression didn't match his tone. "I'll go see if Captain Monroe has, indeed, arrived. But until I know for sure, you stay here."

She attempted to smile. "Not every person who comes here is a suspect."

"We'll see," he said as he turned for the foyer.

"Thom—" she began, but stopped herself just in time.

Because she noticed then that he was armed. He was holding a beautifully crafted new Colt in his right hand. He also looked ready to use it.

27

UH-OH," MABEL MUTTERED UNDER HER BREATH. "LOOK who's back."

Taylor turned to the entrance of the saloon and experienced the same empty feeling Mabel must have. Landon Marshall was back. This was not good news. He'd hoped for another day's break at the very least.

When Marshall's eyes lit on him and then he started sauntering forward, Taylor drummed up a lifetime of experience not to shy away from the man's glare.

Without saying a word, Marshall took the bar stool next to him and pressed a palm on the hammered copper surface. "Whiskey, neat."

"You got it."

When Mabel set the shot glass in front of him with a fake sultry smile, Marshall slapped two bits on the bar. "Thank you."

"Anytime, sugar." Turning toward Taylor, she arched a brow. "You want anything?"

Taylor was terribly thirsty but low on funds since Marshall had reneged on his last payment. "No thanks. I'll wait."

"Give him another anyway, darlin'," Marshall said. "I'm buying."

When Mabel took his glass to refill it, Taylor nodded. "Appreciate that."

"It's the least I can do. Given that you lost one of your partners yesterday."

Remembering how hard it had been to dig even an inch in the hard soil, Taylor pressed his lips together. It had been an ugly job, and Howell didn't seem to have much going for him in the way of upper-body strength. When Mabel set his shot glass in front of him, he drained half of it.

"You got something more for me to do?"

"Yeah. I'm still going to get her to marry me, and I've got something else up my sleeve too. But do something different this time, just as long as it's as threatening to the ranch as killing her cattle."

With effort, Taylor kept his expression impassive, almost glad for the request. The opportunity to change up his scare tactics made a difference when he had no choice but to do what this man wanted. Not only was he too far in to extricate himself, but he had no money and nowhere to go. "Yes, sir."

"Then be on alert. I'm told Baker and Laurel sent a wire to someone earlier today, and I'm thinking something is about to happen."

"Yes, sir. Do you need me to get any assistance?" He hoped Marshall didn't want him to hire Howell again. It was a whole lot easier to take care of everything himself.

"No." After slapping down another two bits on the bar, Marshall got up, sauntered toward a table, and motioned Mabel forward. "Come spend some time with me now, honey."

Mabel picked up the coin and slipped it into the bodice of her dress before visibly steeling herself.

Thinking of Dara, Taylor looked at Mabel with some concern. "You going to be okay with him?"

"Probably not. But why are you even asking?" she whispered, her expression filled with derision. "It ain't like you can do a thing about it."

He threw back the last of his shot and stood up. It was time to leave. He had no desire to witness Marshall mistreat her, because Mabel was exactly right. There wasn't a thing he could do about much anymore.

Even the soiled doves knew it.

⤫

Thomas respected Captain Monroe more than just about any other man on earth. And from the many years when he fought by his side, Thomas knew how his captain liked to do things. He was careful and methodical. He rarely did anything on impulse.

For these reasons, if Thomas were still a gambling man, he would say the chances were slim to none that the captain had decided to ride his horse onto the ranch, dismount, then walk up to Laurel's door and knock as if he didn't have a care in the world.

That wasn't how he did things.

Especially not after receiving a telegram like the one Thomas sent. Instead, his captain would ride to the barn, dismount, and simply wait until he saw Thomas or one of his other men. The captain had always been a man to be assured of his surroundings before making any move.

And that was why Thomas had his new pistol in his right hand at the ready when he opened the door.

"She's got you opening doors for her now?"

He'd been right. It definitely was not his former captain at the door.

"Marshall. To what do I owe this pleasure?"

"Don't play games with me, Baker. I need to see Laurel immediately."

Instead of backing away, he merely raised his eyebrows. "Care to explain why you have brought this pair with you?"

"We live here," Jerome said.

"Not anymore. Don't you recall that conversation? Because I do. I remember it clear as day."

"I recall that you kicked us out of our own home without reason," Jerome said. "I know you have insinuated yourself onto our land and into our lives with the ease of a poisonous snake in tall grass."

"While that's rather colorful, I don't find it to be fitting in this case."

Marshall glared. "Watch yourself, Baker. Laurel's siblings have every right to be here, and you had no right to influence her to drive them out. I've come to help Laurel see that. While you might think you're now someone high and mighty, it is an absolute certainty that you will eventually be nothing more than a dirt-poor criminal again."

Marshall's words stung. But instead of fighting them or pretending they hadn't met their mark, Thomas welcomed the hurt. After all, that was how he had felt most of his life until he'd lived side by side with his friends in the barracks on Johnson's Island. "You may be right," he replied without a bit of animosity in his voice. "Being here is most likely fleeting, and I am nothing more than a poor example of a man. However, the fact remains that I am currently here and you are not."

"Who arrived?" Robert asked as he joined them. His voice and demeanor seemed as if he were greeting Christmas carolers.

Thomas hid a smile. Robert was a master at hiding his true feelings. Thomas had once watched his lieutenant look much the same way when a blowhard major described his excuses for implementing asinine battle plans.

Somewhat eager to see what the man was going to do next, Thomas performed the necessary introductions. "Robert Truax, these are Laurel's stepsiblings, Jerome and Bess. Miss Laurel's already had to kick them out one time since I've been here."

Before their eyes, Robert's pleasant demeanor transformed into something far darker. Actually, he was eyeing them the way one might examine an unwelcome rat in a cupboard. "Interesting." Then he turned to the third visitor standing on the stoop. "And you are?"

Obviously running out of patience, Laurel's neighbor thrust out a hand. "I'm Landon Marshall. I own a sizable spread of land just to the west of here."

After a pause, Robert took Marshall's hand. "Robert Truax. I fought by this man's side during the altercation between the states. And while he might say otherwise, I can say with honesty that he is not some poor criminal. I would watch how you describe him in the future."

Marshall relaxed. "So you're an old friend."

"Of a sort."

Looking just beyond Robert, Marshall took on a wary expression.

The major held out his hand. "Ethan Kelly of San Antonio. I'm a friend too."

"Nice to meet you—" Recognition flew into Landon's eyes. "Any chance you're a relation to the Michael Kellys?"

Ethan nodded. "Michael Kelly is my father."

"He owns one of the biggest ranches in the area."

"The Bar X is one of the biggest ranches in the state," Ethan said, clarifying Marshall's statement.

Thomas couldn't help but stare at Ethan in surprise. He'd known Ethan's family was wealthy and well connected, but he never dreamed they were that well-off.

Marshall's smile was so slick oil could have run off it. "I'd very much enjoy the opportunity to talk to you about your ranch. I have some questions about the train lines and managing a full crew."

"Excuse me," Jerome said. "We are still standing out here on the doorstep." He waved a hand at Thomas. "Step aside now and let us in. Bess and I need to get settled."

"You are not moving back in," Thomas said. "However, I will go ask Miss Tracey if she desires company."

Bess harrumphed. "I fail to see how it is up to her to decide anything. After all, this was our father's house before it became hers."

"Your father ensured this ranch would come to me when he and my mother died," Laurel said quietly from her position next to the staircase.

Thomas gripped the door. "As entertaining as this reunion is turning out to be, I don't believe there's anything more to be said."

"Hold on, Sergeant," Laurel said. "We should let them say their piece."

"Sure?"

Before she could answer, Landon Marshall pushed his way in. "Laurel, I became even more worried when your help relayed that you would not be coming to my home for supper tonight. Please tell me you've reconsidered your decision to manage this ranch and all your troubles on your own. Your siblings and I want to help you."

Sharing a look with Robert and Ethan, Thomas stepped to one side as Bess and Jerome wandered inside too. After looking outside for any sign of Captain Monroe but seeing nothing, he shut the door, then walked to Laurel's side. "You don't need to do or say anything," he said.

Her gaze softened. "While I appreciate your efforts to shield me, I think I should hear what they have to say."

"At last you have regained your senses in that regard," Jerome said. "Let's sit down and discuss why you men are here."

Bess was already walking toward the sitting room. "I'll have some tea, Laurel. With cream and sugar."

"Of course. Please make yourselves comfortable," Laurel said as she walked toward the kitchen.

"What is going on?" Robert said under his breath to Thomas.

"I'm not exactly sure, but I aim to find out. Lead our visitors into the sitting room, would you? I'll go get some answers."

"My pleasure."

Satisfied that Robert and Ethan would keep Laurel's step-siblings and wannabe suitor in line, Thomas followed her to the kitchen.

Laurel had just set the kettle on to boil.

"Why are you serving them tea?" he asked. "You don't need to lift one finger for them."

"I know. But I can't avoid them forever. Jerome and Bess have a way of twisting information and situations to get what they want."

"Yes, I noticed they don't take rejection well."

"They don't take much of anything well. I'm afraid I'm not above using you and your friends to help me get my point across."

"And Landon Marshall?"

"I started wondering if he might be able to give us any helpful information about the problems occurring around here. But I don't want to face him alone either."

"Fair enough. But I'm putting a time limit on this visit," he warned. "They are not staying longer than half an hour."

Setting cups and saucers on a cart, Laurel nodded. "That suits me just fine." After she set out a plate of shortbread cookies, a small pitcher with cream, and a sugar pot, she poured the now boiling water into a fine-looking blue teapot. "You may push the cart, Thomas," she said lightly.

"My pleasure. You know, I do believe this is the first tea service I've ever pushed."

"So far you are doing an exemplary job."

Thomas found himself smiling as they entered the sitting room. As he saw that Bess and Jerome were sharing the sofa, Landon Marshall was ensconced in the largest chair, and Robert and Ethan were standing in front of the fireplace, he raised his eyebrows.

Laurel's grace, on the other hand, seemed to have no limits. Standing at the cart, she politely served everyone tea. Only after they had all been taken care of did she perch on the edge of the remaining chair.

Unable to help himself, Thomas walked to her side.

After casting him a look of gratitude, she said, "Now that everyone has met, I must ask why you have come, Landon. Were you simply escorting Jerome and Bess here?"

"Not at all. There has been talk in town of some problems taking place on your ranch. I heard rumors about more dead cattle and gunshots being fired at you. Is this true?"

"It is," Thomas replied.

"Why would anyone want to harm you?"

"I don't know," Laurel said. "I can only guess that someone who wants me to sell my land is hoping violence might sway me. That is, unless he actually wants me dead."

Thomas noticed Jerome and Bess exchange a look with Marshall. He jumped on that. "Miss Tracey has told me that each of you has been attempting to persuade her to sell."

Bess gasped. "What are you insinuating?"

"It seems fairly obvious to me," Robert said.

Jerome got to his feet. "While it is true that I have been unsuccessfully encouraging my sister to sell, I would never resort to killing animals."

"Or shooting at her?" Robert asked. "If you killed Miss Tracey, your problems would be solved."

"Think what you will, but I am not a murderer."

Thomas agreed. Jerome still didn't look like he had ever held a pistol. And from what Laurel had said, he also didn't have any money to pay someone to do his bidding.

Landon Marshall was a different story.

"What about you, Marshall?" he drawled. "I know you also have been hoping to persuade Miss Tracey to sell."

"That is true."

"Would you resort to violence to get your way?"

"While it is true that I fought in the war, I am still a gentleman." The look he gave Thomas showed he definitely did not consider Thomas to be the same type of man.

Thomas was not affronted. After all, he was no gentleman.

"Where did you serve?" Major Kelly asked.

"I was with the Texas militia unit."

"Oh? Did you fight alongside the Tennessee Army?"

Marshall looked uncomfortable. "No. I was stationed near Dallas. I'm afraid I didn't see much action."

"Ah."

Landon turned to stare at Laurel. "I am becoming concerned about you, Laurel. You shouldn't be here alone, and especially not alone in the company of these soldiers. You need to consider not only your stepsiblings' needs but your own. I would still like to marry you."

Laurel clasped her hands together. "I have told you several

times now that I would like you to stop pursuing me. I also told you the other day that I didn't need you looking out for me."

"But something is going to happen to you."

"Is that a threat?" Thomas asked.

"I am stating a fact. As I told you the other day when Jackson and I stopped by, I have had nothing to do with the attacks on the Red Roan Ranch. Also, don't forget that one of my barns was broken into as well. I am also a victim."

Just then Thomas felt a prickling on the back of his neck. Turning around, he saw Captain Monroe standing in the doorway that led out to the kitchen. "Sir."

Immediately, all the other occupants of the room turned to stare at the newcomer. Everyone wore various shades of surprise.

"Good evening," Captain Monroe said. "I decided to come on in when I saw the doorway was cracked and heard such an intriguing conversation." Looking as if he was harboring a secret, he said directly to Laurel, "I hope you don't mind that I barged right in, miss. I couldn't seem to stay away."

28

It took everything Laurel had not to press a hand to her chest as her latest guest stepped into her sitting room. She'd been so focused on the conversation that she hadn't even realized another person had joined them.

Even more disconcerting was the rush of adrenaline she felt when Captain Monroe turned her way. He had blond hair cut close to his scalp, a ruddy complexion that testified he'd spent most of his life out in the elements, and clear, light-blue eyes that seemed to burn into her very soul.

No part of his face was exceptional. However, the sum of its parts made one want to take a second, more lingering look.

Luckily, he seemed oblivious to her stare.

"Miss Tracey, I presume. Please forgive my rude entrance." Executing a small bow, he said in a deep, almost scratchy voice, "My name is Devin Monroe. At one time I was Thomas's captain."

She stood and curtsied deeply. "Sir, your appearance is most welcome. I hope your journey wasn't too strenuous?"

"I am happy to say that it would take a far more taxing trip to make it a strenuous one."

"May I bring you something to drink or eat?"

He looked at Bess, Jerome, and Landon. "Thank you, but not at the moment."

Major Kelly stepped forward and held out his hand. "Glad you could join us, Devin. As you might have surmised, we were just discussing a few things that have been occurring recently on Miss Tracey's property."

Turning to Landon, Captain Monroe surveyed him from top to bottom. "I overheard much of what was discussed," he said, his voice cold. "Trust me when I say that it would be in your best interests, sir, to conclude your visit at this time."

Landon narrowed his eyes. "What are you insinuating?"

"That while thousands of men were in the Confederacy, few earned the reputation you did."

Landon blanched. "I don't know what you think you heard, but I assure you I served with honor."

"I'm sure you served many women extremely well," Captain Monroe said sarcastically. While Landon sputtered, the captain turned to Thomas. "Thomas, I'd like an update as soon as possible."

"Yes, sir. I will do that presently."

"What a minute," Jerome called out. "Our business is not done."

Before Laurel could step in, Thomas said, "I beg to disagree. I believe it's time to bid you good evening."

"Laurel, are you simply going to stand there and let these men push us out the door?" Bess asked.

Laurel thought Bess looked crestfallen. So much so, she was tempted to ask her, at least, to stay. Though Bess hadn't treated her well, Laurel wasn't proud that she'd sent Bess away. It wasn't a Christian way to behave, especially toward a woman who was essentially on her own in the middle of Texas. Bess was also family. Even though she had neither been grateful for Laurel's sacrifices on her behalf nor lifted a finger to help her, she could change. Maybe she already had changed?

While the men in the room waited on her reply, Laurel pursed her lips. Maybe she should ask the men to move back out to the barn and strive to make it work with Bess and Jerome? Her step-father had been so very good to her. Surely he would be pleased if Laurel took them back.

Her mother would be proud of her too. After all, hadn't she taught Laurel time and again to do good deeds without expecting anything in return? Surely this was in that category.

Having made her decision, Laurel cleared her throat. "Bess, as a matter of fact—"

"Good," Bess said, interrupting. "I'm glad you're coming to your senses. For a moment I was worried you were actually think-ing of continuing this façade."

Laurel blinked. "I'm sorry, I don't understand."

Bess waved a hand impatiently. "Look at you, primping among all these gentlemen."

"Primping?" Laurel looked down at herself. She was wearing a faded and worn calico. No doubt her hair resembled a rat's nest after being pushed off her face for the last ten hours.

When she raised her head, she saw Bess looking her up and down, disdain heavy in her eyes. "You know what I'm talking about. Don't pretend you don't. It's unseemly. And if I may be blunt, embarrassing for you." Raising her chin, she said, "We both know you would never catch the eye of men like these. Why, they were officers."

Mortified that Thomas and his friends were hearing such accusations, she sputtered, "I have not been attempting to catch anyone's eye."

"You need to accept Landon's suit. He is your only chance for matrimony. And he has promised that Jerome and I can live in this house too."

Landon got to his feet. "My offer of marriage still stands, Laurel. I can protect both you and Red Roan Ranch. And if you feel guilty about how you've treated Miss Vance and her brother, I can buy the ranch and you can give them the proceeds."

Oh, but this was awful! Her cheeks burned as Thomas, his captain, Robert, and the major all looked on with varying degrees of distaste. What did they think of her now? She could only imagine.

And though she hated to continue to air her dirty laundry, it didn't seem as if she had much choice. She ignored Landon and turned to her stepsiblings.

"I need to keep the Red Roan Ranch. It's all I have left of my parents. It's all I have left of your father too. Surely that means something to you. He loved this ranch."

"If he loved this place, his affection was misplaced," Jerome interjected in a bored tone. "Besides, if he had truly loved this land, he would have asked Bess and me to come here years ago. He never did."

"Why would he ask you to live here? He and my mother lived on the property he left you. And besides, you two were still in boarding school when he married my mother."

"Yes, I believe you were studying math and whatever while the rest of us were fighting," Thomas murmured.

Jerome folded his arms across his chest. "I was studying business and law while you all, I have learned, were languishing on an island during the end of the war. There's a difference, I think," he said.

Robert Truax's whole posture changed and his fists clenched. Looking at his expression, Laurel realized he was holding on to his temper with care.

Luckily, she was also coming to the conclusion that nothing

was ever going to change her stepsiblings. No matter what she did or said to Bess and Jerome, they were never going to respect her. They also were never going to appreciate the ranch the way she did. To them, it was simply a piece of land that, one way or another, would allow them to continue their rather aimless lives.

It would never be their legacy.

It would never be their home.

That realization bolstered Laurel's resolve. She had to keep the ranch. If she lost this land, she would feel like a failure. She would also feel as if she had lost an important part of herself. She couldn't allow that, not when she'd already lost so much.

Turning to Landon, she said, "I do think you have had my best interests at heart, and I understand you think marrying me will be of help. But I can't marry only for the ranch's future, and I will not sell this land."

"You will regret this," Landon warned.

"I don't think so." As he glared at her, she turned to face Bess and Jerome. "Time and again I have tried to give you both the benefit of the doubt. I have waited for y'all to help me work the ranch. To help me keep your father's legacy alive and well. But you never did. Now it is very apparent that you never will. I have had enough, I'm afraid. Please leave."

That seemed to be all Thomas needed. He turned toward the foyer. "You heard the lady. It's time to go."

Jerome glared at the assembled men, his expression holding nothing but disdain for the war heroes in the room.

Then he turned to Laurel. "From now on, I will cease to know you. You are no better than a soiled dove working the alleys, living the way you are with multiple men. It's shameful and unseemly."

Just as she was about to sputter a reply, Thomas threw out a punch and hit Jerome square in the face.

Uttering a startled cry, Jerome's head jolted back from the force, though he did remain on his feet. After a few seconds, he blinked his one good eye, his other hidden behind one palm. Blood began to pour from his nose. "You will regret this."

"You are full of threats, aren't you?" Lieutenant Truax asked as he grabbed Jerome's elbow. "I've rarely seen or heard the like."

"Are all of you going to allow him to get away with this? He struck me."

"If he hadn't hit you, I would have done the deed myself," the lieutenant said. "There is no way I would stand quietly while you disparaged Miss Tracey. Though I may not have Thomas Baker's size, I can pack a good wallop."

Holding a handkerchief to his face, Jerome merely walked out of the room without a word.

"It is evident that this situation has disintegrated," Landon said. "I'll see myself out."

Bess said nothing, just followed Jerome and Landon and scurried to the front entrance.

After Robert closed the door, he grinned. "Good riddance to them."

Thomas stepped close to her. "Are you all right, Laurel?"

"Yes, of course. Thank you for coming to my defense. Thank you, too, Lieutenant Truax."

"It was my pleasure," he said. "I must say, I always thought having siblings would make my life better and more complete. But after meeting those two, I'm kind of glad I missed out. They couldn't have been harder to bear."

"I'm afraid I've often felt that way myself," Laurel replied. Wanting to get everything out in the open, she looked curiously at Captain Monroe. "Sir, what did you mean about Landon Marshall? I thought he'd served with honor."

"No, he didn't do that. Not exactly. But I'm afraid the things I know are not suitable for feminine ears."

Thomas rested a hand on the middle of her back. "He's right, Miss Laurel. Let it go, at least for now."

Realizing he was right, that there were far more important things to dwell on besides Landon's past, she drew a deep breath. "Gentlemen, would you care for some fresh coffee?"

"That would be much appreciated, miss," the major said. "Thank you."

Just as she left the room, she saw Captain Monroe hug Thomas like a fond old friend. She imagined Thomas was asking how he knew he was in jail and thanking him for his gifts. Thanking him for coming now to his aid.

When all the men started chuckling, then began to talk as though they'd never been apart for more than a day or two, she knew it was a welcome reunion. A needed one.

It was a blessing in the middle of a terrible situation. And because those moments were hard to come by and should be treasured, she decided to take her time with both the coffee and the captain's supper. Some things were far more important.

29

Johnson's Island, Ohio
Confederate States of America Officers POW Camp

MAIL HAD ARRIVED AGAIN.

Thomas knew the routine, and in his more maudlin moments, he resented the men who looked forward to each mail day like the arrival of a long-awaited lover.

Whenever rumors circulated that a boat had arrived with a pack of letters, a new tension would flurry around the camp. The men would rest on their bunks, gazing at the door of the barracks. And while they waited, they would mope and whine and talk about how the hours passed so slowly.

Then their eyes would light up when one of the guards wandered in with a handful of precious correspondence.

It happened again and again, with Thomas never receiving a thing.

Usually he dealt with his disappointment by muttering caustic remarks to whoever was nearby. But this day found him in a more reflective mood. Instead of glaring at the guards or mercilessly teasing the recipients, he sat on his cot and watched.

As usual, Phillip Markham had a handful of letters. Each

one was addressed with care. Each letter of his name was carefully formed, as if his beloved Miranda cared so much about her husband that she needed to make even the letters of his name perfect.

Phillip received so many letters from his wife that he wasn't stingy when he read them. While most men retreated to corners in the barracks or empty spaces on the grounds to read mail, weep, and mourn, Phillip simply sat down on his cot, placed his letters in chronological order as best he could, and read them one right after the other.

Thomas, sitting on his cot next to him, would sometimes sneak a glance and attempt to read some of Miranda's words and phrases. It was hard for him to do. He didn't want to be rude and intrusive.

But he had a whole other more embarrassing reason. It was plain and simple too. He couldn't read well. Not hardly at all.

He liked to tell himself it was most fortunate that he didn't have a sweetheart to write him. If she did write, he'd have to ask another man to read her words. And then he'd have to ask him to write for him too. A man's pride could take only so much.

Therefore, he lay on his back on his cot and made do with feeling the happiness that drifted off the lieutenant.

"Hey, Thomas," Phillip said after almost a quarter hour had passed.

Thomas turned his head to face him. "Yeah?"

"Want to hear part of Miranda's letter?"

He did. He ached to hear the words, to pocket them away so he could one day pretend they had been written for him. But such eagerness would be misunderstood.

So he propped himself up on his elbows. "If you want. What is she pattering on about today? Her daffodils?"

Phillip laughed, the sound lighthearted and sweet. "Not this time. It's . . . it's about our house."

"Don't keep me in suspense," he teased. "Read on."

Phillip cleared his throat. "'I hope you don't mind, but I decided to redecorate some of the downstairs rooms. They seemed so dusty and drab. You know they do, Phillip, dear. Why, your office alone feels like a dark tunnel with those plum-colored velvet curtains and heavy carpets. And the smell! We've had so many fires in that fireplace I fear everything will forever smell like a chimney sweep.'"

Thomas closed his eyes and imagined such a place. Thick curtains, heavy carpets, roaring fireplaces, and a woman living in the center of it all who actually cared what it looked and smelled like.

Phillip inhaled. "Don't fret, Thomas. It gets better. Listen to this: 'With your comfort in mind, dear husband, Winifred and Emerson and even Cook and Belle and I pulled out the rugs and beat them on the front lawn. Then Belle and I—Belle is the new girl from New Orleans, remember?—set to work taking down those drapes. It was difficult. They were so heavy, and they were fastened with those awful brass rings your mother is so fond of.

"'Anyway, just as we were halfway done, a mouse scurried out of the hem of the drape Belle was holding! A mouse had been living there! That was how long it had been living in your office unattended, Phillip. Which, as an aside, means those drapes were in desperate need to be removed.'"

Phillip chuckled as he flipped over the sheet of velum. "Isn't this something, Thomas?"

Thomas's throat was so tight with jealousy he could only nod.

Clearing his throat, the lieutenant continued. "'Well, you must surely imagine what happened next! That rodent scurried toward me! I cried out and jumped on a chair. Belle was stranded, so I pulled her up on the same seat as me! Us in our skirts . . . why, there was hardly an extra inch to breathe.

"'Then, when Belle saw another mouse, we squealed again, so loudly that we startled Mr. and Mrs. Clark, who were out for their usual Friday evening stroll. They came running up the lawn and burst into the foyer without even knocking first.'"

Phillip looked at Thomas. "I never cared for Mr. or Mrs. Clark. They don't have much of a sense of humor, I'm afraid."

"Pity," Thomas muttered, eager to hear the rest of the tale.

"'And . . . oh, Phillip, it was just awful. There they were, standing in the doorway, watching Belle and me clasp each other on top of a chair. When—and I am sorry about this, Phillip, I really am—the chair broke—'"

Thomas leaned forward. "Broke, you say?"

Phillip's face lit up as he continued. "'We fell to the ground, startling the mouse, who went running toward Mr. and Mrs. Clark! Mrs. Clark ran out of the house while Mr. Clark attempted to bash the poor thing with his umbrella. He missed, thankfully.'"

Unable to help himself, Thomas interrupted. "Thankfully?"

Phillip chuckled. "That is one thing you're going to learn when you get yourself a wife, Thomas. Women are fretful creatures. They change their minds on a moment's notice and feel sorry for small furry creatures." He sighed. "I don't know what we men would do without them."

Thomas laughed. "You mean you don't know what you'd do without your Miranda, sir. You, I'm afraid, are well and truly smitten."

Staring down at the letter, Phillip grinned. "I can't deny it. I'm afraid I am."

"What are you going to write to her about all that, sir? Are you upset about the chair?"

"The chair? Of course not. I don't care about the mouse either.

All that matters to me is that she's there at home, waiting for me to return."

"You are a blessed man, sir."

"I know I am. But don't worry, Thomas. When you get back to Texas, I'm sure some gal will claim your attentions too." He laughed again. "I am only going to be sorry that I won't be there to hear the stories about all she puts you through."

"I won't be marrying anyone, sir."

"Don't be so certain. Love and marriage happen to the best of us."

"Not to men like me, I'm afraid."

Carefully folding Miranda's letter into its envelope, Phillip glanced at him again. "That's where you're wrong, Sergeant. It happens especially to men like you."

Not wanting to argue that point, Thomas lay back down. He rested his head on his folded arms and closed his eyes, and finally gave in to the temptation of imagining what it might be like to be Phillip Markham. To have a pretty woman waiting for him in a comfortable house.

But no matter how hard he tried, he couldn't picture it. It seemed such a thing was beyond him.

30

Thomas woke up before dawn. Every nerve in his body felt raw, every sense on alert. Startled, he realized he'd felt the exact same way before going into battle. His stomach was in knots and his head felt clearer than it had in months. Even a faint metallic taste was in his mouth.

He was both bemused and relieved to realize that his body hadn't forgotten how to prepare for war. Maybe a small part of him had missed fighting after all.

After hurriedly dressing, he carefully walked downstairs and stepped out to the kitchen. He hoped he hadn't awakened Laurel. She'd sat with him and the men late into the night, listening while they made plans and answering questions about various parts of the Red Roan Ranch.

He'd been proud of the way she answered each man's questions. She had been both thoughtful and observant, and hadn't acted either rattled or nervous when the men listened to her answers intently. He'd seen many men handle Captain Monroe's questioning less well.

Much later, well after midnight, Thomas had heard Laurel's light footsteps going down the stairs. He'd sat up in bed, waiting to hear her ascend again. It had been a lengthy wait, almost an hour.

While he'd waited, he let his mind drift again, imagining how pleased he would have been to have the honor of taking care of her. If she hadn't been able to sleep, he would have held her in his arms into the night, soothing her worries by reminding her that he and his friends weren't just former soldiers with battlefield experiences. No, they had years of practice tracking men in all sorts of terrain. They each had also fought several battles in hand-to-hand combat. She wasn't going to have to worry about getting hurt.

Unable to stop himself, he'd let his mind wander to places it shouldn't. He thought about pressing his lips to her temple and brow, softly kissing her lips. Imagined whispering things only a lover would. That she was important to him. So important that he would be extra careful when he was out, because he now had someone to come home to.

The bright light of morning reminded him he was a fool. He would never be her sweetheart, her husband, or her lover.

No, he was destined to be only her hired hand, a prisoner in her eyes. A poor man without relatives to vouch for him or money to improve his situation. He was simply a man she would know for only small amount of time. He was expendable.

That was all right, though. Even if he did get nicked by a stray bullet, he wouldn't mind dying to help her live a better life.

After shaking off his doldrums, he entered Laurel's kitchen. By now he knew his way around it well enough to make a pot of coffee. As he boiled some beans and reviewed their plans for the day, he heard footsteps. Turning, he saw the captain was already up.

"Good morning, Thomas," the captain said as he joined him, his blond hair damp and his cheeks freshly shaved. "I was hoping to find you here."

"Just making coffee."

Monroe looked around and smiled. "I never thought I'd say this, but domesticity looks good on you."

"I like to help Miss Laurel when I can. She didn't sleep well." Of course, the moment he said that, he wished he could take back the words. He didn't want any of the men to think he wasn't treating Laurel with anything other than respect.

But if the captain had thought his comment was odd, he didn't dwell on it. "That's understandable. Today is a big day."

"Yes, sir." Pointing to the pot on the stove, he said, "I'll pour you some coffee momentarily. It's almost done."

Leaning against the counter, Captain Monroe shrugged. "No hurry. Have you seen Miss Tracey yet this morning?"

"No, sir. I'm hoping she's still resting."

The captain seemed to relax. "Good. Poor thing. I thought I'd seen everything, but those siblings of hers were rather insufferable."

Thomas grinned. "That they were." Satisfied that the coffee had been boiling long enough, he poured them each a cup. "Here you are, sir."

"Thank you." Smiling at the dark, rich brew, he murmured, "No matter how many years pass, I find I can never take a decent cup of coffee for granted."

"This is certainly better than some of the drinks we ground up and sipped around campfires."

Monroe groaned. "Remember when we tried to make coffee out of ground black walnuts? To this day I haven't tasted a more vile concoction."

"We were thankful for it at the time. I do remember that."

"We were thankful for a great many things. One had to believe that God had our backs, otherwise our reality was too hard to bear." After draining half his cup, the captain looked at him. "How bad is your back, Thomas?"

"From the whipping?"

"Of course."

Hating that Monroe had brought it up, Thomas shrugged. "It's nothing to be concerned about. It's healing."

"Are you sure? Are you in a great deal of pain?"

He certainly wasn't eager to discuss his back with his former captain. "No, sir. Miss Tracey cleaned my wounds. That helped."

"Did she now?" he murmured. Staring at Thomas intently, the captain said, "She's a good woman. Kind."

"She is." After looking toward the door to make sure she wasn't within earshot, Thomas shared what was hard to admit even to himself. "I guess it's pretty obvious that I'm fond of her."

"I did take notice of that." As he filled his mug to the brim again, the captain said, "If the way you stayed close to her side didn't clue me in, the facer you gave her stepbrother demonstrated how you felt."

Now that his own mug was empty, Thomas set it on the counter and folded his arms across his chest. "I don't understand the way those two are constantly putting her down. Laurel is just about the prettiest thing I've ever laid eyes on."

"She is fetching, that is true."

Thomas was rather surprised that the captain's statement didn't sound more emphatic. After all, she was so much more than that. "She's more than fetching, sir. She's beautiful. It's not just me who thinks that either," he rushed on. "Why, when I accompanied her in town, I saw men watching her. I tried not to get too riled up. After all, how could they help themselves?"

"Indeed."

"It's all I can do not to keep my hand constantly on her arm or back," he continued, since it seemed he was unable to stop himself. "People need to know she is not someone to be trifled with."

"I reckon she's grateful to have such a devoted servant," the captain said lightly. "Have you told her how you feel?"

"That I admire her? I have. Not that it really matters."

"Why doesn't it?"

"It's pretty obvious even to me that she deserves someone other than a worn-out ex-prisoner."

"I fear we are all ex-prisoners, Sergeant."

"You know what I mean. She paid money to release me from a cage. She deserves someone a whole lot better than the likes of me."

Captain Monroe walked to the pot, picked up a rag to hold the hot handle, and poured himself more coffee. "Forgive me, but it sounds as though you're having confidence issues."

It was on the tip of his tongue to deny it, but he couldn't do so without flat-out lying. "Maybe I am." He didn't like the thought of that. Men needed to be confident and strong, not full of self-doubt and impulsive. "I'll work on that."

Just as the captain smiled, Robert Truax poked his head into the kitchen. "Good. You're both here."

"I'm surprised you found us," Thomas said.

"I followed the scent of coffee."

"I'll pour you some," Thomas said. "Let me just find another mug."

"That can wait," Robert said with a grim look. "I need y'all to see something," he said, then turned before Thomas or the captain could ask any more questions.

Suddenly realizing that Robert smelled faintly of smoke, and feeling no small amount of dread, Thomas followed Robert into the main house, through the front rooms, and into the foyer. There he saw Ethan Kelly standing by the door, looking grim. His clothes were uncharacteristically rumpled.

"What happened?" Thomas asked.

Kelly opened the door farther so they could see outside without any barriers.

Half expecting another dead animal, what he saw instead made his breath catch.

A sizable plume of smoke was rising from the north pasture. "Fire?"

"Only a small one," Kelly said. "Someone took a barrel, lit a fire on the inside of it, and took off. If Robert and I hadn't seen it when we were shaving, the barrel could have blown, and with the direction of the wind this morning, this house and the barn might have been destroyed, along with all the horses."

"So they've upped their game," Thomas said.

"It seems like they have, but their methods are still confusing. They kill cattle, but only a few. Now they start a fire, but intentionally limit it to threaten these buildings," Robert said.

"They want Laurel afraid, or homeless, but the ranch intact."

"There's one thing more," Ethan said as he handed Robert a sheet of paper. "This was nailed to a nearby mesquite tree."

Thankful that Laurel wasn't there to read this one, Thomas said, "Major, have you read it yet?"

"I did. It says, 'This isn't over.'" Looking intently at Thomas's face, Kelly said, "Does that mean anything to you?"

"Only what it probably means to you. Escalation."

Looking at the other men surrounding them, Ethan Kelly's expression seemed almost lethal. "I don't know how y'all feel, but I sure as heck didn't survive the war and prison camp just to deal with some idiot setting fires while I sleep." His voice rose. "I don't take kindly to someone setting out notes for me to find like it's a bloody game."

Just then, Captain Monroe walked out the front door and

joined them on the porch. "My patience has reached its end," he said. "We need to ride out immediately. Track who did this."

"I'll be ready in ten," Robert said. "Just give me a minute to drink some coffee."

"I'll fish out something for us to eat on the ride while you're doing that," Thomas said. "I think Laurel has some biscuits left over from yesterday."

Kelly shook his head. "Appreciate you getting us some food, but we need to stick to the plan we devised last night. You need to stay here to protect her."

"I can't stand down while the rest of you take care of this business. I'll tell Laurel to stay inside with the doors locked. She has a rifle, and so far no one's tried to come into the house."

"We don't know they won't now, not after this fire. This could be a trap." Major Kelly shook his head. "You don't know what kind of men they are. Not for certain."

Kelly was right. But Thomas couldn't see another way to fight the men. "We need every man on horseback to track and fight. Plus, I know the terrain. You all need me."

"We'll make do," Captain Monroe said. "That lady is going to be scared to death when she discovers what happened. We can't leave her to sit and worry by herself."

"But—"

"You know I'm right." Lowering his voice, he said, "Think about what you just told me in the kitchen."

"That is precisely why I need to go. I can't stay behind while the three of you solve my problems."

Robert placed his hand on Thomas's shoulder. "If it's any consolation, I just went through something like this with my wife." He paused as he looked at Thomas more closely. "Do you really want what's yours left unguarded?"

Thomas exhaled. He didn't dare meet the major's or captain's eyes. No doubt they were amused by his newfound love for such an innocent, sweet girl.

But he couldn't deny his friends' words made sense. If he rode out, he might feel better about what he was doing, but he would also be putting Laurel at risk. She would always be on his mind. And he would never forgive himself if something happened to her while they were all away. "You have a point," he said around an exhale. "I'll go find some food for y'all. And thank you for what you're doing."

"I'm just glad you contacted us," Captain Monroe said. "Whoever is doing this needs to stop."

Thomas turned to walk back inside . . .

And was brought up short by the sight of Laurel standing right inside the open door. Her face was pale, and a question was in her eyes. "Thomas, what happened?" she asked, her voice tremulous.

"There was a fire, but it's out now."

"Where?"

"North pasture. Someone started a fire in a barrel." No reason to tell her what could have happened if the barrel had exploded, nor about the note.

"What are we going to do?" she asked as Robert and the captain joined them.

"You and I are going to stay here while Robert, the captain, and Kelly attempt to track whoever set the fire in your pasture."

She shook her head. "I can't do that."

"You can't do what, darlin'?" Robert asked. When he caught Thomas's glare, he rolled his eyes.

"I can't stay here. I'm sorry, but I can't do it."

Thankful that his friends had coached him, he reached out and rubbed both of her arms. She was frightened to death. Why had he ever thought it would be okay for him to leave her to worry and fend for herself? "You aren't going to be alone, Laurel. I'm going to stay with you. I promise, no one is going to hurt you while I'm nearby."

But instead of looking reassured, she shook her head. "No, I want to go too."

"Miss Tracey, forgive me, but you don't understand," Robert said. "We all rode together for months, if not for years. There's a trust there and a familiarity. If you came along, you would only get in the way."

"I can ride well too. I grew up on a horse." She straightened her backbone. "Plus, I know this land better than any of you could ever hope to. You need me."

While Thomas considered the best way to cut off her argument, she stepped away from him and raised her chin. "I am not going to be scared, and I am not going to slow you down."

"And if someone is shooting at us again?"

"Then I'll do my best to shoot back," she said. Staring at him, she said, "Look at me, Thomas. Really look at me. I am not a spoiled hothouse flower. I, too, survived the war. I am also the same woman who walked through a crowd and bought myself a convict."

Feeling the other men's approval, Thomas exhaled. It seemed there was only one thing to do. "Can you be ready within the hour, Miss Laurel?"

She smiled. "Since I'm nearly ready now, I believe my answer is yes." Turning toward the kitchen, she called out, "I'll gather some food to take with us and meet you in the barn."

"Before you start gathering, may I beg a favor?" Robert said, moving to her side. When she stared at him warily, he offered a sheepish smile. "I'm parched and half asleep. May I have a cup of coffee, Miss Laurel? Preferably right this minute?"

"Of course," she said around a relieved exhale. "I'll be happy to get you anything you need."

When they disappeared down the hall, Thomas met Captain Monroe's eyes. "I'm sorry, sir," he bit out. He hated to disappoint Devin Monroe. "I know you were right, but it seems I am hopeless against her. I couldn't think of another way to encourage her to stay."

But to Thomas's surprise, the captain chuckled. "Don't apologize, Sergeant. She was extremely persuasive. She also happens to be right."

"I never thought I'd hear you say that."

"At one time, I wouldn't have either. However, times have changed. During the war, our women had to take care of themselves without our help. Some even thrived. Now I'm afraid we can't expect them to always be content to sit and wait while we do our best."

"We sure couldn't have expected Miss Tracey to do that. She was determined."

"She made some good points too. I couldn't have said no to her if I'd tried. Buying herself a prisoner, indeed. You got lucky the day she decided to free you."

Trotting up the stairs to get his weapons, Thomas smiled to himself. No matter what happened next, he knew one thing for certain. Laurel Tracey was a woman like no other.

31

Her skin felt tingly. Every one of her senses felt as though it was on alert. Actually, Laurel had never felt more alive, not even when she'd made the decision to walk through a crowded square and claim Thomas Baker as her own.

The reason could be the company surrounding her. The four soldiers were gruff and confident and seemed to be solely focused on implementing the plans they'd made. She'd taken a leap of faith when she made the decision to join Thomas and his friends on their mission, though she'd been fairly certain Thomas was going to refuse her request to join them.

A part of her wouldn't have blamed him. Although the war and the following years had changed her, she was still her parents' daughter. They'd taught her both to mind authority and to know her place. But she'd also witnessed her mother making decisions about their home or about her and her brother that her father hadn't necessarily agreed with.

But time and again he'd bowed to his wife's decisions.

But this felt different. She didn't have people to lean on. She had only herself. And while she might have Thomas for the year, and he claimed he would stay as long as she needed him, the day would come when she would be safe and he would be ready to move on. That day would no doubt come sooner than she was ready for.

Because she had that knowledge, she knew she had to do everything she could to help herself, and to learn too.

After she'd made some bacon sandwiches and served Robert a cup of coffee, she decided to put on her most comfortable riding boots, a brimmed hat, and her sturdiest gloves. She also took her brother's rifle from its resting place.

Then she gathered up the sandwiches and hurried out to the barn. The last thing she wanted to happen was for the men to be waiting for her to make an appearance.

She was pleased to see that only Thomas and Captain Monroe were in the barn when she arrived. They were inspecting their own rifles and storing ammunition.

It was a stark reminder that this ride would likely be dangerous. The men were determined to hunt down the trespassers, and they undoubtedly expected trouble.

"You ready to ride with a bunch of worn-out soldiers, Miss Tracey?" Captain Monroe asked when he spied her lurking at the barn door's entrance.

She rolled her eyes. "I doubt there's a person in Texas who would describe any of you men in that fashion. But to answer your question, yes, sir, I am ready."

"I admire your gumption, but don't forget that gumption and fortitude can get one only so far. Be sure to stay close to Thomas's side."

The captain's blue eyes were solemn. Looking in Thomas's direction, she noticed that he, too, was looking at her in complete seriousness. "I'll do my best to keep up with you, Sergeant."

But instead of smiling at her, he shook his head. "That ain't good enough. You need to promise you will."

She didn't believe in promising what she couldn't be sure she could do, but Laurel understood his point. She needed to set her mind on success, not just hopes and dreams. "I promise to keep up with you. I will."

"Good. I need to know you're going to be there, no matter what. The other men would no doubt rather have us stay here while they fan out and look for your intruder. We have both allowed our vanities to go against our better judgment."

Laurel felt a chill run down her spine. She believed in herself and knew she wanted to do everything in her power to help save her ranch. That included joining these men and helping out however she could.

Just as important, she needed to prove to herself and her parents' memories that they'd been right in leaving the ranch to her. She loved the land as much as they had. She was willing to make sacrifices for it too.

However, she also didn't want to risk putting other people in harm's way to feel good about herself. "Gentlemen," she asked hesitantly, "am I being foolish?"

"You are not," Captain Monroe said. "All of us need to put ourselves in harm's way at one time or another for something we believe in. If a person wants to be a person of worth, that's part of the territory."

His words reinforced her resolve. "Thank you for understanding," she murmured.

"Oh, I certainly do understand," he said with a kind smile. "However, I beg you to be honest with us. If you are having second thoughts, say so. There's no shame in letting a group of men do what they are trained to do."

"I'm not having second thoughts," she answered, though she was certainly a bit more nervous about what was going to happen next.

Thomas's reassuring hand on her arm drew her eyes to him. "It will be all right," he said. "I'll look after you. Plus, chances are better than good that we'll ride out and see nothing."

Relieved, she gave him a tremulous smile.

"Uh-oh, looks like our sergeant has brought out his game face," Major Kelly called with a touch of humor in his eyes as he and Lieutenant Truax walked into the barn. "Don't let that scare you, Miss Tracey."

She giggled. "I'm afraid I don't know what 'game face' means."

Lieutenant Truax answered that one. "Thomas here was known to put on a fierce persona before each battle or skirmish. He'd march up and down the line and spur our poor privates on, leaving them shaking in their boots."

Thomas grunted. "Hardly that." Holding up a canteen, he appeared eager to drop the subject. "We all have water. Let's ride out."

Immediately, Lieutenant Truax and the major became serious. "We following last night's plans, Devin?"

Captain Monroe nodded. "Thomas and I talked some more just now. Robert and Ethan, you head south and west. Thomas, Miss Tracey, and I will ride north and east. If you spy trouble or need assistance, shoot three bullets into the air. Otherwise, we'll convene back here in five hours."

"What if we don't see anything in five hours?" Laurel asked as she handed Major Kelly one of her food pouches.

"We probably won't. But that's long enough to keep the horses out in this heat. Plus, we'll need to check with each other and report findings."

Major Kelly swung onto the saddle of his fine-looking Tennessee Walker. "Gentlemen, miss, I suggest we get on our way."

"We'll see you at noon. God be with you," Captain Monroe said as he led his own horse out of the barn.

After helping Laurel onto her saddle, where she secured the other food pouch and her rifle, Thomas mounted Yellow, then directed the horse to follow Captain Monroe. Taking one last look at Laurel, he said, "You ready?"

She inhaled. Exhaled. Then finally answered, "I am."

"Then let's go." He smiled before motioning Yellow into a good clip.

Doing the same with Velvet, Laurel gripped her reins with one hand and her hat with the other.

They were off.

∽

They'd been riding for three hours. With the exception of a few broken branches and a vague feeling in his gut that they were close to trouble, Thomas had nothing to report. Though he had known their hunt wasn't going to be easy, he felt disappointed for Laurel's sake.

It didn't help that as the sun rose higher, the faint wisps of clouds that usually formed in the sky vanished. The sky was now a vivid shade of bluebonnet blue, coloring the sky and making it possible to see for miles across the horizon. Because of that, Thomas was very aware that any movements they made could be observed by whomever they were after.

He also couldn't seem to stop worrying about Laurel. Though she was an excellent rider, he found himself concerned with the sun burning her nose, the heat burdening her, whether she was thirsty or becoming too tired.

Every thirty minutes or so, Thomas would slow his horse and make sure she was all right.

Captain Monroe no doubt noticed his inattention to his

surroundings, but he didn't say anything. Instead, he constantly moved from the front of their group to the back, circling his horse expertly. Taking up Thomas's slack.

When they came to the area by the creek where he and Laurel had come under gunfire, Thomas showed the spot to the captain. "They came from that bluff," he said, pointing. "Laurel and I ended up crouching next to the creek bed."

"Looks as good a place as any to make a quick stop, I think," Monroe said. "Let's stretch for a minute and let the horses get some water."

After Thomas dismounted, he walked to Laurel's side. "Here, honey, let me help you," he drawled, no longer caring that he was uttering a number of endearments. He was glad she didn't refuse his aid. Instead, she merely murmured her thanks and rested her hands on his shoulders as he swung her out of the saddle.

"You feeling all right?" he asked quietly as she held on to him a little longer than was necessary. He wondered if she was trying to get her bearings or was simply tired.

"I'm fine." Looking nervously around, she said, "This spot brings back bad memories, doesn't it? It feels a bit vulnerable."

"It does, but we're well prepared now," he replied, hoping he spoke the truth. "Before, we never would have imagined that someone would fire at us. Now we know better."

Laurel looked warily at Captain Monroe, who had also dismounted but was gazing around them with an alert expression, his rifle at the ready. "I hope the other men are faring better than we are."

"If something happens, we'll hear three shots. If not, it will be no more than we expect." Leaning closer, Thomas said, "Now I'm going to see to the horses. You take a rest or move your legs a bit. They'll thank you for it."

Laurel looked at Thomas gratefully as he walked Yellow, Velvet, and the captain's dark quarter horse to the creek. The captain's horse seemed able to follow the smallest command with high-stepping elegance. Velvet and Yellow looked ill trained by comparison.

However, she couldn't deny they had conducted themselves with honor so far that day. As had she, she reflected as she moved a bit to the side and stretched her arms over her head. When they'd first set out, she had been a nervous wreck. She'd been just as afraid of proving the men right by not controlling Velvet well or getting in their way as she was of encountering their attackers again.

But as they'd split up and quietly continued on, focusing on any faint shadows they spied on the horizon or noises heard in the distance, her body had relaxed. While she might not have been able to lead the search party, she had certainly been able to keep up.

"I must say you're doing a fine job, Miss Tracey," Captain Monroe said as he approached. "I have never been on a mission with a woman before, and I have to admit I was a little worried about how you'd do. But you are proving to me that you can handle just about anything."

"Hardly that," she said. "This has been hard, but even though we're out in the open, I feel safer with you and Thomas out here than I would at home, even if one of you had stayed with me."

"I'm glad you aren't there too."

After realizing Thomas was now taking watch, she smiled her thanks at the captain. "I was just coming to the conclusion that I was glad I had accompanied you," she admitted. "Now I'm torn between hoping we see those men and praying we do not."

He smiled in return. "I would be lying if I said I haven't experienced those same thoughts more than once this morning."

"Really?"

"Absolutely. It's the danger of the unknown that reminds a man he's only human. After all, only the Lord knows our future."

"Indeed." As she drew in a breath, ready to ask the captain about some of his past missions, Thomas cocked his gun.

Both Laurel and Captain Monroe froze.

"Report," Captain Monroe called out.

"Three o'clock," Thomas replied.

She had no idea what that meant. "What—"

Immediately, the captain pulled out his pistol. "Go to the creek, Laurel," he ordered. "Go there and crouch low. Now."

She didn't waste time arguing. She ran as fast as she could to do as he bid. And had just fallen to her knees on the soft, cool ground when a gunshot rang out.

She covered her head and prayed as Captain Monroe fired into the air three times.

It seemed their prey had become their predators.

32

Thomas had always clung to his faith. He'd clung to it when he'd been hiding during the Indian raid that had killed his parents and brother, and during the hard, lonely years when he'd suffered so much on the streets of Fort Worth.

He'd trusted in the Lord to get him through each battle and mission he'd fought during the war and had prayed for strength and grace when he'd been imprisoned on Johnson's Island. In short, he'd always hoped and believed he was never completely alone.

But he'd never feared being forgotten by the Lord as he did at that very moment.

Standing by the captain's side, he watched two men scramble forward, their pistols drawn. One was a stranger. A wiry fellow with a desperate, almost scared expression on his face.

The other man was Laurel's neighbor, Landon Marshall.

Marshall looked grim and determined. Deadly determined.

While the captain raised his Colt, Thomas attempted to talk some sense into the man. He absolutely did not want Laurel to have to witness him killing Marshall. "That's far enough!" he called out. "Lower your guns. We can talk this through."

"I'm done talking!" Marshall yelled right back. And though his steps slowed, he continued forward.

He could sense Monroe closing one eye beside him. "Right or left, Baker?" he murmured, already choosing a target.

"Left," Thomas replied instantly. "But give me a minute."

"You got thirty seconds."

Only because he knew Laurel was witnessing their actions, Thomas attempted to get Marshall to talk. "What is this all about, anyway?" he asked. "We should be able to talk. There's no reason for you to be firing at us."

Marshall sneered as he stepped forward. "Of course there is. Haven't you learned anything in your sorry life? Some matters simply can't be settled without a show of force."

"I agree, but this ain't one of them," the captain said. He'd lowered his gun slightly. In fact, the pistol looked as if it were hanging limp in his right hand. "Now, what exactly do you want?"

"This land. I tried courting Laurel for it. I've even tried to scare her. Killing her cattle, staging property theft, that fire this morning . . . all so she'd sell it to me, if not marry me so I could control it. But nothing has worked. And now she's got you hunting us down."

"It's only one thousand acres," Thomas reasoned. "I was told you have over double that amount."

Landon nodded as he continued to approach, one slow step at a time. "I do. But this property here has two water supplies. Around here, water is more valuable than gold."

"You threatened to poison the creek."

"If I had, the water would have run clear after a matter of days. I need it."

Landon Marshall still wasn't making sense. "Why?"

"Rumor has it that the railroad has plans to come through this way. Anyone who can cater to the railroad is destined not only to survive but to prosper."

Monroe narrowed his eyes. "I was a Ranger before I was a captain. You and I both know a man can't go around staking his claim through poison, bullets, and fires."

Marshall ignored that statement. Glaring at the horses, he said, "There are two of you and three horses. Where's your other rider? Who else is with you?"

"No one you need to be aware of," Thomas said. There was no way he was going to give up Laurel's position if he could help it.

Marshall raised his pistol again. "How about you try answering me again?"

"Lower your weapon," the captain ordered. "There's no need for you to start murdering more people."

"More?" Marshall asked.

"Yeah. You already took down one of my men," Monroe said, lying easily. "You or your partner there shot him."

Marshall's pistol wavered. "Show him to me, Baker."

"If you want to see him, you'll have to dismount and check him out on your own. No way am I leaving my friend alone with you."

Marshall turned to his partner. "Orr, go down to the creek and take a look."

Without a word, the man started heading down the sloping hill toward the creek. Toward Laurel.

Thomas's heart was beating so hard he felt as though the other men could probably see it pounding in his chest. Not daring to even look in that direction, he prayed that Laurel had followed the captain's command and hidden herself well.

The air felt thick and cloying as the three of them watched the man disappear into the brush around the creek. Soon all they could hear was the snap of twigs as he searched.

While Monroe looked a bit bored, Thomas stared at Marshall and attempted to think of reasons not to simply fire a shot into his heart right that minute.

"You're looking a little tense, Baker," Marshall jeered. "What's wrong? Is freedom not suiting you? Or is it that you are coming to realize that Laurel Tracey ain't worth the effort?"

"If I'm tense, it's because I'm trying to convince myself not to kill you for the trauma you've put her through."

"I wouldn't have put her through anything if she'd agreed to marry me in the first place."

"She can't marry you. She deserves better."

"Why?" His voice was filled with thick sarcasm. "She's nothing. She's nothing more than a plain, quiet woman with too much land and too high an opinion of herself."

The captain shifted one foot forward, resurrecting an old move that he'd perfected during the war. Inconspicuously following the direction of his boot, Thomas could see Robert and Kelly approaching from the south. They were on foot and walking stealthily enough not to attract Marshall's attention.

Thomas knew he needed to keep Marshall talking until the other men got close enough to help take him down.

With that in mind, he lowered his gun. "Laurel might have a high opinion of herself, but that don't mean her cattle deserved to be slaughtered."

Landon stepped closer. "Slaughtered? All Orr did was poison them. Half a dozen cows and one calf are hardly worth thinking about."

"Most men value livestock a bit better," Monroe drawled.

"Most men are too afraid," Marshall scoffed. "Most men aren't willing to do whatever it takes to get what they need."

Thomas saw that Kelly and Robert were less than fifty yards

away now. They had separated and were approaching Marshall from either side. With luck one of them would be able to take him by surprise before he could fire.

Knowing he needed to goad him a bit, Thomas smirked. "Unfortunately, your plan didn't go so well. You were no closer to obtaining Laurel's land than before. I'm starting to understand why you didn't see much action during the war."

"I saw enough."

"Of the cathouses," the captain scoffed. "That's where you rescued those women, isn't it? Because you were with the harlots instead of with your regiment."

"I was doing what I needed to do."

Monroe's gaze was filled with pure loathing. "No. You were doing what you—"

"Marshall," his partner called out. "I found something, but it sure ain't a dead man."

Thomas's heart sank as he turned to the thicket of brush and saw Orr holding Laurel's elbow in a death grip. She looked shaken and frightened . . . and mad.

"Laurel!" he called out. When she turned her head his way, he pleaded with his eyes not to give up. He also sent a quick prayer to the Lord for his help. He needed to caution Laurel to keep quiet and meek-looking. Thomas needed her to do whatever it took to stay unharmed.

"You've been standing there lying to me?" Marshall yelled. "What do you think I am? Some pitiful, gullible, weak-kneed opponent?" He raised his pistol, but it hung limply in his hand. "Just because I didn't—"

The rest of his speech was cut off when, without a word, Robert knocked the gun from Marshall's hand from behind, pulled him to the ground, and subdued his protests with a solid blow to his jaw. Seconds later, he had him facedown on the ground and was calf-roping him. Marshall writhed in pain.

Meanwhile, Monroe had turned to Orr. "Let loose of the woman and you'll live."

The man looked wild-eyed, but he didn't let go. "This weren't my fight. I was only doing this for the money. I owed him money. And . . . and he killed a man. George Irwin, after Irwin poisoned the cattle by the creek and shot at her. So did Foster Howell."

"I'd venture to say you don't owe him anything no more," the captain said, his voice smooth and reassuring. "Landon Marshall isn't going to be harming anyone anytime soon, and neither is this Howell. Let go of Miss Tracey."

Orr's eyes widened as he turned to Laurel. He gulped as he stared at her, almost as if he couldn't figure out how he'd met her in the first place.

"Please," Laurel begged.

At last he lifted his hand.

The moment she was free, she started running toward Thomas. He walked down to meet her halfway and pulled her into his arms. "It's okay now," he soothed. "You're safe."

Kelly strode over, and as he tied Orr's hands behind his back, Laurel closed her eyes and burrowed her face into Thomas's chest. "I was so afraid."

"I know. I was too," he admitted as he stared at the other men. Robert now had Marshall sitting against a rock and Kelly was maneuvering Orr to a spot against an old pine tree.

The captain was facing Thomas and Laurel with a pleased look on his face. "It's over."

Relief flooded Thomas. He felt like he was on the verge of tears. "I'm beholden to you," he said to his best friends in the world. "I couldn't have done this on my own."

"You never should have thought you had to, Sergeant," Monroe replied. "We wanted to help."

Still tucked safely in Thomas's arms, Laurel looked up at all of them with shining eyes. "I'm so grateful. Gentlemen, I hardly know how to convey my thanks."

"No thanks are needed," Robert said. "We're only glad you're all right."

His expression now all business, the captain moved toward his horse. "I'm going to ride into town and tell the sheriff what transpired and get some assistance. Robert and Ethan are going to stay here with these men. Thomas, I think it might be best if you took Miss Tracey home."

Thomas couldn't agree more. Running a hand down the curls of her hair, free of its bonnet, he murmured, "How does that sound, angel? Do you feel like you can handle riding Velvet home?"

She nodded. "I can, but I don't want to leave here. Not yet."

Thomas wasn't eager for her to hear Marshall say any more harsh words against her. But he knew it was just as important that he let her see this through. She'd been dealing with this man's destructive behavior since before he'd met her, and she'd be dealing with the consequences of his actions long after he was put in jail.

Looking at both men tied up and silent, he sighed. "If you'd like to stay a bit longer, we will. But now is not the time to talk to Landon Marshall, you understand?"

She nodded. "I don't want to talk to him ever again."

"I think that can be arranged. You won't have to talk to Howell again either."

"I'll be back when I can," Monroe said, then set off toward town.

After helping Laurel get situated in a cleared spot near the creek, Thomas walked over to Kelly and Robert to see if they needed anything.

Each man shook his head before Thomas could open his mouth. "We're fine, Thomas. You know we are," Ethan said.

But that was their way, he knew. They would stay where they were needed for hours or until their captain or whoever was in charge said otherwise. Until that time, they would remain vigilant and silent.

Feeling satisfied that there was nothing else to do for the time being, Thomas returned to Laurel and sat down beside her. Then he took her hand, carefully pulled off her glove, and cradled her hand in between his. She didn't offer a single word of protest.

They sat and waited. No words were said.

That was just as well. Not a single word could be said that would make a bit of difference.

33

No matter how hard Laurel tried to get her body to comply, she couldn't seem to make it stop shaking. Fortunately for her, Thomas didn't notice. Or perhaps he had.

While the other men stayed a respectful distance away, allowing them to have a small semblance of privacy, Thomas had moved from holding her hand to holding her close in his arms, then pressed his lips to her temple and brow.

"Easy now," he murmured for what must have been either the sixth or the sixteenth time. "It's over. I promise, it's all over."

She'd kept her hand resting along the expanse of his chest. Her palm was flat against the soft cotton. Underneath the fabric, she could feel the line of his muscles, and underneath those hard planes, she could feel the beat of his heart.

It beat steadily, centering her. As the minutes passed, she was able to draw strength from its constant beat. She was alive, and Thomas was too.

Little by little, she once more became aware of the oppressive heat of the sun, the faint scent of soap, the gentle whickering of the horses in the meadow. She began to feel more secure, calmed by Thomas's heartbeat, his warm embrace, his soft assurances.

But even all that couldn't alter the fact that her world had just been shaken up. Yet again.

"I can't believe Landon was the man behind everything," she said at last. "I don't understand it."

Thomas sighed. "I know you don't, sugar. But that's okay."

"How can it be all right?"

"If you did understand such things, you wouldn't be the woman you are."

That statement felt as cryptic as any she'd ever heard. Lifting her head at last, she studied him carefully. "What about you? Do you understand it?"

His blue eyes, usually so bright, were cloudy with regret. "To an extent I do." Looking a little sad, he continued, "Marshall wanted everything to stay the same. He thought if he possessed this land and you, it could be."

"But marrying me would have changed everything."

"For you, it would have. For him? He would have gained the water he was fixated on. He would have had better access to the rail line people are talking about coming in the future. He would have even gotten your family's home and any money you had in the bank."

"He was willing to kill to get it all."

"Men kill for such things all the time."

She scoffed. "Thomas."

"It's true. People kill and hurt and maim for security and money. Sometimes even for a woman's love." Lifting one finger under her chin, he tilted it up so she would look into his eyes. "Those things are what dreams are made of. I know I sure dreamed of having such blessings many a time."

"I suppose. But Landon already had so much."

"Landon Marshall's problem was that he couldn't see beyond what was lacking in his life to realize what he already had."

Thomas sounded so sure. "Did you ever do that? Feel like

you needed to put other people in jeopardy to get what you needed?"

"Maybe I did. There have been a lot of times when I would rather eat than starve or sleep instead of suffer. Or kill, rather than be killed."

"That was different, though, wasn't it? Because it was during the war."

Gazing at her, one corner of his lips turned up, he nodded. "Yes, Laurel," he said as he smoothed a lock of her hair away from her face. "It was different. It was a matter of life or death, and I don't mean that in a dramatic, over-the-top way. I mean it was because I had no choice."

"Thomas, I remember the night before my brother and father left for the war. Landon and his father were over, and we were all in our sitting room watching the blaze in the fireplace." She remembered feeling as if she'd known exactly how her life was going to play out. She'd felt safe too.

She hadn't felt that secure or safe again until Thomas appeared in her life. "Landon promised my father he'd look out for me."

"Did he ever do that?"

"For a time. But then he left. When he came back, his personality was different. Altered."

A shadow filled his gaze. "War can change people, I'm afraid."

"I guess that's what happened." Thinking of the many men and women she knew and had known, she sighed. "I guess everyone is destined to change in one way or another. Do you think so?"

He shrugged. "Maybe. I know I have."

"Landon did. And when he did, the things he used to think were important—family, honor—didn't seem to matter anymore. I can't help but think about his poor mother and sister. This will devastate them."

Thomas changed positions and kicked his legs out. "Laurel, it does us no good to try to understand why a man like him did something like he did. You are right. War changed everything. Our land, our homes. People too. However, most of us clung to our values and our hearts. We stayed true to those."

Laurel nodded. Realizing she was no longer shaking and holding off tears, she dropped her hands and exhaled. "You're right. It is over. And it was foolish of me to wonder why he valued different things than he used to. After all, no one really keeps their promises anymore, do they?"

"What? Of course they do."

He sounded so indignant, she almost smiled. "I meant, besides you."

"Look at the captain and the major and Robert. They came here because of a promise we once made."

"They came here because you are a man worth helping."

"I'd like to think I am, but I also know they're honoring something we shared one night in the prison camp."

Lifting his chin, he let his gaze drift over the horizon. "We had just buried Rory MacDonald. He'd been younger than all of us. So fresh and young. So full of promise. We were all feeling the pinch of our confinement."

"I'm so sorry, Thomas."

"While we were all standing there, worrying over what was going to happen next and wishing our circumstances would somehow get better eventually, Captain Monroe had us all make a promise to each other. We promised to look out for each other the rest of our lives."

"That's why they came when you sent word you needed them."

"Yes, that's why. The only reason why. It wasn't because I

deserved it or I had earned their efforts. It was because they'd made a promise. A vow."

"They are truly good men."

"They are."

"You are worth it, you know," she said softly. "Even if you had to ask for help for yourself, not me, it would have been the right thing to do. You're worth it too."

"I'm beginning to think I am at that," he said lightly as he got to his feet.

Bending down, he reached for her hands. "Now, don't you think it's time I got you home? The major and Robert can wait for Sheriff Jackson here. If he needs to speak with you, he'll find you. Let's go home."

She loved how he referred to her house as his home. It was going to be a difficult day indeed when he left, when his year was up and she was the only one who lived in her house again. Thomas didn't seem like someone who would ever settle down if he didn't have to, and she felt sure he was the kind of man who probably never would, no matter how he felt now.

As Laurel placed her hands in his, she made a vow to herself to show her love for him as well as he showed his to her, for the time she would be allowed to do so.

No matter what happened in the future or how much she yearned for him to always stay by her side, she, too, could honor a promise. She could let him go.

Secretly, she knew her reasoning had nothing to do with honor and glory. It was simply because she loved him.

She loved him enough to one day encourage him to leave.

34

THOMAS WATCHED IN DISMAY AS HIS THREE BEST FRIENDS in the world packed their duffel bags in their rooms. After Marshall and Orr were safely jailed in town, along with Foster Howell, they had brought the sheriff and Judge Orbison to the house. And because the two officials wanted to meet with everyone involved individually as well as in a group, the three men divided their time between eating a light meal of cold pork and fried potatoes and bathing off the sweat and grime of the day.

Thomas had also checked on Laurel frequently. As far as he could tell, she was handling all that had happened as well as anyone could have expected. However, he had known many a green recruit in battle who had broken down from the shock of it all hours after seeing such violence and bloodshed. Thomas feared that such a thing would happen to Laurel as well.

He'd been hoping the other men could help him find the words to comfort her. He knew they'd all had more experience soothing tattered nerves than he did.

But less than an hour after Orbison and Jackson left, Thomas discovered the three of them preparing to leave.

"Surely y'all aren't planning to leave right now?" he asked.

Captain Monroe nodded. "I need to get to Fort Worth before it gets too late."

"I had hoped y'all would stay at least until morning. We could catch up."

Major Kelly flashed a smile. "As much as I would enjoy that, I'm afraid that's not possible, for me at least. I need to get back to San Antonio. I need to see to an issue at the Menger Hotel."

Ethan's voice held a note of desperation in it. "Are you in trouble?" Thomas asked.

He shook his head. "Of course not. My, uh, concerns have more to do with a woman than anything else."

Robert chuckled low. "Concerns, hmm? Perhaps I'm not the only one to be falling in love."

"I didn't mention love, Lieutenant," Ethan retorted sharply. "What Lizbeth and I have is just"—his voice lowered—"friendship. At least I think it could be categorized as that."

"Lizbeth sounds like a name to remember," Robert mused.

Feeling a little desperate, Thomas turned to Robert. "I didn't even get to hear the whole story about you and Miranda."

"There were some problems and threats . . . well, it all worked out for the best," Robert said easily. "Once we let our guards down, Miranda and I discovered we had room in our hearts for something more."

For the life of him, Thomas couldn't imagine how Robert and Miranda had fallen in love, but now it seemed he wasn't likely to learn the ins and outs of it anytime in the near future. "I see."

Robert laughed. "I know you don't see at all. But I'm thinking you will see what I'm talking about very soon."

"I suppose you need to leave tonight as well?"

"I do. Miranda doesn't do well without me nearby." Looking a little self-conscious, he added, "I don't do too well away from her either."

Thomas finally brought himself to look at Captain Monroe.

The captain was staring right back at him. However, unlike Ethan and Robert, he wasn't smiling. Instead, he was wearing a solemn expression that spoke volumes. "I have other pressing concerns as well. I am sorry."

"I feel like things are at loose ends." No longer caring that he sounded like a sulky child, Thomas added, "Captain, I haven't even thanked you properly."

Devin Monroe brushed off his words. "Like Robert said out on the range, no thanks are needed. They are never needed. We made a promise, remember?"

"Yes, sir." But still, Thomas knew this was a case where a mere thank-you wasn't good enough. He was going to need to do something more to convey his thoughts and gratitude, even if it was in the form of a letter. "Are you going back to Galveston? Is that where you'll be?"

"No." Looking a bit uncomfortable, Monroe said, "There's a small town out west, almost to the New Mexico territory. I've had my eye on it for some time. I thought I'd head out that way and maybe make a home."

"What are you talking about?" Kelly asked. "Big Spring?"

"None other."

Realizing that the other men were as much at sea as he was, Thomas dropped the subject. "I'll leave you to finish your preparations, then."

"Don't worry, we'll tell Miss Tracey good-bye before we depart," Captain Monroe said.

After going downstairs and ascertaining that the main house was quiet, Thomas looked for Laurel in the kitchen. He wanted to check on her again and let her know about the men's plans. As he walked, he was mentally trying out ways to let her know the men who had helped her so much were about to take their leave.

But she was nowhere in sight.

"Laurel?" he called.

Not hearing a reply, he glanced outside the kitchen door, hoping she was taking a break on the back porch, as she sometimes did. However, there was no sign of her there either.

After checking the bathing room and finding it also empty, he strode up the stairs and tapped lightly on her bedroom door, then turned the doorknob.

If she was sleeping, he would close the door again and tell the men he would convey their good-byes.

Peeking in, he saw that she was, indeed, lying down. But instead of seeing her resting peacefully, he saw her staring back at him.

He was so startled that he gripped the door for a moment to gain a few seconds. "I'm sorry to disturb you, but I couldn't find you downstairs. I thought you might be asleep."

"I probably should be." Moving into a sitting position, she shrugged. "I just thought I'd take a few minutes to gather myself." Her gaze warmed. "Someone keeps telling me I try to do too much and I should rest more."

"Sounds like a very smart man with good advice."

"I think so."

Her light response made him flush. "The men will be leaving soon. They'll be coming down to tell you good-bye. I thought you might want to see them off."

She sat up abruptly. "They're leaving right now? I was hoping they'd stay for a while. I wish they would."

"I asked for the same thing. Unfortunately, they couldn't be persuaded."

Pressing her palms to her cheeks, she said, "I'll freshen up and be down presently."

"I'll let them know. Thank you," he said as he edged out of the room and closed the door behind him.

As he walked back down the stairs, he realized things were about to change between him and Laurel. Now that she was no longer in danger, he needed to go back to his rightful role on the ranch. He needed to put some distance between them and move back to his room in the barn.

Funny, but he had a feeling that, in some ways, he was about to tell her good-bye too.

35

TELLING THE MEN GOOD-BYE HAD BEEN EASIER THAN Laurel thought it would be. No doubt it was because they looked so eager to be on their way. After another light but hasty meal, they each bowed over her hand and wished her well. Then they each shook Thomas's hand, gave him a hug, said a few words, and went to fetch their horses from the barn.

Thomas seemed to handle their departure in a stoic manner. He stood beside her on the front porch as they turned their animals and rode out.

Watching their forms change to faint silhouettes to eventual faint clouds of dust, Laurel felt Thomas's dismay. Though of course he didn't say anything, she knew he was no doubt disappointed that he'd be bound to her for another eleven months. That he couldn't be off on his own adventures, live his own life.

"They are good men," she said when there was nothing left of them to see. "I'll always be grateful for their help."

"I know I've said it before, but they are the best."

Now that they were alone again, she felt a little awkward. After all, what did you say to a man who had saved your world? "Would you care for something more to eat?"

"No, Miss Laurel." He pursed his lips. "Actually, I was thinking I would go get settled back in the barn."

"Why?"

"You know as well as I do that it ain't seemly for me to be living in the house with you. People will talk."

"Surely we don't have to worry about what other people say anymore." Her reputation had undoubtedly been ripped to tatters the moment she'd walked through the crowd and paid good money to make him her servant.

Still staring straight ahead, he said, "Eventually Marshall's betrayal will fade and you will get lonely. When a man comes courting, he's not going to be real pleased to discover me sleeping down the hall."

"You moved into the house for my safety," she pointed out. "You were down the hall to protect me."

"I was there for that reason, but you're safe now. You don't have any need for me to be so close to you at all times."

She supposed he was right. Oh, not about her entertaining suitors, but about the other thing. She was safer now. At least, her head knew that.

But her heart and nerves did not. She did need him. She wanted him nearby. She wanted him as close as possible.

"Can you please wait a couple of nights, Thomas?"

"Miss Tracey . . ."

She hated that he was speaking to her in such a formal way again. Hated that he was putting up a wall between them that she wished didn't exist. "Please don't do this," she pleaded. "Don't push me away. Don't pretend we're nothing more than employer and employee. We've come too far for that."

"I agree." He looked pained. "But it's because we are more to each other that I feel we should return some of that distance between us."

"I disagree."

"Miss Tracey, please. Allow me this. I'm trying to do the right thing by you. I'm as far from a gentleman as a man can get, but I know at least this much."

"All right."

"Good."

"But not yet," she said quickly. "Stay down the hall two more nights. Please, Thomas? I already know I won't be able to sleep much tonight. Don't make it worse."

He stared at her for a length of time. Lifted his hand as though he wanted to curve it around her cheek, then let it drop to his side. "All right," he said around a sigh. "I'll stay in there for two more nights. But no longer."

"Thank you, Thomas."

"Don't thank me for this, Miss Laurel," he said in a low tone. "I'm doing this because I can't bear to say no to you. But that don't mean I'm doing either of us any favors."

"I understand."

"Good. Now, I'm going to go check the barn and see what kind of mess the men left for me."

"You think they left you a mess?"

"They're good men, not perfect," he replied with a dry smile before walking away.

Watching him walk away, she realized what she needed to do.

❧

When she came back from town the following afternoon, tears were in her eyes. She could only hope Thomas wouldn't notice.

"I have something for you," Laurel said the moment she found him working in her garden, his sleeves rolled up and a disgruntled expression on his face.

Sitting back on his haunches, he looked at the paper curiously. "What do you have there? I thought you were going for more supplies. Did you get mail too?"

"Stand up and I'll show you."

After stretching his arms, he slowly got to his feet. "You came in the nick of time," he teased. "I was about to tackle these bean plants. Now you can help me with them."

Noticing the stage of growth the beans were in, she said, "What were you going to do? None of them are ready to be picked."

"They aren't? Huh. Well, in that case, it seems your arrival saved them from certain death."

In spite of the lump in her throat, she giggled. But that was always how it was with him. He brought light into her world even when she knew there shouldn't be anything but clouds or darkness. What was she going to do without him?

Almost immediately, she pushed that question away. It didn't matter what she was going to do or how she was going to feel. All that mattered was him. Thomas Baker needed to start living for himself.

"Now I know two things about you. You don't like chickens and you don't know anything about gardening."

Pulling the paper out of her hand, he flashed her another one of his brilliant smiles. "Well, I definitely do not like chickens, but I did learn something about gardening in that prisoner of war camp," he countered. "Just maybe not enough. I'd better be careful or you aren't going to think I'm worth keeping around."

That was as good an opening as any. She leapt on it. "I might have already come to that conclusion."

"Hmm?" he asked as he unfolded the paper and scanned through the writing. His right hand gripped the paper, wrinkling it slightly as he scanned the words again. "Laurel, what did you do?"

"I got you your freedom," she said, hoping she looked more triumphant about what she'd done than she felt.

"What? How?"

"I did pick up a few supplies, but this is the main reason I went into town. I talked to Judge Orbison and Sheriff Jackson about you and what you did for me. For Sweetwater, actually."

"For Sweetwater," he echoed.

"Yes. I reminded them that you helped prevent what could have been a horrible situation. If Marshall and his men hadn't been stopped, who knows what else they would have done to my cattle and my ranch, not to mention people could have lost their lives." Lifting her chin slightly, she added, "I was fully prepared to do whatever it took to convince them I was right, but it turned out I didn't need to do much convincing at all."

"No?" He still held the paper in one hand, looking for all the world as though he hardly cared what was written on it.

"Not at all. Actually, they agreed that such a service needed to be rewarded."

"So you got me my freedom."

She smiled. "Yes. A man like you never should have been an indentured servant in the first place. You're free, Thomas. You can leave me whenever you want."

His face turned expressionless, but then his lips curved up slightly. "Free to leave you, hmm?"

She wasn't sure she liked how that sounded, or the glint in his eyes that looked suspiciously like pain. "That was a slip of the tongue. What I meant to say is that you are free to leave the Red Roan Ranch."

"If I leave, how will you manage? This is a big ranch, Laurel. It would be a lot for a man to handle on his own, let alone a woman by herself."

She knew he was right. But some things were more important than even a family legacy or a home to live in. She was willing to sell the ranch if she had to. Nothing was more important than ensuring Thomas's freedom. "I'll make do."

"How?" he scoffed. "Are you planning to hire someone else?"

"Maybe. I'm not sure." Stuttering a bit, she added, "I don't know what I'll do." She was feeling defeated. How could she feel so optimistic one moment and so deflated the next?

"If you do try to hire someone else, what will you pay them with? I know you put the majority of your cash on me. Even convicts cost money."

"I know." Not liking the harsh way he was looking at her, she took a step backward.

"Laurel, did the judge give you your money back?"

"Of course not," she sputtered.

His gaze was cool. Cold. "So you have almost nothing."

That was where he was wrong. "I have a lot. I have my pride. I have my safety. I'm no longer afraid for my future." She was only sad that her future was going to be a lonely one.

He stared at her for a long moment, then seemed to come to a silent decision.

Dropping the paper onto the dark soil, he reached for her. "You're right," he drawled, his lips brushing her ear. "Those are all real good things. But still . . . what you have won't be enough."

His hands were covered with a light dusting of soil. He was hot and sweaty and was holding her so close she could practically feel frustration pour off him.

Yet she also sensed the way he made her feel so secure. The warmth of his breath against her skin. The faint smell of soap mixed with leather and earth and everything that was Thomas. And because of all that, he still felt right. So right.

Which was why she knew she had to do the right thing too. Firmly, she pushed away from him so she could look into his eyes. "You need to let me give you your freedom. I want you to be able to get away from here."

"No."

"What? Thomas, if you read that letter again, you'll see it says—"

"I can't read all that well. But that hardly matters to me at the moment. I know everything I need to know right here, right now."

"What is that?" she asked, dreading his answer. Her heart felt as though it had stopped beating.

"That I belong with you. I need to be with you, Laurel Tracey. And not as your worker. Not even as your protector. I want to be your husband." Lowering his voice, he said softly, "I want to be yours."

Her pulse jumped as she got warm all over. Was he truly saying what she thought he was? "You sound so sure."

The corners of his mouth lifted as he reached again for her hands. "Oh, I am. I don't know a lot of things. I've actually spent most of my life wishing I knew far more than I do. But one thing I know without a bit of doubt is that I want you forever."

He swallowed. "Laurel, I love you. If I promise to give you the best of myself, if I promise to work hard and care for you and work your land and do my best to protect you from the bad things life can bring . . . will you have me?"

"I will . . . if you can promise me one more thing," she said, now feeling as though her heart was pounding so hard in her chest that he could surely hear it.

"Anything. Name it."

"Will . . . will you promise to still love me tomorrow?"

"I promise, honey. And the next day. And the day after that," he said before his lips crashed down over hers.

He kissed her with no finesse, little gentleness, and complete fervor. His arms held her tightly, his body strong and solid next to hers. This, she realized, was Thomas.

Passionate and strong. Impulsive and sure. Everything that had been lacking in her life until he'd come. And everything that had happened since he'd stepped into her life.

She held on to his strength and reveled in his love.

Suddenly, they had a future.

Suddenly, they had each other.

And when they had all that, nothing else was needed.

They had enough.

DISCUSSION QUESTIONS

1. What do you hope to discover when you read historical fiction?
2. This novel centers on various interpretations of protecting. Protecting land, values, other people, one's heart. Which kind of "protecting" are you most familiar with? Which theme in the novel resonated with you?
3. What do you think of Thomas Baker? Is he truly a hero? Why or why not?
4. What about Laurel? Was she actually in need of protection?
5. It might be obvious that my favorite parts of these novels are the scenes back in the prisoner of war camp on Johnson's Island. Did you care for them? Why or why not? What hero are you most intrigued by?
6. All of the characters in the novel have been marked by tragedy in some way. Each is attempting to come to terms with that and move forward. What has helped you recover from difficult situations in your life?
7. I loved the scripture quote from Zechariah: "I promise

this very day that I will repay two blessings for each of your troubles." I thought it described the storylines of the main characters in the novel very well. When have you received two blessings for each of your troubles?

8. Which Lone Star Hero are you most interested in reading about in the last book of the series?

Acknowledgments

THOUGH MY NAME IS ON THE BOOK'S COVER, THERE ARE SO many people who worked very hard to guide this novel to publication! First and foremost is the amazing team at HarperCollins Christian Publishing. Not one but two editors helped me fine-tune this novel! Thank you to Becky Philpott and Karli Jackson! Huge thanks also go out to the amazing Jean Bloom, who somehow manages to locate every discrepancy! Jean's honesty and humor make working on this book for the fifth, sixth, and seventh time almost enjoyable.

I also owe a debt of gratitude to Lynne, my first reader, as well as my assistant Laurie Smith and my wonderful street team, the Buggy Bunch. Since writing is a very solitary job I'm so grateful for these ladies' (and men's) support!

I also owe so much to my own Thomas, my husband Tom. He spent a weekend with me on the shores of Lake Erie and stood by my side as I plotted and chatted with historians about Johnson's Island. He also very patiently explored the Confederate Officer Cemetery with me, taking pictures of almost every tombstone! Tom also spent many hours with me plotting each hero's journey. He knew how important they became to me, which says a lot, given that his ancestors fought for the Union while mine fought for the Confederacy.

Finally, I am eternally grateful to God for being with me while I write. He has answered many a prayer while I fussed and worried over these characters. I'm so grateful that even in my basement office, I'm never completely alone.

ABOUT THE AUTHOR

Photo by The New Studio

SHELLEY SHEPARD GRAY IS A *New York Times* AND *USA Today* bestselling author, a finalist for the American Christian Fiction Writers' prestigious Carol Award, and a two-time HOLT Medallion winner. She lives in southern Ohio, where she writes full time, bakes too much, and can often be found walking her dachshunds on her town's bike trail.

She also spends a lot of time online. Please visit her website: www.shelleyshepardgray.com.

Find her on Facebook at Facebook.com/ShelleyShepardGray.

Enjoy Shelley Shepard Gray's

Chicago World's Fair Mystery Series

Available in print and e-book.

The Chicago World's Fair Mystery Series
is also available as an e-book collection!

Available in e-book only May 2016.